BEHIND THE CURTAIN
AN ECHO FALLS MYSTERY

PETER ABRAHAMS

BEHIND THE CURTAIN

AN ECHO FALLS MYSTERY

LAURA GERINGER BOOKS
An Imprint of HarperCollins *Publishers*

To Rick Starke

Behind the Curtain: An Echo Falls Mystery
Copyright © 2006 by Pas de Deux
For information address HarperCollins Children's Books,
a division of HarperCollins Publishers, 1350 Avenue of the Americas, New York, 10019.
www.harpercollinschildrens.com

Library of Congress Cataloging-in-Publication Data
Abrahams, Peter, date
Behind the curtain : an Echo Falls mystery / Peter Abrahams.— 1st ed.
    p. cm.
Summary: An avid Sherlock Holmes fan, eighth grader Ingrid Levin-Hill is kidnapped while
investigating mysterious happenings in her home town.
    ISBN-10: 0-06-073704-2 (trade bdg.) — ISBN-13: 978-0-06-073704-7 (trade bdg.)
    ISBN-10: 0-06-073705-0 (lib. bdg.) — ISBN-13: 978-0-06-073705-4 (lib. bdg.)
    [1. Mystery and detective stories.] I. Title.
PZ7.A1675Beh 2006   2005017774
[Fic]—dc22   CIP
                                                                          AC

Typography by Hilary Zarycky
1 2 3 4 5 6 7 8 9 10

First Edition

BEHIND THE CURTAIN
AN ECHO FALLS MYSTERY

BEHIND THE CURTAIN
AN ECHO FALLS MYSTERY

ngrid Levin-Hill sat
ing pleasantly. She h
back of the outside
as could be from the
Middle School stood
about a mile upstream
something interesting t
were in the habit of n
like how the water ruff
and a big black bird dri
under its chin, and—

"Ingrid? I trust I ha
Ingrid whipped aro

her through narrowed eyes, and her eyes were narrow to begin with.

"One hundred percent," said Ingrid, in the faint hope of pacifying Ms. Groome with math talk.

"Then I'm sure you're excited about MathFest."

MathFest? What was Ms. Groome talking about? The word didn't even make sense, one of those contradictions in terms.

"Very excited," said Ingrid.

"Just in case Ingrid happened to miss any of this," said Ms. Groome, "who wants to sum up MathFest?"

No one did.

"Bruce?" said Ms. Groome.

Brucie Berman, middle row, front seat, class clown. His leg was doing that twitchy thing.

"MathFest be my guest," said Brucie.

"I beg your pardon?"

Brucie tried to look innocent, but he'd been born with a guilty face. "Three lucky kids from this class get to go to MathFest," he said.

"And MathFest is?"

"This big fat fun math blowout they're having tomorrow," said Brucie.

"Not tomorrow," said Ms. Groome. "Saturday morning, eight thirty, at the high school."

"Even better," said Brucie.

Ms. Groome pursed her lips, totally focused now on Brucie. There was lots to be said for having Brucie in class. Ingrid tuned out, just in time to catch that big black bird disappear around a bend in the river. No way this had anything to do with her, no way she'd be one of the chosen three. She shouldn't even have been in this section, Algebra Two. There were four math classes in eighth grade—Algebra One for the geniuses, Algebra Two for good math students who didn't rise to the genius level, Pre-Algebra, where Ingrid should have been and would have been happily, if her parents hadn't crawled on their knees to Ms. Groome, and Math One, formerly remedial math, for the kids out on parole.

Math blowouts on Saturday morning. Who thinks these things up? Grown-ups, of course, the kind with a sense of humor like that warden in *Escape from Alcatraz*. Ingrid was half aware of Ms. Groome scrawling long chains of numbers on the blackboard, all dim and fuzzy. She wrote a note—*What's the word for stuff like giant midget or MathFest?*—balled it up, and tossed it discreetly over to Mia's desk across the aisle. Mia was the smartest kid in the class, should have been in Algebra One, but she and her mom had moved from New York last year and the school had messed up.

Mia flattened out the note, read it, wrote an answer. The sun, one of those little fall suns, more silver than gold, shone on Mia's hand—her fingers, skin, everything about her, so delicate. She rolled the note back up, flicked it underhanded across the aisle. Ingrid reached for it, but all at once, so sudden she wasn't sure for a moment that it had really happened, another hand darted into the picture and snatched the note out of the air. Nothing delicate about this hand, skin scaly, knuckles all swollen.

"What could be so important?" said Ms. Groome, unfolding the note. "I'm dying to find out." The sun glared off fingerprints on her glasses, hiding her eyes. She read the note, stuck it in her pocket, returned to the front of the class. Her mouth opened, just a thin sharklike slit. Some withering remark was on the way, but at that very moment, like a message from above, the bell rang.

Class over! Saved by the bell! Chairs started scraping all over the room as the kids got up. Hubbub, and lots of it. Thanksgiving couldn't come soon enough.

"Just a second," said Ms. Groome, not so much raising her voice over the bedlam as cutting through it like an ice pick. Everyone froze. "We still haven't chosen our MathFest team."

Brucie raised his hand.

"Thank you, Bruce. Congratulations."

"Oh, no," said Brucie. "Wait. I was just going to say let's do it tomorrow."

Ms. Groome didn't seem to hear. "Any volunteers

for the other two spots?"

There were none.

"Then the pleasure will be mine," said Ms. Groome. She smiled, if smiling meant the corners of the mouth twisting up and teeth making a brief appearance. "Mia. Ingrid. Everybody wish our team good luck."

"Go team," said everybody, in a great mood because it wasn't them.

"But wait," said Brucie.

"I could get sick," Brucie said on the bus ride home.

Someone snickered.

"What if I forged a note?" Brucie said. "With Adobe Photoshop I could make it look like a doctor's—"

"Zip it, guy," said the driver, Mr. Sidney, his BATTLE OF THE CORAL SEA cap slanted low over his eyes, like a ship captain in rough seas. Brucie zipped it; the other choice was walking the rest of the way, as Brucie had learned on the first day of school last year and then had to relearn again just last week.

Mr. Sidney stopped in front of Ingrid's house.

"See you, petunia," he said. Girls were petunia to Mr. Sidney, guys guy. Things must have been a lot different when he was growing up.

Ingrid stepped off the bus, started up the brick path to her house. Ninety-nine Maple Lane was the only place she'd ever lived. Not the biggest, newest, or fanciest house in the neighborhood, Riverbend, but there were lots of good things about it. Such as the breakfast nook in the kitchen with windows on three sides, where the family—Mom, Dad, Ingrid, and her brother, Ty, a freshman at Echo Falls High (home of the Red Raiders)—ate just about all their meals; and the living-room fireplace, the bricks set in zigzags that matched the brick patterns in the chimney and front walk, a nice touch in Ingrid's opinion; and maybe most of all her bedroom at the back, overlooking the town woods—the smallest room in the house, excluding bathrooms, and the most peaceful.

Ingrid went around to the side, unlocked the mudroom door. Nigel ambled out.

"Hey, boy," said Ingrid, reaching down to pat him.

Nigel loved to be patted, maybe his second favorite thing, next to food. But now he changed course, making a kind of slow-motion swerve that took him just out of reach of her hand.

"Nigel?"

Nigel, crossing the lawn, swiveled his head around in her direction, walking one way, looking another. He had a jowly face and tweedy sort of coat, just like Nigel Bruce, who'd played Dr. Watson in the old black-and-white Sherlock Holmes movies; Ingrid, a lover of Sherlock Holmes, had them all on DVD. Her Nigel, like Dr.

Watson, could be slow on the uptake. Unlike Dr. Watson, he wasn't always reliable.

For example, the way he was now avoiding eye contact and had resumed his course, headed for the road. Nigel wasn't allowed on the road. Ingrid, with a book in hand called *Training Even the Dumbest Dog*, had spent hours with Nigel, teaching him not to leave the property, rewarding his eventual success with a pig-out of Hebrew Nationals, his hot dog of choice.

Nigel paused at the edge of the lawn, right forepaw raised in the attitude of one of those clever pointing dogs that understand commands in several languages. Was he remembering those hot dogs, even maybe just a little bit?

"Nigel?"

He stepped onto the street, a dainty little movement— like Zero Mostel in the *Producers* movie, one of Ingrid's favorites—that still surprised her and always meant no good. The next moment he was picking up the pace, pushing himself into that waddling trot, his top speed.

"Nigel!"

Ingrid dropped her backpack, hurried after him. Nigel tried to go faster—she could tell from the furious way his scruffy tail was wagging, slowing him down if anything. He reached the other side of Maple Lane, sniffed at the Grunellos' grass, and then made a beeline for the stone angel birdbath that stood by their front door.

"Don't you dare," said Ingrid, running across the lawn.

Too late. Nigel raised his leg against the birdbath. Ingrid grabbed his collar and dragged him away, trailing a golden arc all the way back to the road. Nigel didn't like the Grunellos, a quiet middle-aged couple who were kind to animals, never bothered anybody, and spent a lot of time away. Like now, please God. At the edge of the driveway he snatched up the Grunellos' copy of *The Echo*.

"Put that down."

But he clung to the rolled-up newspaper with all his might until they were back at the mudroom door. Then he dropped it in a casual sort of way and scrambled inside.

"Kiss those hot dogs good-bye," Ingrid said. She could hear him panting in the kitchen as though he'd just performed some incredible feat.

Ingrid picked up *The Echo*, kind of drooly and tattered now. She'd have to make a trade, dropping their own copy back on the Grunellos' lawn. But the delivery kid had missed them today.

Ingrid went inside, glancing at the front page. The big story was SENIOR CENTER OPENS WITH A BANG, accompanied by a photo of some white-haired people laughing their heads off around a flowerpot. Below that was something about new rules from the Conservation

Commission, pretty much chewed through, and below that, under a headline that read ECHO FALLS NEWCOMER, was a photo of a striking woman who looked to be a little younger than Mom. She actually resembled Mom—dark hair, big almond-shaped eyes—but although Mom was beautiful, you couldn't call her striking. Ingrid gazed more closely, saw the prominent cheekbones, the fine shape of the lips, everything perfect, if a bit severe; maybe not like Mom after all.

> *Ms. Julia LeCaine, formerly of Manhattan, has moved to Echo Falls to take the position of vice president of Operations for the Ferrand Group.*

Hey. Dad worked for the Ferrand Group. And he was a vice president too.

> *Ms. LeCaine, a graduate of Princeton University with an MBA from the Wharton School of Business, founded an Internet company. A former outstanding soccer player, she was a Team USA alternate in 1992. Welcome to Echo Falls, Ms. LeCaine!*

Ingrid went into the kitchen, took a Fresca from the fridge. Bliss, essence of. Whoever invented Fresca was a genius. Could that be an actual job, inventing sodas? A whole new career possibility arose, handy backup in case her number-one choice, acting and directing on stage and screen, didn't pan out.

Ingrid drained the can to the last drop, opened the trash cupboard under the sink.

"That's funny," she said.

At the top of the trash bag—which needed to be replaced, Ty's job—lay *The Echo*, today's *Echo*, still rolled up. How could that be? Mom and Dad were at work, wouldn't be home for a couple hours at least, and Ty was at football practice, the only freshman on the varsity. Ingrid glanced over at Nigel, lying by the water bowl with one paw over his eyes in that way he had, as if warding off the light. Nigel—getting out of the locked house, retrieving the paper, depositing it in the trash, locking himself back in? Only in an upside-down universe.

Ingrid heard a footstep somewhere upstairs. Oh my God. She recalled a moment like this once before, when she'd helped Chief Strade solve the Cracked-Up Katie case. A creepy moment that led to all sorts of scary things. She stood motionless by the kitchen sink. Another footstep, right overhead. That would be Mom and Dad's

office, the extra bedroom on the second floor. And was there something familiar about that footstep? Did footsteps have a sound unique to every person, like fingerprints but much harder to distinguish? Ingrid didn't know; but she thought she recognized that footstep.

She went into the front hall, up the stairs, turned left toward the office. The door was half open. Ingrid peeked in.

Dad was at the desk, his back to her. The computer was on and he wore a suit—all Dad's suits were really nice, with sleeve buttons that you could actually unbutton—but he wasn't working. Instead he was slumped forward, his head on the desk.

"Dad? Are you all right?"

He sat up quickly and swiveled around. Ingrid caught a glimpse of his face as she rarely saw it—pale and anxious. Then came a smile and in a second he looked more like himself, the handsomest dad in Echo Falls.

"Hi, cutie," he said. "What are you doing here?"

"Me?" said Ingrid. "I'm home from school."

"Oh," said Dad. "Right."

"Everything okay, Dad?"

"Sure," said Dad. He glanced at the computer, switched it off. "Just punched out a little early. All work and no play—" He paused, waiting for her to finish.

"Makes Dad a dull boy," Ingrid said.

He laughed.

The computer was blank now, but Ingrid had quick eyes and they'd grabbed that last fading screen: Jobs.com.

TWO

"Anyone seen *The Echo*?" Mom said, setting the take-out cartons from Ta Tung on the table. "I need to check the listings." Mom was a real estate agent at Riverbend Properties and also wrote all their advertising, which *The Echo* didn't always get right.

Dad, coming in from the living room with a glass in his hand, paused for an instant, a tiny wave of golden liquid slopping over the rim. Ingrid concentrated on laying out the plates and silverware, plus chopsticks for herself. Ty, in his chair, waiting with fork in one hand and knife in the other, was the only one who responded.

"Did you get the Mongolian ribs?" he said. Not an answer, exactly, but Ty loved Mongolian ribs.

Mom pointed to one of the cartons, at the same time kicking off her heels and sliding into her sheepskin slippers. They sat down to dinner.

"How was everyone's day?" she said.

"Great," said Ingrid.

"Anything special happen?"

"Nope."

"What are you reading in English?"

"Nothing."

"Nothing?"

"We're doing adverb packets," Ingrid said. "We're supposed to use lots of adverbs."

"You are?"

"Incessantly," said Ingrid.

Mom laughed. Dad had a big gulp of his drink. Ty said, "Any crispy duck?"

Mom passed him a carton. "How about you, Ty?"

"Me what?" said Ty, stabbing the biggest piece of duck.

"Your day," said Mom.

Ty shrugged.

Dad looked up. "How was practice?" he said.

"Not bad," said Ty, pouring plum sauce over everything on his plate.

"Who've you got on Friday?"

"Rocky Hill."

"With that quarterback B.C.'s going after?" Dad asked.

Ty, his knife in that stabbing grip he always used no matter how often Mom corrected him, cut off some crispy duck and started chewing, mouth open. "B.C.?" he said.

"Boston College," Dad said, his tone sharpening. "A D-One school, in case you hadn't heard. He's got a gun for an arm. Didn't the coaches tell you?"

"Maybe," said Ty, stabbing another piece. "I don't remember."

Dad slammed his hand on the table, so unexpected it made Ingrid jump. "Damn it," he said. "You think that's good enough?"

"Huh?" said Ty.

"Because the world doesn't work that way, buddy boy." Dad rose, picked up his drink, left the room.

"Mark?" said Mom.

He didn't answer. Ingrid heard his footsteps in the front hall, then up the stairs.

"What's he so pissed about?" said Ty.

Mom had beautiful skin, the darkest in the family and very soft, the only flaws being two vertical lines on her forehead, just between the eyes. Sometimes they were hardly visible; at other times—now for example—they deepened. Ingrid thought of them as a measuring device, like a barometer, for predicting the weather in Mom-world.

"Excuse me," Mom said, folding her napkin. Her footsteps faded fast, those sheepskin slippers making almost no sound at all.

Ty and Ingrid looked at each other. "What does Dad do, exactly?" Ingrid asked.

"Huh?" said Ty. "Works for Mr. Ferrand, you know that. Pass those egg rolls."

"How much are you going to eat?"

"Got to get my weight up." Ty bit off half an egg roll. "These are the best," he said, or something like that— hard to understand him with his mouth so full.

"It's because of the ends," Ingrid said.

"The ends?"

"The way Ta Tung egg rolls have those browned ends," Ingrid said. "No one else does that."

Ty examined the remaining end of his egg roll. "Browned," he said. "Cool." He gave her a quick look. "How do you know stuff like that?"

From Sherlock Holmes, of course, who believed in the importance of observing small things. But one small thing Ingrid had noticed was the way most people's eyes glazed over when she got started on Holmes. She just shrugged and said, "What does Dad do for Mr. Ferrand?"

"They develop things," Ty said. "Invest. Dad's the

number-two guy, vice president."

"How many vice presidents are there?"

"Just Dad. Gonna eat that last one?"

Ingrid passed Ty the last egg roll.

Somewhere upstairs a door closed. Dad's voice rose for a moment. Then Mom said something and Dad got quieter. The whole house grew quiet, except for Ty's chewing.

Time to clean up.

"Rock paper scissors," Ingrid said.

Ty nodded. They made fists. Their eyes met. They tried to read each other's minds.

"One, two, three," said Ty.

They pumped their hands. He was going for rock, beyond doubt. There was no one Ingrid knew better than Ty. She flashed spread fingers—paper.

And Ty: scissors. Scissors? He never did scissors. "Don't forget the countertops," he said on his way out.

Ingrid cleaned up. First came scraping off the plates. That meant opening the trash cupboard and again setting eyes on *The Echo*—two copies now, theirs and the Grunellos'. *Ms. Julia LeCaine, formerly* blah blah . . . *vice president of operations.* Did that make Dad vice president of everything else? Maybe it was a good thing. Maybe the richer the company, the more vice presidents. Microsoft probably had thousands, all of them with money piling up faster than they could count. If they got rich, the four of them, this family, the first thing she'd buy would be . . . what, exactly? Ingrid, loading the dishwasher, was trying to come up with the perfect kickass something when the doorbell rang.

Ingrid went to the hall, switched on the outside light, opened the door. Sean Rubino? Sean was the older brother of her best friend, Stacy, and had dropped Stacy off at the house once or twice, but he'd never come to the door.

"Yo," he said.

Ingrid peered past him. His car, a dinged-up old Firebird with a HELL ON WHEELS bumper sticker, was parked on the street, no one in it.

"Hi," Ingrid said. Had he come to pick Stacy up? "She's not here."

"Who?" said Sean.

"Stacy." And come to think of it, wasn't his license suspended because of that DUI thing on Labor Day?

"I'm looking for Ty," Sean said.

"Ty?" Sean and Ty weren't friends. Sean was two years older for one thing, a junior at Echo Falls High, and also not into sports, although he was pretty big.

"He in?" said Sean.

Ingrid gazed up at him. Sean looked a lot like his sister: same broad face, same color hair—although hers wasn't gelled up like that—but the feeling you got from seeing them was very different. "I'll get him," she said.

He came in, stood in the hall, glanced around.

Ingrid went upstairs. Mom and Dad's door was closed, Ty's open. He had a pile of books on his desk but was playing a video game.

"Sean Rubino's here to see you," Ingrid said.

Ty turned away from an exploding worm creature. "Yeah? Tell him to come up."

Ingrid paused. "You want Sean Rubino to come up?"

Ty's eyes got that squinty look she knew so well. "What's your problem?"

Ingrid went downstairs. Dad's golf clubs stood in the corner by the door. Sean was over there, examining the putter.

"He says go up," said Ingrid. "Second door on the right."

Sean slid the putter back into Dad's bag and went upstairs. She didn't like the way he put his hand on the rail, which was crazy.

Ingrid got her backpack and sat down at the kitchen table, her first choice homework venue. She closed her eyes, pulled out a book. Whatever it was, she'd do first. Except it turned out to be math. She tried again. English. That was better.

The assignment: Write ten complete, grammatical sentences using two adverbs in each.

Ingrid went to the fridge, snapped open a Fresca. Ah.

1. This corpse has been frozen recently, said Sherlock Holmes icily.

2. Holmes stepped into the hansom cab handsomely as the horse neighed nasally.

3. Dr. Watson coughed harumphingly when the woman in red—

Ingrid heard footsteps coming down the stairs. The front door opened and closed. She went to the hall, looked out the window in time to see Sean driving off in the Firebird, one taillight out. He turned right on Avondale and disappeared. Ingrid was about to return to her homework when headlights flashed down the street. A second car drove by, also turning right on Avondale. This one read ECHO FALLS POLICE on the driver's door, and in smaller letters: CHIEF. But Ingrid would have recognized Chief Gilbert L. Strade anyway, just from the massive silhouetted form behind the wheel.

Homework all done, at least to her satisfaction. Sometimes Ingrid was easily pleased. Up in her room, she went online, sent an IM to Stacy.

Gridster22: sean was here

Powerup77: ???

Gridster22: to see ty

Powerup77: sean my stupid bro?

Gridster22: yup

Powerup77: wha for?

Gridster22: i'm asking u

Powerup77: dunno—wanna come over after the game?

Gridster22: sounds goooooood—i'll—

Ty poked his head in the door.

"Got a minute?" he said.

Gridster22: cul8tr

"What?" said Ingrid.

"Need a safety," he said.

"What about Dad?"

"They went to bed."

"Why so early?"

"Do I look like a search engine?" Ty said. "You gonna help me or not?"

Ingrid went to the basement with Ty. They had practically a whole gym down there—StairMaster, treadmill, slant board, bench press, and machines for leg curls, leg extensions, leg presses, ab crunches, delt thises and pec thats, none of which Ingrid ever used. She'd read in a magazine—on the letters-to-the-editor page, actually, just a letter from some reader who didn't even have an MD after his name, but it did get printed—that thirteen was too young for weight training. No sense taking chances.

Ty went to the bench press, slid a forty-five-pound plate on each end of the bar, then added two twenty-fives. Forty-five plus forty-five was ninety, plus fifty made one thirty, and don't forget the weight of the bar itself, forty-five more: one eighty-five. Wow. The most she'd ever seen him do was two twenty-fives on each end—one forty-five—and that had been only a few weeks ago. Those iron plates: so big.

"What are you looking at?" he said.

"Nothing."

Ty lay down on the bench. Ingrid stood at the end, ready to help if he had trouble raising the bar back up to the cradle. But what kind of help could she be with one eighty-five? Ingrid weighed ninety-four pounds.

Ty gripped the bar, his fingers wriggling around for the spot that felt right. He planted his feet on the floor, first wriggling them a bit, too. Then he took a deep breath, jerked all that weight up out of the cradle, lowered it to his chest, pushed up again.

"One," said Ingrid.

Down. Up.

"Two."

He grunted.

"Three."

The grunts got louder. His face got red. His eyes bugged out. He looked like a freak. But he did ten. Ten at one eighty-five, and lowered the bar into the cradle with no help.

"Hey," Ingrid said.

Ty lay on the bench, chest rising and falling, the muscles stretching his T-shirt. RED RAIDER FOOTBALL it said on the front. BIGGER, FASTER, STRONGER.

"What was Sean doing over here?" Ingrid said.

"Nothing," said Ty, reaching up for the bar. He took a few deep breaths. "Ready," he said, and lifted on the last exhale.

"One," said Ingrid. This was what being a slave master in a Roman galley must have been like, easy work but boring and a bit smelly. Ty grunted louder, got redder and more bug-eyed, but did ten more.

"Good job," she said.

He got up, rubbing his shoulder. Ingrid turned to go. "One more set," he said. He fetched two tens from the weight stack, added them to the bar.

One eighty-five plus twenty? That made—"What are you doing?" Ingrid said.

"Just three reps," said Ty.

"Whoa," said Ingrid.

"Did I ask for your opinion?" said Ty.

He lay on the bench, grasped the bar, planted his feet, took a huge deep breath, pushed. The bar lifted off the cradle. Ty lowered it to his chest, grunted, tried to heave the weight back up, a vein popping out in his neck, all blue and throbbing. Slowly, oh so slowly, the bar rose. Ingrid heard his teeth grinding, got ready to say *one.* But at that moment, the bar still maybe six inches below the cradle, Ty's arms started shaking and the bar stalled.

"A little help," he said, almost in a normal tone of voice.

Help? What was she supposed—

"Help!" This time not normal at all.

Ingrid stepped forward, grabbed the bar, her hands between his, his upside-down face, purple now, right under all that iron. She bent her legs, drove up with all her might. The bar didn't budge, except for the quiver from the way Ty's arms were shaking.

"Damn it," said Ty. "Lift."

Ingrid found a little extra. Now she was grunting too. They grunted together, fighting the weight of that bar. It rose, inch by inch, up to cradle level and clanged into place. For a second she felt lighter than air, as though she could float up to the ceiling.

"That was lucky," Ingrid said.

"You don't know what the hell you're talking about," Ty said.

"Huh?"

He sat up, pulled off his T-shirt, mopped his face. "I'm so damn weak."

"Maybe mentally," Ingrid said.

His voice rose, that deep man voice he sometimes had now. "You're such a jerk," he said, throwing the T-shirt at her.

Ingrid ducked. For just a second, a scary second, she thought he might hit her. They'd had an incident or two like that in the past. Instead he turned and drove his fist into the padded bench, very hard, making a sound that boomed through the house. He was acting so weird. What was wrong with him? And his back: Ty had always been one of those lucky acne-free kids, and his face still was smooth and unblemished. But under the ceiling lights, she could see dark-red pimples all over his upper back. He rose and started stripping off the weights.

In the morning when Ingrid went downstairs, Mom and Ty were already gone. Echo Falls High started half an hour before Ferrand Middle, and Mom went right by it on her way to work. That meant Ingrid and Dad ate a lot of breakfasts together, Dad never going in before his nine-o'clock meeting with Mr. Ferrand. Dad would read her little snippets from *The Wall Street Journal*, and Ingrid would eat the kind of things she ate when no one was paying attention. But today *The Wall Street Journal* was still in its plastic wrapper and Dad was already packing his briefcase, tie knotted, suit jacket on.

"Morning, Dad."

"Morning," he said, barely looking up. "Going in a little early today."

"Something special happening?"

"Probably be going in a little early for the foreseeable future."

"How come?"

"Globalization, if you want to put it in one word."

A word that was in the air, even if Ingrid didn't really understand it. "What does it mean, anyway?"

"Means we're all going to have to work harder," Dad said. "Including you."

"Me?"

"Not just you," said Dad. "Kids in general."

"Kids have to work harder?"

"That's the future. Big forces are on the move."

"What kind of forces?"

"History will judge."

Dad poured coffee into a thermos—he never did that, always enjoyed his second cup at home—and headed for the door that led from the kitchen to the garage.

"I like your shirt, Dad." A beautiful deep blue with white collar and cuffs, but Dad, already out the door, didn't hear. For the first time in her life, Ingrid felt a little nostalgic. History would judge how hard she was working? The future sounded grim.

THREE

Ingrid had health last period on Fridays. Time slowed way, way down in health class, just when you wanted to be out of the building so bad, but otherwise Ingrid had no complaints. Mr. Porterhouse, the gym and health teacher, whistle hanging around his neck, would read for a while from the textbook, and then say, "I know all you sports"—Mr. Porterhouse called everyone sport—"got work to do." Then he would settle down to the *Hartford Courant* crossword puzzle and the kids could a) do their homework, b) talk quietly, or c) go to sleep. Getting a head start on weekend homework made the most sense, but come on. And had it been first period, Ingrid would have slept, but her sleepiness always wore off by midmorning. So she almost always chose B, talking to her friends, and she had a lot of them in health class, including Stacy, Mia, and Joey Strade.

Today's subject seemed to be drugs, pretty much as usual. There were a lot to cover—heroin, PCP, cocaine, meth, LSD, ecstasy, marijuana, hashish, plus all those nicknames like crank, crack, spliff, weed, grass, smoke, uppers, downers. Ingrid's favorite—as a name—was hashish because it sounded so exotic. Without even smoking it, she could call up clear pictures of caravans, camels, casbahs. So: Why bother smoking it?

All those drugs were bad; Ingrid didn't dispute that for a second. The problem was that maybe they all weren't quite as bad as the textbook said, a discrepancy that raised doubts in the minds of some kids. Getting the facts right was important. As Holmes told Watson in "A Case of Identity," "Never trust to general impressions, my boy, but concentrate yourself upon details." You could learn a lot from Sherlock Holmes, and Ingrid had. On the other hand, he could be unpredictable, like when he went on cocaine jags from time to time. Maybe if he'd run into Mr. Porterhouse, who was now droning on about—

". . . anabolic steroids mumble mumble synthetic hormones mumble mumble make muscle." He glanced over the top of his reading glasses. "We all know what hormones are by now?"

No one disagreed.

Mr. Porterhouse went back to the text. He wasn't a fast reader but it seemed that way, maybe because he ignored punctuation. Plus all that mumbling. ". . . exaggerating the mumble mumble testosterone on the body such as increased mumble mumble muscle mass and deep voices steroids are illegal and can cause stunted mumble irreversible liver mumble violent mood mumble facial hair on girls and women as well as male-pattern mumble and bad acne."

He glanced up at the wall clock, where the minute hand still had a huge distance to travel before they were free. "That about covers it," he said. "Any questions?"

No questions. Mr. Porterhouse reached for the crossword. Quiet talk started humming around the room.

Joey Strade, sitting across the aisle, said: "Going to the game tonight?"

Ingrid turned to him. Joey, son of Chief Strade, was someone she'd sort of known for years. He'd always been a quiet, pudgy kid, his only uniqueness being a stubborn cowlick that stood up like a blunt Indian feather. Now he wasn't so quiet or pudgy—although the cowlick was still happening—and she knew him better. They'd gone to a couple of dances at the Rec Center and she'd been to his house, where he'd demonstrated the catapult he built for the science fair, winning honorable mention. He also had this new direct way of looking at you. And they'd kissed two times, no point leaving that out, although how important it was Ingrid didn't know.

"Of course I'm going," she said. "Did he say acne?"

"Acne?" said Joey. "There was something about liver. I hate liver anyway."

School sucked in many ways, but the goofy part came close to making it all worthwhile. Ingrid restrained a crazy impulse to pat that untamable Indian feather thing at the back of Joey's head. Up front, Mr. Porterhouse did some erasing on his puzzle, then chewed on the pencil, deep in thought. Ingrid remembered she still hadn't learned the word for giant midgets. And that almost reminded her of something else, something maybe important. Oh, yeah, MathFest. Mustn't forget.

A kid with his face painted red ran through the parking lot by Red Raider Field waving a red banner and screaming, "Are you ready for some football?"

"What happens in other countries on Friday nights?" said Stacy. "Like Norway."

"I guess they just sit around," said Ingrid. She stood by Mr. Rubino's top-of-the-line Weber, grilling the last of the burgers for the Booster Club. Dad, former Red Raiders star quarterback, was president and Mom was treasurer.

"I always liked the sound of Norway," Mia said.

Over on the field, the band struck up "The Star-Spangled Banner." Spangled: Ingrid loved the word. Maybe it didn't make sense, but that was America to her, summed up. She got rid of the rest of the burgers at fire-sale prices, gave freebies to Stacy and Mia, shut off the gas. They were in their seats—top row, fifty-yard line on the home side, right above Mom and Dad—in time to see Rocky Hill run the opening kickoff all the way to the Echo Falls thirty-yard line.

"Nice shade of blue," Mia said. Rocky Hill did wear sparkling sapphire-blue pants, but was that the point right now? Mia really wasn't much of a football fan.

A fact Stacy picked up on right away. "Do they have football in New York?" she said.

Mia rubbed Stacy the wrong way sometimes. Most of what they had in common was being friends with Ingrid.

"Not that I ever saw," Mia said, which was probably the simple truth. But Stacy thought Mia was giving her attitude—Ingrid could tell just from the way Stacy let out her breath.

The defense ran onto the field. "Hey," Ingrid said. "Ty's starting." There he was, number 19, in the secondary on the near side, bouncing up and down.

"Bobby Moran rebroke that arm yesterday," Dad said.

Ingrid spotted Bobby Moran, one of the stars of the team, on the sidelines in a sweatshirt and jeans. His cast, attached at an awkward angle to a chest harness, went from shoulder to fingertips. His eyes were on Ty.

"Ty's just as fast, maybe faster," Ingrid said.

"Takes more than speed," Dad said.

"For a corner back against a passing team?" Ingrid said.

"They won't be passing tonight," Dad said.

"Why not?"

Rocky Hill came to the line of scrimmage. "Sweep," said Dad, more to himself; he was uncanny about knowing what was about to happen in football games. "Going at him right off the top."

Rocky Hill's quarterback took the snap, handed off to the running back. Sweep to the near side, the running back following a huge lineman, number 61, both of them kicking up clods of dirt. They turned the corner. Ty came up to meet them, hardly hesitating at all. That was bravery. Ingrid understood at that moment how much Ty loved football, like nothing else in his life. The lineman knocked him down and then the running back ran over him. Touchdown. Ty jumped right back up.

"Going to be a long night," said Dad.

The very next time Rocky Hill got the ball, they tried that sweep again. The lineman bowled Ty over. The running back stepped on him on his way by. Ty got up, not so quickly.

Dad shook his head. That pissed Ingrid off. "The linebacker's not even getting there, Dad," she said.

Mom glanced back in surprise. "So it's not Ty's fault? How do you know that, Ingrid?"

Ingrid shrugged. But this wasn't rocket science or brain surgery, the two jobs people always used for defining braininess, leaving out for some reason detective or criminal mastermind. This was just football, and she'd been watching lots of it—all Ty's games this season and, just lately, Joey's Pop Warner games as well.

"Forget about the linebacker," Dad said. "Ty's got to fight off that block."

But what about the end? Ingrid thought. Where was the Red Raiders end, that enormous kid from the Flats, son of the crabby guy at the Sunoco, number 88? Shouldn't he be out there, trying to slow down 61? Wasn't he supposed to push 61 wide, giving the linebacker a lane?

The coaches were talking on the sideline.

"They're going to move Ty to the weak side," Dad said.

Next series, they moved Ty to the other side.

"As if they won't be able to find him," said Dad.

Mom turned, gave him a look. Dad, gaze fixed on the

field, didn't catch it, but Ingrid did. It wasn't an angry or irritated look—she'd seen looks like that going back and forth between her parents, what kid hadn't?—but more puzzled, as though she didn't quite know him.

Toward the end of the second quarter—Rocky Hill 14, Red Raiders 7—they found Ty again. A sweep to the weak side, 61 still leading it, untouched. This time Ty was a little more hesitant coming up—Ingrid wanted not to see that but couldn't help herself. He plugged the hole, in a crouch, hands up, tried to slide off 61, spin around in time to tackle the running back. Ty was so quick it almost worked. But 61 was pretty quick too, especially for someone his size. He lifted Ty right off the ground. Ty landed flat on his back just as the running back ran over him one more time.

Ty lay there for a moment, then rolled and pushed himself up. He took a few wobbly steps toward the wrong sideline, turned, walked to the Red Raider bench, actually recovering enough to jog the last few steps. The coach met him on the sideline, put a hand on Ty's chest. He yelled something, his nose practically touching Ty's face mask. For a moment, Ingrid thought he was yelling encouragement, like nice try or not your fault, or not entirely one hundred percent your fault. Then she saw spit droplets flying from the coach's mouth, silver under the lights, and realized he was beside himself with fury.

He stayed there in Ty's face, some of his words—like "piss poor"—carrying all the way up to the top row. Ingrid felt herself turning red, as though she were on the receiving end. She saw that Mom had reddened too. A lumpy muscle jumped in the side of Dad's face. Ty went to the end of the bench, sat there, head down. No one talked to him.

"Can you punt for a field goal?" Mia asked.

Ingrid rode to Stacy's house in the Rubinos' pickup. RUBINO ELECTRIC read the gold lettering on the door. NO JOB TOO BIG OR SMALL. A great slogan, in Ingrid's opinion. Said it all. And true: Mr. Rubino was a genius when it came to electricity. He'd turned the Rubinos' family room into a kickass entertainment center complete with a real popcorn machine and a robot that rolled around with a tray of drinks. Even the sound system in the pickup, now playing a song about strawberry shortcake and broken hearts—Mr. Rubino loved country—rocked. Mr. Rubino was also lighting director for the Prescott Players, famous in local lighting circles for how he'd handled the Cheshire Cat's smile in *Alice in Wonderland*.

"How's the script look, Ingrid?" he said.

"Haven't seen it yet," said Ingrid. Every year, the Prescott Players put on The Xmas Revue at the high school, directed by Jill Monteiro, the leading drama teacher in Echo Falls and a genuine off-Broadway actress, with kids from the school system in all the roles. There was lots of singing and dancing, plus a scene from a play or two. This year the High School Theater Club was doing a sword fight from *The Mask of Zorro* and the kids from Ferrand Middle the scene from *The Wizard of Oz* where Dorothy and her friends finally meet the wizard. Did Ingrid have the title role? Yes, she did, but the truth was there hadn't been much interest in *The Wizard of Oz*, the kids preferring a spoof of the balcony scene in *Romeo and Juliet* that Brucie Berman had written, or rather claimed to have written, although it came off the Internet and was nixed by Jill Monteiro in any case; and in the end no one else auditioned for Dorothy.

"That sword fight's gonna be awesome," said Mr. Rubino. "Bobby Moran stuck one of those suckers right through the auditorium wall."

"Bobby Moran's in the play?" Ingrid said.

"That's how he rebroke his arm," said Mr. Rubino.

"Not football?"

Mr. Rubino shook his head. "Swordplay."

The Rubinos lived in the Lower Falls neighborhood, not as nice as Riverbend but they had a great house with lots of additions Mr. Rubino had built himself, sprawling all over the place. Just as he pulled into the driveway, the Firebird pulled out, the tires squealing as it sped away.

"Now where the hell's he going?" said Mr. Rubino. He watched the Firebird till it vanished around a bend, his forehead wrinkling up. Mr. Rubino had a round friendly face with a big bristly mustache. Ingrid had never seen it worried like this. For a moment he looked like someone she didn't know. "And I told him three times to stick a bulb in that taillight."

They went inside, Mr. Rubino first straightening a garden elf in a flower bed by the door.

"Ellie," he called, "where's Sean off to?"

No answer.

"She's back on four to midnights," said Stacy. Mrs. Rubino was a nurse at the hospital, up by the soccer fields.

"Oh," said Mr. Rubino. "Right." His body sagged, as though he felt tired all of a sudden. He popped open a can of Bud from the fridge, sat at the kitchen table, but didn't even have time for a sip before the phone rang. He listened for a few seconds, then said, "Did you try the circuit breakers?" He listened some more and said, "It's that box under the cellar stairs." And some more, before saying, with a little sigh, "Be there in ten minutes." He put the beer back in the fridge.

Stacy and Ingrid went down to the entertainment center, reclined on the recliners. They watched *Ferris Bueller's Day Off*, one of their favorites, on the gigantic screen. The popcorn machine made popcorn with tons of butter. The robot brought a Coke for Stacy, Fresca for Ingrid.

"This is the life," said Stacy.

"Wouldn't change a thing," said Ingrid. She and Stacy went all the way back to before they could even walk and talk. There was a photo to prove it: two tiny girls splashing around in a tiny plastic swimming pool, not wearing bathing suits for some reason. What was that all about? Did people get stupid the moment they had kids?

"I love this part," said Stacy, "the car going through the window."

Ingrid loved it too, but something about the scene made her say, "What's up with Sean these days?"

Stacy bit her lip. "You think something's up?" she asked, her voice quieter than normal. Normally it was kind of booming, but she just wasn't the same person when it came to her brother. "Like what?"

"I'm asking you."

"I don't know," Stacy said. "He's flunking every course. And the DUI thing cost my dad a thousand bucks."

"Your dad paid?"

"Sean's broke. All the money he made last summer goes into that stupid car."

The *Ferris Bueller* credits scrolled by. "How about

Happy Gilmore?" Ingrid said.

"Sure," said Stacy.

But they couldn't find it.

"Maybe it's in Sean's room," Stacy said. "He got a new DVD player."

"Your parents gave him a DVD player?"

Stacy shook her head. "Some friend of his didn't want it anymore." She pressed a button and the robot came over.

"I'll go look for the DVD," Ingrid said.

"Okay," said Stacy, reaching for another Coke.

Ingrid went upstairs. Sean's room was at the end of the second floor. Like Ty's, it was a horrible mess, the smell a little off. But there were differences. For example, posters of sports heroes covered Ty's walls. Sean's were bare, except for bits of masking tape where posters had once hung. Just a little thing, a trifle, but it had to mean something. Sherlock Holmes's whole method was based on the observation of trifles.

Where to even begin a search in this squalor? Ingrid chose the bottom drawer of Sean's desk. Was that really where he'd keep the *Happy Gilmore* DVD? Probably not. There was just something about that bottom drawer, the hardest to get to.

The bottom drawer of Sean Rubino's desk was

crammed—packets and packets of wrinkled homework, most undone or partly done; old magazines, all of them about cars and drag racing; and down at the bottom a baseball glove. Ingrid remembered that Sean had once played Little League. Wasn't there some story about the field getting torn up late one night? She took out the glove, put it on, went to punch her fist in the pocket.

Ingrid paused, fist in midair. A roll of money lay in the pocket of the glove. A big fat roll, like a gambler might have in some movie. She counted it: $1,649.

"Hey," called Stacy, coming down the hall. "You find it?"

Ingrid saw herself as others, even a best friend, would see her now—a snoop—and made a snap decision not to tell Stacy, at least not yet. Maybe all that money was somehow perfectly innocent. And if not, wouldn't it be better to first get a few more facts? Theorizing without data was a capital mistake, as Holmes told Watson in "A Scandal in Bohemia."

Ingrid folded the glove around the wad of money, stuck it back in the bottom of the drawer, exactly as she'd found it.

"Let's watch something else," Ingrid said.

"*Fawlty Towers*?" said Stacy, coming into the room.

"Sounds good."

Stacy went over to Sean's TV, popped a DVD out of the player. "*Happy Gilmore*'s right here," she said, looking at Ingrid in surprise.

"Oh," said Ingrid, all at once feeling very bad.

FOUR

I ngrid had a dream she dreamed over and over, all about being in a snug boat on seas that sometimes got rough. She was dreaming it now, maybe a little late even for a Saturday morning, when her door burst open.

"Phone," said Ty, and then came a thump on the pillow.

Ingrid opened her eyes. The portable phone lay on the pillow and Ty was gone. Beside her on the bed, Nigel opened his eyes too, saw how light it was, and quickly closed them. Mister Happy, her teddy bear and no favorite of Nigel's, was jammed into the tiny space between the bed and the wall. She was kind of jammed there as well. Nigel had plenty of room.

Ingrid reached for the phone. "Hello?"

"Ingrid? It's Chloe."

Ingrid sat up. Chloe Ferrand calling her? Had this ever happened before? No. They'd been friends years ago, back in the time of being too young to make phone calls. In fact, Mister Happy was a present from Chloe, who had an identical teddy bear she'd named Mister Bumpy. But that was then. Now Chloe, the most beautiful thirteen-year-old girl in Echo Falls, with genuine modeling jobs to prove it, went to Cheshire Country Day and they seldom saw each other. Plus when they did, there was even some bad feeling between them, like on the set of the *Alice in Wonderland* production, when Ingrid ended up with the title role.

"Hi," Ingrid said.

"Busy today?" said Chloe.

"Huh?"

"Your schedule."

Ingrid didn't really have a schedule on Saturday, except for soccer. "I've got soccer at two," she said.

"Is that ridiculous hardware store guy still the coach?" Chloe said.

"Mr. Ringer's still the coach," Ingrid said. Maybe Mr. Ringer was kind of ridiculous, but she suddenly felt loyal to him.

"We'll make it for after the game then," said Chloe.

"Make what?" said Ingrid.

"This invitation," Chloe said.

"What invitation?"

Chloe's tone sharpened. Ingrid had a pretty good ear for tones. This one was all about trying to keep impatience under wraps, like Ingrid was a little slow. "That's why I'm calling, Ingrid. To invite you over for a swim. After the game. At your convenience. Whatever."

A swim. The Ferrands had an indoor pool lit by a huge crystal chandelier from France, installed by Mr. Rubino. Word was that Mrs. Ferrand swam a mile every morning in the nude. Ingrid made one of those quick decisions that felt totally right.

"Oh," she said. "I just remembered."

"What?"

Ingrid searched her mind for some excuse she could have just remembered. And then out of the blue came a memory of something she *should* have remembered, namely MathFest. Oh my God. MathFest, Saturday morning, 8:30. What time was it now? She checked her watch—Fossil, bright red, red being her favorite color, the only one that said COLOR in capital letters. Twelve minutes till noon. Till noon? How could that have happened? By now MathFest was finished, all that wacky number fun a thing of the past. As for the future: Ms. Groome.

"Well?" said Chloe.

"MathFest," said Ingrid.

"What are you talking about?"

What was that saying about if life hands you a lemon make lemonade? In this case, she'd handed herself the lemon. "A school thing," Ingrid said. "Right after soccer till God knows when."

"They chose you for math?" said Chloe.

"Crazy, I know," said Ingrid. "But thanks for the invitation. Would have been great."

Chloe clicked off, no good-bye.

Ingrid went downstairs, leaving her door open in case Nigel ever decided to get up. A very sharp kind of light filled the kitchen, making everything seem more real than real, like in some modern paintings Mom had dragged her to see at the museum in Hartford. Outside, the sky was a hard, cold blue, the trees in the town woods out back all bare now, winter around the corner. Dad was at the table, punching numbers on a calculator.

"Hi, Dad," said Ingrid. "Where is everybody?"

"Mom's got a showing," he said, eyes on the calculator screen. "Ty's gone for a run."

"Thought you had golf today," Ingrid said. Dad belonged to the Sandblasters, a fanatical bunch of golfers at his club who played at least one round in every month of the year.

"Work comes first," he said, "as you should know by

now." Uh-oh. Some kind of mood. He jotted a few quick numbers on a yellow legal pad. "Who was on the phone?"

"Chloe."

Dad looked up. "Chloe Ferrand?"

What other Chloes did they know? Was there even another Chloe in the whole state? But Ingrid sensed it wasn't the moment for an answer like that, and just said, "Yes."

"What did she want?"

"Me to come over for a swim."

"Really?" said Dad, putting down his pen. "When?"

"After soccer. I told her I was busy."

"You said no?"

"Nicely."

"You said no?"

"Yeah," said Ingrid. "No."

That jaw muscle of Dad's got all lumpy. "And why was that, if you don't mind telling me?"

"We're not friends, Dad. I didn't feel like it."

"Is that any reason to be rude?"

"I wasn't rude. I did it nicely, like I said."

"How did that go, exactly?" said Dad.

"Huh?"

Dad's tone sharpened just as Chloe's had done, impatience yearning to be free. "I'm asking what your excuse was. Wake up, Ingrid."

"My excuse?"

"For blowing her off," said Dad.

Her excuse. Yikes. The whole MathFest thing, now starting to loom up like one of those shape-changing monsters. Other people, lots of them, could tell the odd lie from time to time and move on, no problem. But whenever Ingrid told a lie, she immediately stepped onto a tightrope of lies, each one slippier than the last. Telling the truth now would lead to the whole MathFest confession, and Dad was big on math, had a thing about her staying on the calculus track all the way to Princeton, where Ferrands had gone since the Ice Age and where she and Ty were going too, no discussion. Telling a lie led into the three-ring circus.

"Um," said Ingrid, "I just said I was busy."

"Doing what?"

Doing what? How about—"Going to the mall with Stacy."

"You told her you were going to the mall with Stacy?"

"Uh-huh." On the tightrope already.

Dad's eyes shifted slightly, like he was checking a rearview mirror, a thing he did when he was having a sudden thought.

"No reason it couldn't fall through," said Dad, "a plan like that."

Ingrid didn't get that at all. It wasn't even a real plan.

She wasn't going to the mall with Stacy, so there was nothing to fall through. She studied Dad's face. He didn't look like himself: skin pale, purple smudges under his eyes, plus red veins crisscrossing the whites. And he'd missed shaving in that little cleft in his chin.

"And if it did fall through," Dad went on, "would there be any reason not to call Chloe and tell her you'd still like to come over?"

"Huh?"

Dad gave her an angry look. Ingrid didn't remember many looks like that from him. "Damn it, Ingrid," he said, "can't you simply do what I want without arguing for once?"

"You want me to go over to Chloe's?"

"I do."

"But why?"

"Because she asked you," Dad said.

Ingrid didn't understand. Through the window behind Dad's head, she saw a dark bird rise up out of the town woods and fly away.

When Dad spoke again, his voice was quiet, not angry at all, even kind of lifeless. "This isn't the time to piss off the Ferrands," he said, his gaze no longer on her but on the legal pad instead. What was going on? Ingrid had no idea. All she knew was that she didn't like seeing him like this, in fact preferred him angry.

"Okay," she said. A swim at Chloe's—how bad could it be? "But the invitation won't be good anymore. I know Chloe."

Ingrid went up to her room, called Chloe in private, making up a brand-new lie about MathFest being postponed.

"See you after soccer, then," said Chloe.

Ingrid hung up. Maybe she didn't know Chloe after all.

"Gonna give it to you in three words," said Coach Ringer.

The girls' U13 A travel team stood by their bench on soccer field one, up by the hospital. The sun was not far above the treetops, and the wind was picking up, ruffling all their ponytails. Coach Ringer, not much taller than the girls and maybe three times as wide, wore his black-and-gold Towne Hardware jacket with that slogan—SCREWS FOR YOUSE SINCE 1937—on the back and clutched an unlit cigarette between his nicotine-stained fingers.

"Have your attention?" said Coach Ringer. A few of the girls nodded. Most, including Ingrid, just stared blankly across the field. "Three words: All. The. Marbles."

Coach Ringer paused to let the three words sink in.

Now all the girls' faces were blank. *What the hell was he talking about?* Ingrid thought. All the marbles? This was just the first game of the play-offs. Marbles—Coach Ringer was losing his.

Over at midfield the ref tapped his watch. The girls from South Harrow were already in position.

"Any questions?" said Coach Ringer.

"Yeah," said Ingrid. "Where's Coach Trimble?"

Assistant Coach Trimble had played for a UConn team that went all the way to the NCAA finals. She was an amazing athlete, could probably jump right over Coach Ringer if she wanted; and the parents couldn't wait till he retired down to Florida so she could take over.

Coach Ringer shot Ingrid a quick look: not the kind of question he had in mind. "Assistant Coach Trimble's in Tokyo," he said. "Business trip. Won't be back till Christmas."

Business trip? Ingrid realized she had no idea what Coach Trimble did for a living. None of the kids had ever asked, and Coach Trimble, who didn't say much, had never mentioned it.

"What does she do?" Ingrid said.

"Some kind of foreign business," said Coach Ringer. "But in the meanwhile I got us a new helper."

He waved at a woman standing about ten yards away on the sidelines. A tall woman, although not as tall as

Coach Trimble, and strong-looking, the way Stacy was going to be when she grew up. She wore running tights, dark glasses, and a short jacket made of—hey!—fur. Really nice dark-brown fur with black streaks, like maybe mink, absolute—what was the word when something was a complete no-no? anathema?—to Mom.

The woman came over. Ingrid was just thinking there was something familiar about her when Coach Ringer said, "Listen up. This here's our temporary assistant, Julie LeCaine."

"Julia," said the woman.

Julia LeCaine, new vice president at the Ferrand Group. Up close, she looked even more striking than in the *Echo* photograph, but that might have been an effect of her shades, some new European style, the coolest Ingrid had ever seen.

Coach Ringer didn't appear to have heard the correction. "New in town," he said, "but as for soccer credentials—look out. Actual alternate on Team USA, 1999."

"1992," said Julia LeCaine.

"Personal friends with Mia Hamm, ain't that right, Ju—Ms. LeCaine?"

"We met," said Ms. LeCaine. "I wouldn't say friends."

"Anything you want to tell the team?" said Coach Ringer.

Coach Trimble always said "Play hard and play to

win," making an important distinction it had taken Ingrid two years to understand. Ms. LeCaine said, "I'll just be observing today."

"Oh, come on," said Coach Ringer, "give them a little pep talk."

Julia LeCaine took off her shades. She had green eyes, not just a browny-blue but real green. Ingrid had never seen that before. Those green eyes made a quick scan of the girls, came to rest on Ingrid. "Very well," she said, "a pep talk. How's this?" She licked her lips—her tongue was one of those very pointy ones—and said, "Whatever it takes."

There was a little silence. Then the ref blew his whistle. Something made Ingrid glance over at the stands. Dad was watching from the top row, eyes on Julia LeCaine, jaw thrust forward in an aggressive sort of way that reminded Ingrid of those stupid *Rocky* movies.

FIVE

inal score: Echo Falls 2, South Harrow 1. Should have been easier than that, but Ingrid missed a wide-open net in the first half and hit the post on a penalty kick early in the second. The girls gathered around Coach Ringer, the sun behind the trees now and purple clouds sailing fast across the darkening sky.

"Skin of our teeth," said Coach Ringer, "but—a W is a W. On two, now. One. Two."

"TEAM!"

"Practice Wednesday, four o'clock, field two, no excuses either way." Mom, who'd memorized all kinds of poems, said that poetry was language stripped of extras, plus a little magic thrown in. Coach Ringer was like that sometimes, pure poetry. He shuffled off the field in that crablike, hunched-over way of his, had a cigarette going before he reached the sideline.

Dad came out of the stands. "Nice job, girls."

"Thanks, Mr. Hill."

Ingrid walked off the field with her father.

"Pretty good game, Ingrid," he said.

"Thanks," said Ingrid. She heard that unspoken *but*. Uh-oh. Another one of Dad's postgame critiques was coming. Ingrid was starting to get tired of them.

They crossed the parking lot. Dad drove a silver TT, a very cool car, but parked next to it was an even cooler one, longer, lower, wider. A Boxster, Ty's dream car. She'd never seen one close up before.

"Got open once or twice," Dad said.

"Thanks."

"But," said Dad. She waited. "You didn't close the deal. Any idea what that's all about?"

"Nope."

"That's all you've got to say? Nope?"

Ingrid said nothing.

"Got to get your head in the game, Ingrid."

"A W is a W," she said.

Dad's voice rose. "What did you say?"

Now what? Were they really going to get into a fight about this stupid soccer game? All she wanted was to relax for a while. Why did Dad have to take sports so seriously?

"I asked you a question," Dad said.

"You heard me," Ingrid said. Oh my God. Did she really say that?

Dad was stunned. His jaw actually dropped. Then his face got red and that muscle in his jaw clumped up. At that moment, the door of the Boxster opened and Ms. LeCaine stepped out.

"Hello, Mark," she said.

Dad composed himself, his face assuming a mask of calm, but not with the kind of speed Ingrid could manage. Drama was her passion, and she practiced quick expression changes just about every time she faced the bathroom mirror.

Dad nodded. "Julia."

"I didn't realize this little speedster was your daughter," said Ms. LeCaine. "The coach was telling me all about her. Ingrid, isn't it?"

"Yeah," said Dad. "Ingrid."

"Interesting name," said Ms. LeCaine.

That was one way of putting it. Would Ingrid have gladly traded first names with any other girl in the whole school, with the exception of LaTrina Welles? Yes.

"I'm going to be helping out with the team," Ms. LeCaine said.

"So I see," said Dad.

"The least I can do," said Ms. LeCaine. "This little town is so friendly."

Dad usually drove in a casual kind of way, just one hand, or maybe no more than a couple of fingers on the wheel, but now, driving down from the soccer fields, he was using Mom's two-handed grip. He didn't speak. Was he getting ready to blast her about the you-heard-me remark? Ingrid kept her mouth shut, concentrated on the route from soccer to the Ferrands' house. If Sherlock Holmes had lived in Echo Falls, he'd have made it his business to know every inch.

Hill to Main. Main, past Nippon Garden, Ingrid's absolute favorite restaurant in Echo Falls, to Bridge. Bridge to River. North on River, the bike path running alongside, where sometimes you might see Joey out blading. But with the wind blowing so hard now, dead leaves flying all over the place, there was no one on the bike path. Except . . . one person, just coming around the bend. An unflashy blader, with a short, steady stride that chewed up a surprising amount of ground very fast—yes, Joey. The blunt Indian feather thing came into view, and then the features of his face. Joey loved blading, always by himself. What did he think about while he—

Dad spoke. "You didn't ask how I know Julia LeCaine."

Uh-oh. Totally unexpected. And un-Dad-like. That wasn't him, following a long, silent thread. It was actually more like her.

She glanced at him. His eyes were on the road. She could bring up that whole business of *The Echo* in the trash, leading right to why he threw it away before anyone had a chance to read it. Or. "Um," she said, "oh yeah. How do you know her?"

One good thing about being a kid: You could pretend to be a dunce and no one batted an eye.

Dad glanced at her. She caught the look. It said *Still got a long way to go, kiddo.* Out loud he said, "Julia's a new hire."

"Yeah?" said Ingrid.

"Probably not long-term," Dad said.

"No?"

Silence.

"You're vice president, right, Dad?"

"Right."

"Meaning you do, like, what?"

"I make the numbers work," Dad said.

"And what does Ms. LeCaine do?"

Dad took a deep breath. "Tim's looking to upgrade

long-range planning. Makes sense—stand still in business and you get trampled."

"So Ms. LeCaine's in charge of long-range planning?"

"I wouldn't say in charge," Dad said. "Not in sole charge."

Long-range planning but she wasn't going to be there long-term? Ingrid tried to make sense of that.

"How did it come about, Dad? Her getting the job."

"Princeton connection, of course. Haven't you got it in your head yet how important those things are?"

He was squeezing the wheel real tight. What was wrong with him? Ingrid didn't reply. Anything she said would probably lead to SATs, the calculus track, MathFest, Ms. Groome. She got the feeling she was way out on the tightrope already, no net.

The Ferrands owned the biggest house in Echo Falls, if you didn't count Prescott Hall, where no one lived anymore. The last of the Prescotts died off long ago, something about canoeing and getting swept over the falls, but before that one of them had married a Ferrand, which was how the Ferrands got their start in being rich. You could actually see Prescott Hall from the Ferrands' place. They stood on hilltops on opposite sides of the river, Prescott Hall a towering brick thing with turrets and gargoyles, the Ferrands' house more sprawling, made of stone and glass.

Dad drove up the long circular drive, gravel crunching under the tires. A young man pushed a wheelbarrow across a long, sloping lawn, the grass somehow still green, even in the fall. Dad stopped by the entrance, big black double doors at the top of broad stone steps.

"Call when you're ready," he said.

Ring. Ingrid would have said it out loud, but she knew he wasn't in the mood.

Dad drove off. Ingrid, bathing suit, towel, and hairbrush in a plastic bag, climbed the steps and knocked on the door.

A dark-skinned woman opened it. She wore a plain gray dress and a white apron. "Yes?" she said, the Y sounding a little like a J.

"Is Chloe here?" Ingrid said.

"Momentito," said the woman. She turned, crossed a stone-floored hall with a tall vase of purple flowers in the center, and disappeared around a corner.

An actual maid. Ingrid hadn't been in this house in years, didn't remember any maid. Mrs. Velez came to clean 99 Maple Lane once a week, but Ingrid didn't think of her as a maid. A maid was a servant.

Chloe came through the archway. If people could be

summed up in one color—Ingrid being red, for example, at least in her dreams—then Chloe was gold. She glowed from the top of her blond head to the tips of her bare tanned toes. Tanned toes? That would be Chloe, sporting a tan at a time of year when no one else did. But too uncool to comment on.

"Hello," said Chloe.

"Hi," said Ingrid. "Where'd you get the tan?"

Just popped out, uncool or not. But maybe the answer would be the Tannerama across from Blockbuster.

"Anguilla," Chloe said. "Just a weekend getaway."

Ong Willa? What the hell was that? "Oh," Ingrid said.

"Been there?" said Chloe.

Not to her knowledge, but wasn't there a suburb of Buffalo that sounded like that? She'd been to Buffalo. November tanning in Buffalo? "Nope," said Ingrid.

"Not missing much," Chloe said. "You want the truth about the Caribbean?"

"Sure."

"It's one big slum when the sun doesn't shine."

Could that be true? Ingrid had been to the Caribbean once, a Christmas vacation to an all-inclusive in Jamaica, the best week of her life, bar none. Bob Marley had been her absolute favorite ever since, and once when the piped-in music at her orthodontist, Dr. Binkerman, had played "No Woman No Cry," she'd gotten a bit teary.

"Close the door," said Chloe. "There's a chill."

They swam in the indoor pool, a big rectangular pool lined with deep-blue marble, so the water was deep-blue too, sparkling with reflected light from that amazing French chandelier hanging above. After a while, Ingrid got out, did a silly dive off the board, her legs bent and sticking out in a diamond shape. Kicking up to the surface, she was surprised to see Chloe laughing at the other end. And then even more surprised when Chloe ran out on the board and did a silly dive of her own. Pretty soon they were both doing silly dives, making huge splashes, laughing, swallowing water, choking, and laughing some more. Ingrid had vague memories of them playing like this long ago.

"Fun, huh?" Chloe said.

Ingrid didn't know whether Chloe meant doing silly dives, swimming in general, or living the life of Chloe. But whatever it was, the answer was clear. "Yeah."

They sat together by the side of the pool, feet dipped in the water. Chloe's were kind of ugly and bony, another surprise. Ingrid considered her own feet just about her best feature.

"What's the name of that little beach below the Falls?" Chloe said.

"Black Beach," said Ingrid.

"Remember swimming there when we were little?"

"Yeah." The memory sharpened in Ingrid's mind—clear water bubbling by, the falls going *shhh* not far away.

"A cool spot," said Chloe.

"Yeah."

They fell silent. Through the tall windows on the other side of the room, she could see a gravel road winding between some outbuildings toward the river, and across it Prescott Hall, silhouetted against a sunset sky. The man with the wheelbarrow stood by the side of the road, little puffs of smoke rising above his head.

"Who's that?" Ingrid said.

"Carl Kraken the third," said Chloe. "Grandson of Carl Senior, caretaker since forever."

"And son of Carl Junior?"

"You got it."

"The whole family works here?"

"Not Carl Junior. He works at the high school."

"Teaching what?" said Ingrid.

"Carl Junior teaching? That's a good one," said Chloe. "He's the janitor."

"Are you going there?"

"Where?"

"The high school," said Ingrid. "Next year."

"The high school?" said Chloe. "I'm staying at Cheshire C.D."

"What's it like?"

"Thinking of transferring?"

"We couldn't afford it."

"Really?" said Chloe.

She slid into the water, glided down. In the distance, Carl Kraken the third turned suddenly as though hearing a sound. Ingrid watched. A car appeared on the gravel road, moving toward Carl the third. Not just any car, but a dinged-up old Firebird. Too far away to read that HELL ON WHEELS bumper sticker, but Ingrid could make out the sticker itself. The Firebird stopped. Carl the third got in. The Firebird kept going, around a bend and out of sight, moving toward the river.

Ingrid turned back to the pool. Chloe was treading water, watching her.

"Do you know Sean Rubino?" Ingrid said.

"No."

"His father put in your chandelier."

Chloe didn't even glance at it. "True?" she said. "There are so many workmen in and out. I never know the names."

Ingrid gazed back at Chloe. None of her friends would ever say something like that. Did Chloe even know how snobby she sounded? Maybe it was just the simple truth—so many workers that you finally stopped noticing. It suddenly struck Ingrid that Chloe might be lonely.

"How about something to eat?" Chloe said. "I'm starving."

SIX

Something to eat turned out to be dinner in the Ferrands' formal dining room, just Ingrid and Chloe, plus the maid, who served. Ingrid had never been served before, except in a restaurant, and this was different. In a restaurant, the waiter brought the plates with the food already on them. Here the empty plates were on the table and the maid came through a door from the kitchen with the food—lobster bisque, duck à l'orange with wild rice, a mesclun salad—in bowls or serving platters, and then stood just to the left of you while you half twisted around and tried to serve yourself without messing up. Turned out the aristocratic life was harder than she'd thought.

But not without a lot of bonuses. Take the plates, blue and white, with delicate scenes of Chinese people in strange landscapes. Or the silverware, so polished and heavy. And there was a fireplace, with a crackling fire. Plus the food tasted great, better than in any restaurant Ingrid knew.

"This is good," she said, taking seconds of that rice, all buttery and nutty.

"Thank you, miss," said the maid. "I tell the cook." She offered more to Chloe. Chloe shook her head, a brusque little shake, and the maid went back to the kitchen.

How about mixing this tiny pool of orange sauce into the rice? Ingrid tried it. Not bad at all. Meanwhile Chloe was pushing bits of food around her plate, in fact hadn't eaten much. Their eyes met.

"So," said Chloe, "how's your grandfather?"

"Which one?" Ingrid said. She had two. She didn't see much of Mom's father, Grandpa Bert, a retired account- ant who lived in Florida with his girlfriend and played in several shuffleboard leagues. But then there was Grampy. Grampy lived on a farm across the river, the last farm left inside the boundaries of Echo Falls, although he didn't do any farming anymore. Grampy had had it up to here with a lot of things, including farming, and his fields now lay fallow, all the animals gone.

"The one with the farm, of course," said Chloe.

"Pretty good," Ingrid said. Last time she'd seen him, he'd been standing on a monster woodpile he'd chopped for the winter, the wind whipping at his thick white hair.

"How old is he?" Chloe asked.

"Seventy-eight."

"And he lives alone?"

"Yeah."

Chloe dabbed at the corners of her lips with her napkin; even the napkins were beautiful, thick and creamy. Ingrid had the crazy idea of stealing one. She'd never thought of stealing anything in her entire life.

"Would you say you're close to him?" Chloe said.

Ingrid, her mind still on this revelation of the depths of her own depravity, didn't follow. "Who?" she said.

Chloe's lips pinched together, which should have made her look a little less spectacular but didn't.

Oh, she meant Grampy. "I guess you could say we're close," Ingrid said. "The thing with Grampy—"

The kitchen door opened. Not the maid this time, but an old man. He wasn't a Grampy-type old man with muscles and ramrod posture. This old man was bent and creaky. He carried two birch logs.

"I bet Carl knows your grandfather," Chloe said.

Carl—had to be Carl Kraken Senior—turned to

them. He had a beaky nose, a pointy chin, big flat ears with lots of sprouting hairs.

"Carl," said Chloe, "do you know—what's your grandfather's name, Ingrid?"

She had to think for a second, she was so used to just that simple Grampy. "Aylmer Hill."

Carl Senior's eyes—beady, if that meant the size of really little beads—homed in on Ingrid and got smaller still. His hand went to his nose, which was bent to one side as well as beaky. "Nuh," he said. He tossed the logs on the fire, jabbed at them with the poker as though trying to inflict pain, then left the room.

"Guess not," said Chloe.

"Tell me about all these Carls," Ingrid said.

"What's lower—moron or cretin?" said Chloe. She dipped a finger in her water glass, stirred the ice cubes. "An actual farm inside Echo Falls," she said. Long pause.

"Yeah, the last one," said Ingrid, feeling a little proud of the fact for the first time.

"Don't you think that's weird?" Chloe said.

"How?" said Ingrid.

The ice cubes swirled around, faster and faster. "It's the twenty-first century, Ingrid," Chloe said.

"There still have to be farms," Ingrid said.

"In cities?" said Chloe.

"Echo Falls isn't a city."

"Not yet," said Chloe. "What do you think his plans are?"

"Plans?"

"For the farm," Chloe said, her tone sharpening.

"I don't know," said Ingrid. How Grampy supported himself now that he no longer worked the farm was a family mystery. One thing was sure: He didn't want anyone messing with the farm. Mom and Dad had found that out when they'd tried to get Grampy interested in building condos on the hill behind the old tractor shed. Come to think of it, wasn't the Ferrand Group part of that deal? Ingrid lifted her gaze from that ice cube whirlpool, a bit mesmerizing, and saw Chloe's eyes, the irises glinting with golden flecks, watching her, nothing friendly about that look at all. A strange physical sensation swept over her, chilling the backs of her neck and shoulders, heating up her face. Even without really understanding what was going on, she felt like a fool. This little playdate wasn't about friendship.

"Am I being nosy?" Chloe said. "I'm only trying to help."

"Help what?" said Ingrid. "How?"

"Everything changes," Chloe said. "Even this stupid town."

Ingrid didn't think Echo Falls was stupid at all.

"What do you mean?" she said. Her tone sharpened too.

The maid came in, bearing an amazing-looking dessert, a sort of pyramid of glistening round things topped with chocolate, completely unfamiliar to Ingrid. "Pro-feeta-rolls?" she said, or something like that, some foreign word Ingrid had no idea how to spell.

Chloe waved her away. "Maybe later," she said. The maid backed into the kitchen. "Let's go up to my room," Chloe said.

Ingrid didn't want to go up to Chloe's room. She wanted to go home. But—she was curious. If this wasn't about rekindling friendship, then what was the purpose, exactly?

Chloe led Ingrid up a broad curving staircase that reminded her of old black-and-white movies. From above came voices.

"Why don't you simply fire him now?" said a woman.

"Just let me handle this," a man replied. "For once."

"You handle this?" said the woman. "That defines oxymoron."

Oxymoron: there it was, the word for contradictions in terms, like giant midget. Life could be so weird some-times—for example, this quest or whatever you wanted to call it for the oxymoron definition leading to the whole MathFest disaster, and now comes this ghost answer from these bodiless voices.

A woman appeared at the top of the stairs. Ingrid hadn't seen her in years, but it was Mrs. Ferrand, no doubt about that. Mom was really pretty, Julia LeCaine was striking, but Mrs. Ferrand? She was something else, with that platinum blond hair, worn up now with a comb—a diamond-studded comb?—features like something carved by a genius ice sculptor, flawless pearly shoulders, a tight floor-length silver gown, silver shoes with diamond bows. Mr. Ferrand, in a tuxedo, came up behind her. They started down the stairs, meeting the girls about halfway.

"Have you had dinner, Chloe?" said Mrs. Ferrand.

"Yes."

"Your father and I are going out."

"Have fun," said Chloe.

"It's not that kind of evening," said Mrs. Ferrand. She glanced at Ingrid.

"You remember Ingrid?" said Mr. Ferrand.

"Certainly," said Mrs. Ferrand, showing no sign of recognition at all. She smelled incredible.

"Dinner was great," said Ingrid, holding out her hand.

"Really?" said Mrs. Ferrand. After a slight pause, she noticed Ingrid's hand sticking out there and shook it, very briefly, her own hand surprisingly hot.

"My room's this way," Chloe said.

Chloe's room was actually a suite, with a sitting room about the size of the living room at 99 Maple Lane, a sleeping area with a king-size bed up a few steps, and off that a bathroom with a gigantic shower that converted to a sauna.

"Where's Mister Bumpy?" Ingrid said.

"Mister Bumpy?"

"The teddy bear."

"Oh that," said Chloe. "Long gone."

A door from the bathroom opened onto a private deck with a hot tub, overlooking all those sloping lawns to the river. It was night now, a few lights shining in some of the Ferrands' outbuildings, Prescott Hall a dark shape across the river.

"Been to Rome?" Chloe said.

Rome. Of all the cities in the world, Rome was the one she wanted most to see. "No," said Ingrid. "You?"

"A few times," Chloe said.

"What's it like?"

"Maybe you can see for yourself," said Chloe.

"Someday," said Ingrid. She had a vague idea that in college there was something called junior year abroad.

"How does spring break sound?" said Chloe.

"Huh?"

"Still a little on the cold side, I know," said Chloe, "but you know what that means."

"What?" said Ingrid. She was getting pretty confused.

Chloe did that pinched-lip thing again. "No tourists, of course."

"Oh," said Ingrid. Tourists, uncool. But also uncool not to travel. How did that work?

The windows of the most distant outbuilding went dark. The wind came up, stirring bare branches, rattling dead leaves across the stone terrace below.

"Do you get what I'm talking about?" Chloe said.

"You're inviting me on a trip to Rome?"

"All expenses paid. In return, you've got to help your grandfather."

"How?" Grampy didn't need help from anybody; nothing was clearer than that.

"Just by explaining the situation," Chloe said.

"What's the situation?"

"Are you listening?"

Ingrid felt that chill again. "I'm listening," she said.

"One, that farm's never going to be worth more than it is right now," Chloe said. "Two, how long can this Grampy character take care of it? Three, here's his last chance to do the right thing for his family. Four, you're closest to him."

"Who told you that?" Ingrid said. In fact, how did Chloe know any of this stuff? The one two three four thing—where did that come from? Ingrid gazed up at her. Chloe was a lot taller, way better-looking, of course, a straight-A student at C.C.D., where things were a lot harder than at Ferrand Middle; plus she seemed so much older. Ingrid started getting mad. "He's not a character," she said.

"So sorry," said Chloe. "But do you get it now?"

"What's to get?" said Ingrid. "You want me to talk him into selling the farm."

A slight nod.

"So the Ferrand Group can get even richer," Ingrid said.

"Where does your father work again?" said Chloe.

Ingrid was silent.

"But it's not just for us," Chloe said. "It's for the good of the whole town."

"The good of the whole town?"

"There are plans for Echo Falls."

"What kind of plans?"

Chloe sighed. "Have you been anywhere at all, Ingrid?"

"What do you mean?"

"I don't know—New York, maybe?"

"Yeah," said Ingrid. "I've been to New York."

Twice—once with Mom to see *The Producers*, once with the whole family to do the Empire State Building/Statue of Liberty thing, but she'd been only three or four that time and didn't remember.

"Then you know that Echo Falls is a pissant little place," Chloe said.

"Not to me," said Ingrid.

Chloe sighed again. "Let's not argue," she said. "But how can it hurt for you to have a little talk, ask him to at least listen to the offer. Maybe explain the fun of retirement to Florida."

Ingrid laughed.

"What's so funny?" Chloe said.

"Grampy in Florida."

"Arizona, then. But how can it hurt?"

Headlights appeared far down the gravel road that wound by the outbuildings, came closer. When they neared the house, powerful outdoor lights flashed on, lit the car: the dinged-up Firebird. Sean Rubino was behind the wheel, his head bobbing along to whatever was playing on his sound system. The Firebird went by the house, and the outdoor lights blinked off.

"How?" said Chloe. Her voice got quiet, almost inaudible. "How, for God's sake?" Then something very surprising, almost shocking, happened. Those golden eyes filled up, overflowed. Chloe didn't make a sound;

tears ran down her face in silence.

Ingrid backed away. She didn't like the Ferrands, didn't like Chloe, didn't even like Chloe's room. But just asking Grampy to listen to the offer—she didn't see how that could hurt.

"All right," she said.

SEVEN

"Phone."

Whiz.

Thump.

Ingrid opened her eyes in time to see Ty leaving the room, wearing boxers and his Red Raider T-shirt. BIGGER, FASTER, STRONGER.

The phone lay on her pillow. She picked it up.

"Hi," she said.

"Did I wake you?" said Mia.

Ingrid cleared her throat. "Have to get up pretty damn early to do that," she said.

"A quarter to eleven early enough?" said Mia.

Ingrid glanced at the clock: 10:46. And out the window: drizzle, wind, charcoal sky. A dismal day. She remembered MathFest. Math, Monday, first period: monster looming in the very near future.

"What happened at MathFest?" she said.

"They forgot to call me," said Mia. "They didn't call Brucie either."

"Who?" said Ingrid. "What?"

"Whoever called you," said Mia.

"Huh?"

"Are you still asleep, Ingrid? Whoever called you to say MathFest was canceled."

"Canceled?" What was that line Mom sometimes quoted—"like to the lark at break of day arising"? Her heart lifted just like that. "MathFest was canceled?"

Mia got it right away. "You slept in?"

"Yup."

"What do you do to deserve this kind of luck?"

"I'm pure in word and deed," Ingrid said. "Canceled? Are you sure?"

"Postponed till next Saturday," said Mia.

Ingrid bounced out of bed. Griddie—that was her cool nickname, unused by anyone but her—Griddie the good luck queen. "How come?" she said.

"The high school was locked," Mia said. "The

janitor never showed up."

"Carl Junior?" said Ingrid. "Was that the name of the janitor?"

"I didn't stick around for the postmortem," said Mia. "I was pretty tired, what with getting up at seven on a Saturday morning for no reason."

"Poor you," said Ingrid.

Mia used a bad word.

Griddie the good luck queen went down to the kitchen. Dad, gulping coffee, was wearing his bright-green pants. That meant the Sandblasters were going out.

"How was Chloe's?" he said.

"Fine."

"What did you do?"

"Swam."

"How's Chloe doing?"

"All right."

"What did you talk about?"

"Nothing much."

"Was Tim around?"

"They were on their way out."

"Did you talk to them?"

"Just said hi."

"Where were they going?"

"I don't know, Dad." He looked like he was about to

ask another question, but before he could, Ingrid headed him off with one of her own. "You're playing golf in this weather?"

Dad's face relaxed a little. "Want to come?"

They both knew that was a joke. Playing golf made Ingrid giddy. Last visit to the club, several years ago, her conduct on the practice green resulted in a letter from the membership committee.

"You're wearing that jacket with those pants?" she said.

"Why not?" said Dad. "Red goes with green."

"You think that's red?"

But Dad was already out the door.

Ingrid popped some waffles into the toaster, mixed up a nice blend of maple syrup and melted butter for filling up those tiny waffle squares. Waffles were a brilliant invention. She whipped up some hot cocoa to go with them.

Eating happily away in the breakfast nook, light rain fogging up those lovely windows on three sides, Ingrid made a mental list of great inventions, the ones that changed the world. Waffles, for sure. Pillows. Snow days. Gift wrapping. Theater curt—

Mom walked in with a cardboard box in her hands. "Morning, Ingrid."

"Morning, Mom."

"Sleep well?"

"Yeah," said Ingrid. Mom herself looked a bit tired, those two vertical lines between her eyes pretty deep. "What's in the box?"

Mom put it on the table, sliced through the packing tape with scissors, opened the flaps. Ingrid knelt up on her chair, peered in.

"Statues," she said. "Cool."

Mom took one out—a plastic man, about a foot high, bearded and long-haired, wearing a robe. There were eleven more in the box, all the same.

"Who is he?" Ingrid said.

"St. Joseph," said Mom. "A freebie to any client who wants one."

"I don't get it," Ingrid said.

Mom smiled. She picked up St. Joseph and gave him a close look. "Some people believe if you bury St. Joseph upside down in your yard, the house sells quicker."

Wow. People were amazing. "Don't give one to the Goldbergs," Ingrid said, the Goldbergs being a new listing of Mom's in Lower Falls.

Mom laughed, tousled Ingrid's hair. "That's what you're having for breakfast?" she said. "Different forms of sugar?"

Ingrid took another St. Joseph out of the box. "What if you buried him right side up?"

Mom thought for a moment. "I guess your house would never sell."

"Can I have one?" Ingrid said.

"Why?"

"I don't know. Just to have."

Mom shrugged. "Sure. And Nigel could use a walk."

Nigel, dozing by his food bowl in the corner, didn't look like exercise was on his mind.

"He's sleeping," Ingrid said. But the words were hardly out of her mouth before Nigel suddenly lurched to his feet, eyes opening in slow motion.

"And it's miserable out there," Ingrid said.

"This is New England," Mom said.

"That makes you a New England dog," Ingrid said through gritted teeth, dragging Nigel, who'd changed his mind about the whole thing the moment he'd stepped outside, across the backyard. He didn't start self-propelling until they entered the town woods, acres and acres that stretched all the way to the river.

Ingrid let him off the leash. Twenty or thirty yards along the path, rain dripping down off bare branches overhead, Nigel paused and sniffed the air. After that he wanted to trot around in circles.

"Whatever you're doing, make it quick," Ingrid said.

He kept circling. Just ahead and slightly off the path

stood a thick oak with a kind of double trunk bearing the remains of the tree house that Ty and Ingrid had built—and Dad had rebuilt more safely—years ago. Nigel trotted over and rubbed his head against the bark.

"Any idea how you look right now?" Ingrid said.

He kept doing it, only now there was some drool.

"Evidently not."

She moved closer to the tree. When had she last been up there? Ingrid couldn't remember. The tree house had somehow just slipped away.

The footholds Dad had nailed into the trunk were still in place. Ingrid ran her hand over one. Just a scrap piece of pine or something, but it had a special feel that brought her back. The next thing she knew, she was climbing up the tree.

The entrance to the tree house was a round hole in the floor, twenty feet up. Ingrid pulled herself through. Inside was a small square room, moss growing on one of the walls, a pile of leaves in one corner, everything damp. But the two stools, red for Ingrid, blue for Ty, were still there, and so was the sign Ty had painted: THE TREE-HOUS. OWNR TY. ASISTENT INGRID. They'd played a game called Dark Forest Spies, consisting mostly of hiding out from imaginary intruders, talking in whispers, and dropping Ping-Pong balls that were actually grenades over the side when things got menacing. Their deadliest enemy was the Meany Cat. When Ty thought he heard it coming, he'd tell Ingrid to hide behind the stools and close her eyes. "I'll protect you," he'd say. After that, she'd hear him making little explosion sounds, and soon the coast would be clear.

Ingrid gazed out the window. Outside was a high-up world she'd forgotten. A gray squirrel stood motionless on a nearby branch, an acorn in its mouth. White mushrooms grew from a hole in a tree trunk. A brown oak leaf drifted by.

Ingrid turned to go, spotted something half hidden in the leaf pile. Could it be? Yes. A Ping-Pong ball. She reached for it and, as she did, felt something else under the leaves.

Ingrid brushed the leaves away, picked it up—a little plastic bottle, empty. It was the kind vitamins might come in, although the label said nothing about vitamins, at least nothing she could understand. The writing was all in Spanish, the words at the bottom reading *Fabricado en México*. The only other words she knew were halfway down: *Anabolic Steroids*. Ingrid placed the bottle back in the leaf pile, covered it up.

Back at home, she found a note on the fridge: *At the office, won't be long. Mom.*

"Ty?" she called. "Ty?"

No answer. She checked the mudroom. The Red Raider varsity jacket, with TY on one sleeve and his number 19 on the other, wasn't hanging on his hook. She was alone in the house.

Ingrid went upstairs. The door to Ty's room stood open. She went in. Chaos. She looked around, not knowing what she was looking for. Maybe just some sign that everything was all right. What she saw were clothes all over the place, four or five copies of *Sports Illustrated* scattered on the bed, lights blinking from all the electronic stuff on Ty's shelf—TV, CD player, VCR, DVD.

Something was bothering her, but what? She stepped over some damp towels, switched on the TV. ESPN. She pressed Play on the CD player. Rap. She popped open the drawer of the VCR. *Jerry McGuire*. What was wrong? Some little thing, some trifle.

What trifle was she looking for? She reached for the DVD player, popped open the— Only she didn't. The DVD player was gone.

Dust balls lay on the shelf where it had been. A cable hung unattached. That was all data. Impossible to reach conclusions unless you had enough of it, according to Holmes. She could think of one more bit of data: Sean Rubino had a new DVD player. What did Stacy say? *Some friend of his didn't want it anymore.*

Ingrid stood in her brother's room, very still, waiting

for some idea to arrive. She was still waiting when a horn honked on the street.

Ingrid peered out the window. A pickup was parked outside. A bright-red pickup, pretty old, but spotless.

Another honk, longer this time. Grampy didn't like waiting.

EIGHT

"Hi, Grampy," Ingrid said through the open window of the pickup. "No one's home."

"What does that make you?" said Grampy. "A ghost? Hop in."

"Where are we going?"

"Questions, questions," said Grampy.

"That was only one question," said Ingrid.

"What if the answer was ice cream?"

"At Moo Cow?" Moo Cow had the best ice cream in Echo Falls.

"Where else?" said Grampy.

"I'll just leave a note," Ingrid said.

* * *

They drove off in the pickup. A cold day, the clouds dark and heavy, but Grampy kept the windows open. He wasn't wearing a jacket, just a T-shirt, old corduroys held up with suspenders, and filthy work boots. The wind ruffled his hair, white as chalk but very thick. He looked pretty happy about something.

"Hey," said Ingrid.

"What?"

"Isn't Moo Cow down that way?"

"How did that happen?" said Grampy. "We'll swing by after."

"After what?"

"You'll see," said Grampy.

He crossed the bridge, the river flowing fast and black down below, and turned up Route 392 on the other side. After a while the farm appeared on the right—brown fields, bare apple trees in the orchard, and the sheds, barn, house, all painted red that might have been bright at one time.

"How old's the farm, Grampy?"

"We stole it from the Indians," Grampy said.

"Very funny," said Ingrid.

Grampy did not reply.

He parked by the barn, led her out back, where a

stack of boards and a toolbox lay waiting.

"Just hold things steady while I hammer," Grampy said.

"What are we building?" said Ingrid, holding things steady.

"A box," said Grampy, hammering. He hammered hard and fast, his arm muscles like stiff cables under his skin.

"A box for what?" said Ingrid. The look in his eye reminded her of a recent project she'd helped him with, a sort of ecological renovation down below the orchard that had involved dynamite and rare toads.

Grampy plugged a power saw into an outlet on the barn wall, started sawing. "Can't hear you with all this noise," he said.

He worked faster and faster, almost reckless, never took a single measurement, but after a very short time there stood a perfect box, about six feet square and three feet high, with a hinged door and even a roof.

"Forgot the windows," he said, changing saw blades, and zip, zip, cut out three round windows. "Know the story about Giotto?" he said.

"Who's Giotto?"

"Some painter guy trying out for a job," said Grampy. "The pope says let's see how good you are, so what does Giotto do?"

"What, Grampy?"

"Draws him a little circle," said Grampy. "But perfect."

How did Grampy know something like that? He'd never shown any interest in art. She looked at him closely. He caught the look and said, "Not this pope, of course. Earlier."

"Did he get the job, whatever his name was?" Ingrid said.

Something about her question made Grampy smile. "No idea," he said. "Ask your mom."

"My mom?"

"Head on her shoulders, your mom," said Grampy. "She's the one told me the story." He handed Ingrid a pitchfork. "Get some of that hay into the box." He picked up the tools and went into the barn.

Ingrid tossed a few forkfuls of hay through the hinged doorway. From the barn came some high-pitched squeaks. Grampy came out with a squirming pink thing in his arms.

"A pig, Grampy? You're going to have animals again?"

"Just the one piglet for now," said Grampy, stooping to shove it into the box. "Tax purposes."

The piglet poked its snout through one of the round windows, made miserable noises.

"Ugly little fella," Grampy said.

"I think he's kind of cute," said Ingrid. "What does

tax purposes mean, Grampy?"

Grampy took a Slim Jim from his pocket, peeled off the wrapper, offered it to Ingrid.

"No thanks."

He bit off a piece, held the rest out for the pig, who scarfed it up with one snort. "All on paper, the tax situation," he said, and set off toward the house, Ingrid following. The pig started whining before they were out of sight.

"Should we give him a name?" Ingrid said.

Grampy shook his head. "Only makes it harder in the end," he said.

Grampy had a great kitchen with wide-plank pine floors and a huge fireplace—big enough for roasting grown-up pigs, Ingrid recalled, which used to happen long ago. But he didn't have a fire going and it was cold. Ingrid touched a radiator.

"Is the heat on?" she said. At 99 Maple Lane, the heat went on by the middle of October; earlier if Mom had her way.

"Not till Thanksgiving," said Grampy.

He stood by the table, searching through the mail. There were piles and piles of it. Ingrid went over. Piles and piles of mail, almost all unopened, going back for weeks.

"Here we go," he said, pulling out an envelope. It had

one of those green Registered Mail stickers, meaning the mailman had stuck around for Grampy's signature. He handed her the letter.

> *Dear Mr. Hill,*
>
> *It has come to the attention of the Echo Falls Board of Assessors that your property on Route 392, town lots 103 A through T, is no longer a working farm. Accordingly, your tax category for the upcoming fiscal year has been changed from D to A. You have thirty days to appeal this ruling.*
>
> *Sincerely,*
> *Scrawled Signature*

"What does it mean?" Ingrid said.

"Means they're bloodsuckers," said Grampy. "Pure and simple."

"Who?"

"All of them," said Grampy, waving his hands. He was getting agitated, all at once seemed older. "The whole town."

"I don't understand."

He jabbed at the letter. "Farms are D. Houses are A. Get it now?"

Ingrid didn't. "Sorry, Grampy."

He looked angry for a moment; then his face softened. "Farms don't get taxed. Houses do."

"Oh."

"And the more acres you got, the more you pay. I own more acres than anybody in town."

"You do?"

"Know how much the taxes are going to be?"

"How much?"

"The earth," Grampy said.

"But it's going to be all right," Ingrid said. "You've got the pig. We'll appeal."

"Takes more than one pig," Grampy said.

He sat slowly in a chair. Mail cascaded off the table. Ingrid bent down, started picking it up. Under the table, she could see his legs. They were shaking.

Ingrid rose, began arranging the mail in neat stacks. "We'll have to get more, that's all."

Grampy nodded, but not an energetic sort of nod.

"Where should we get pigs from?" Ingrid said.

"There's places," he said, but his eyes had a faraway look and he didn't really seem to be listening. Raising pigs was going to demand a lot from Grampy. Hadn't he had it up to here with farming? Why couldn't the board of assessors have just left him alone? Maybe Chloe was right: selling the farm might be the best thing for Grampy. *How long can this Grampy character take care of it?*

She sat down beside him. "Grampy?"

He turned to her. "What is it, kid?"

"Do you think that maybe . . ." The flow of words dried up.

"Maybe what?"

She licked her lips. "Maybe it's time to sell the farm."

Energy came rushing back into Grampy's body. He seemed to get bigger and redder, and just like that he was on his feet, a neck vein throbbing. "You too?" he said.

"No, Grampy, I'm only saying that since—"

He pounded his fist on the table, Ingrid's careful stacks all tumbling back down. "Never," he said. "Is that clear?"

"Yes."

He gazed down at her. "With me or against me?"

"Me, Grampy?" There were all these questions, taxes, pigs, how long he could live here by himself. Ingrid ignored them. "With you," she said.

Grampy nodded. "Then let's roast up some marshmallows," he said.

Grampy built a roaring fire. They roasted marshmallows, Ingrid getting those perfect golden-brown crusts on the outside, Grampy burning most of his although he didn't seem to care. The house warmed up. Grampy practically went through the whole bag of marshmallows by himself, like he'd been starving.

"We'll have to get those pigs pretty soon," Ingrid said.

Grampy popped another blackened marshmallow into his mouth. "Thing with bullies," he said, "you got to punch 'em right in the nose."

"Won't just filing the appeal be enough?" Ingrid said.

The flames flickered in Grampy's eyes. "I learned about bullies when I was—how old are you again?"

"Thirteen."

"When I was even younger than you. Just a little guy back then, didn't get my strength till I was eighteen, went to Wyoming and worked on a ranch."

"You worked on a ranch?"

"But this was before, right here. Those days there were still lots of farms around, including a small one the Prescotts had right across 392."

"There were still Prescotts then?"

"Yup."

"How long was this before the accident at the falls?"

"You know about that?" said Grampy. "Four or five years, maybe. But that's not the point. The Prescotts didn't live on the farm—they had tenant farmers, the Krakens, a rotten family from way back, and the Krakens had a boy a few years older than me. Liked to play cowboys and Indians. I was the Indian." He stared at the fire for a long time. "Always ended up in their barn, somehow," said Grampy, "me with my hands tied, noose around my neck."

"A noose?"

"He was good with ropes. Noose around my neck, strung over the rafters, standing on a box. He'd threaten to kick the box out from under me 'less I spilled the beans."

"About what?"

"Where the gold was hidden, whatever it was, the game we were playing. Didn't matter what I said, he wouldn't believe it. After an hour or so, he'd get bored and untie me."

"Oh my God, Grampy. Did you tell your parents?"

Grampy shook his head. "No one can protect you," he said. "Got to protect yourself. So one time, when he untied me, it finally dawned—here I am up on the box at eye level. And I popped him a good one on the nose."

"And he ran away?"

"Ever had your nose broken?"

"God, no," said Ingrid.

"Stings," said Grampy. "Plus there was lots of blood. Naturally he put his hand right up to his face, feeling around. That's when I kicked him in the . . . in the place where sometimes you got to kick a guy. Ol' Carl never came near me after that."

"Carl?" said Ingrid.

"Still alive," said Grampy. "I keep checking the obituaries."

Ingrid took a guess. "Does he work for the Ferrands?"

Just the mention of the name changed the expression on Grampy's face. "The Krakens went over to them after the Prescotts died," he said. "Vultures of a feather."

Ingrid laughed. Then she remembered how Carl Kraken Senior had said "Nuh" when Chloe asked if he knew Grampy, and felt his bent old nose, and she stopped laughing.

"Here," he said, offering her the last marshmallow. She roasted it to perfection and gave it to him.

"My lucky day," he said. He polished off the marshmallow, tossed his stick in the fire.

"So what's the plan?" Ingrid said.

"Plan?"

"Won't we need a lawyer?"

"Lawyer?"

"To handle the appeal."

"Lawyers'll screw you six ways from Sunday."

"But—"

"No lawyers," said Grampy. "Real pigs will do the trick."

Chloe called that night. "I talked to my parents about that Rome trip. Looks good."

"Yeah?"

"Not definite yet. But possible. Depending."

Depending. There was a silence. Then Ingrid said, "I talked to my grandfather about the farm."

"And?"

"The answer's no," Ingrid said. "Never."

More silence.

Workout sounds rose from the basement.

"Three more, Ty," said Dad. "Come on. Push. Push. One more. All you got. Push! Push! YES!"

"Chloe?" Ingrid said. "Did you hear me?"

But Chloe was gone.

NINE

Tuesday, a day of the week Ingrid would just as soon have done without, but this particular Tuesday was teacher development day. Teacher development at Ferrand Middle meant that the kids got freed at noon while the teachers went to the Holiday Inn conference room near the interstate on-ramp in East Harrow to develop.

"Wanna come over?" said Stacy on the bus ride home. "My dad reprogrammed the satellite card, picks up everything."

"Etchings over at my place," said Brucie.

Stacy turned in her seat, stared at him. "You wouldn't know an etching if it punched you in the nose."

He shrank back. Stacy could break him in two. "Like Etch A Sketch?" he said.

"Zip it, guy," said Mr. Sidney from the front.

"Maybe later," Ingrid told Stacy. That punch-in-the-nose remark made her think of something.

The *Echo*'s office was on Main Street, right across from Town Hall. Ingrid leaned her bike—Univega, bright red—against the window. Gold-leaf letters on the plate glass read THE CENTRAL VALLEY'S SECOND OLDEST NEWS-PAPER, ESTABLISHED 1896—THE WHOLE TRUTH AND NOTHING BUT. Mr. Samuels, owner, editor, and publisher, was watching from his desk. Ingrid knew him from the Cracked-Up Katie case. She went inside.

The *Echo* office had its own smells—ink, wax, dust, mold. Stacks of yellowed newspapers lined the walls from floor to ceiling. Mr. Samuels sat behind a low railing, wearing his green eyeshade.

"Speak of the devil," he said in his high, scratchy voice.

"Hi, Mr. Samuels."

"I'm working on an item about you at this very moment."

"About me?"

"Not you specifically," said Mr. Samuels. He was a little guy with a long nose, lively eyes, and ink stains on his shirt even though he wore a pocket protector. "About this outrage at Ferrand Middle."

Oh my God—steroids: Was it true?

"What's so strange?" said Mr. Samuels. "You're the one gave me the tip."

"Never," said Ingrid.

Mr. Samuels peered at her from under the eyeshade. She could almost feel his mind probing around. "Are we failing to communicate here, Ingrid? I'm talking about the budget cuts that wiped out the student newspaper."

"Oh, that," said Ingrid.

"What other outrage could there be?"

"None," said Ingrid.

Mr. Samuels made a curt nod, the kind that said they were on the same page, kindred spirits. She and Mr. Samuels? At that moment, Ingrid had a very weird thought: I'll have to leave this town one day.

Mr. Samuels turned to his screen, stuck reading glasses on the end of his nose. "How's this for an opening graf?" he said. "'Question: What kind of town is too cheap even to put up the measly funding for a middle school student newspaper? Answer: Echo Falls. Yes, readers, this picture-perfect little town of ours, or so those good folks over at the Chamber of Commerce would have us believe. Very quietly—some might even say on the sly'"—Mr. Samuels glanced up at Ingrid, gave her a significant look—"'the School Committee cut *The Clarion*, voice of Ferrand Middle School, out of the budget three years ago. My question to you, school committee: What the heck were you thinking?'" He swiveled around in her direction, an aggressive look on his face, like he'd just challenged someone to a fistfight. "Well?" he said.

"Um," said Ingrid. The truth was she couldn't have cared less about *The Clarion*. Teachers always supervised student newspapers, meaning the fun got squeezed out. But Mr. Samuels didn't want to hear that, so Ingrid said, "Pretty hard-hitting, Mr. Samuels."

"They'll have to lump it," said Mr. Samuels. "I'm not changing a syllable. Some of the powers that be in this town could use a good smack upside the head."

"Does that include the board of assessors?" Ingrid said.

He took off his glasses, peered at her. "Don't tell me you've got something on them?"

"Oh, no," said Ingrid, "it's nothing like that."

"Too much to hope for," said Mr. Samuels. "Let me guess—this is about your grandfather."

"Yes."

"Now he's locking horns with the board of assessors."

"Not exactly," said Ingrid. She told him the whole story.

"So he plans to get some pigs and file an appeal?" said Mr. Samuels.

"Yes," said Ingrid. "Without a lawyer."

"Goes without saying," said Mr. Samuels. He put his hands together like a church steeple, poked his nose over the top. Ingrid assumed he was considering the lawyer question, but she was wrong. "I wonder how this got started," he said.

"How what got started?" said Ingrid.

"The whole reassessment," said Mr. Samuels.

"It's true," Ingrid said. "Grampy hasn't done any farming for years."

"Exactly," said Mr. Samuels. "Then, after all that time—boom, reassessment."

"Maybe one of the assessors happened to drive by," Ingrid said, "saw how bare everything was."

Mr. Samuels shook his head. "Doesn't work that way," he said. "Not in Echo Falls." He picked up the phone, dialed a number, covered the mouthpiece, whispered to Ingrid, "Polly Porterhouse. Just the clerk, but she runs the show."

"Porterhouse?" said Ingrid. "Any relation to the gym teacher?"

"Wife," said Mr. Samuels. He uncovered the mouthpiece. "Polly," he said, "Red Samuels, over at *The Echo*."

Red? Ingrid looked at him closely. What he had for

hair were a few wisps on his head and eyebrows, all white. Polly Porterhouse said something that made him laugh. He said something about mill rates that made her laugh. Then he started talking about farms in general and soon Grampy in particular. All of a sudden he straightened up.

"Really, Polly?" he said. "And who would that be?" He wrote something on a pad and said good-bye. Turning to Ingrid, he said, "Always a neighbor in cases like this."

"What cases?"

"Where someone gets reassessed out of the blue," said Mr. Samuels. "Some neighbor with a grudge makes a call to the board of assessors." He rotated the notepad so she could read what he'd written.

FRD Properties.

"What's that?" Ingrid said.

"Name that whoever owns those cottages across 392 from your grandfather's place hides behind," said Mr. Samuels.

"Are you talking about the old Prescott farm?" asked Ingrid. "Where the Krakens lived?"

"How'd you know a thing like that?" Mr. Samuels said.

"Grampy told me," Ingrid said. She stared at the notepad, tried to make sense of things. "Can we find out who FRD Properties is?"

"Just watch me," said Mr. Samuels.

He started tapping at the keyboard, nose inching closer and closer to the screen. "Hmm," he said. "FRD seems to be owned by DRF Development . . . registered in Delaware."

"Someone in Delaware tried to get Grampy's taxes raised?" Ingrid said.

"*Registered* in Delaware," said Mr. Samuels. "Red flag, far as I'm concerned. If they think that's going to stop me, they don't know who they're dealing with."

"Why is it a red flag?" Ingrid said.

But Mr. Samuels was typing fast now, his eyes shining with light from the screen, and didn't hear. Ingrid let herself out.

"Welcome, everybody," said Jill Monteiro at the first rehearsal for The Xmas Revue. "We're off to see the wizard."

Everyone laughed. They sat in a circle on folding chairs on the auditorium stage at Echo Falls High, five kids from Ferrand Middle and Jill. Jill was a genuine artist who'd actually performed off-Broadway and had had a brief speaking role—she'd said "Make that a double"—in *Tongue and Groove*, a home-renovation spoof with Will Smith and Eugene Levy that had gone straight to video.

"Ingrid I know," she said, her big dark eyes taking them all in, "but not the rest of you. Why don't you introduce yourselves, tell us a bit about your acting experience. Let's start with the Cowardly Lion."

"That's me," said Stacy. "Stacy Rubino. No experience. Ingrid dragged me into this."

Jill laughed, her black curls glistening under the light. "Exactly how I got my start," she said. "Kicking and screaming. Scarecrow?"

Mia raised her hand. "Mia McGreevy. Back at my old school I was in lots of plays."

"Where was this?" asked Jill.

Mia bit her lip. "New York." She and her mom had moved to Echo Falls after the divorce, but her parents still kept fighting, mostly by e-mail that sometimes got mistakenly copied to Mia.

"And what do you think of Echo Falls?" Jill said.

Ingrid knew the answer to that: Mia was bored to tears. But what Mia now said surprised her. "It's so beautiful. And the kids are great."

Jill gave Mia a smile—a strange one, Ingrid thought, almost sad. "Tin Woodman?" she said.

Joey mumbled his name, incomprehensibly.

"Missed that," said Jill.

"Joey Strade," said Joey. Jill's gaze went to that stubborn cowlick at the back of his head. "No experience," he added. Ingrid was still amazed that Joey had come out for this in the first place. All he'd told her was "Why not? It's just one little scene."

"Can you supply an ax, Joey?" Jill said.

"An ax?"

"As a prop for the woodman."

"Oh, yeah," Joey said. "We got axes."

"Ingrid's Dorothy," Jill said. "So that just leaves the wizard."

"C'est moi, amigos," said Brucie Berman.

"Our scene is the one where Dorothy and her friends meet the wizard," said Jill, handing out the scripts. Everyone leafed through.

"Hey," said Brucie. "Where's the singing?"

"No singing," said Jill. "I adapted this from the book."

"Book?" said Brucie.

"It was a book first," said Jill, "written by—"

"But what about me singing 'Over the Rainbow'?" Brucie asked.

"The wizard doesn't even sing 'Over the Rainbow,' you dweeb," said Stacy.

Brucie gave her what he must have considered a withering look. "I was going to rap it," he said.

"You know something?" said Stacy. "You're totally—"

"How would that go, Brucie?" said Jill. "Your 'Over the Rainbow' rap."

Brucie's eyes lit up. A second later he was on his feet, grunting into his fist as though it were a mike.

> *"Unh uhn where ha—*
> *ppy unnh unnh, blue blue*
> *blue birds fly unh unh*
> *unnh unnh*
> *beyon unnh da rai yayn*
> *bow wow wow why unnh*
> *can't*
> *unnh*
> *yo."*

"Wow," said Jill.

"So I can do it?" said Brucie.

"It would fit beautifully," said Jill, "in some future production."

"Huh?" said Brucie.

"But unfortunately not this one," Jill said. "First, let's talk about what the scene is actually trying—"

An alarm went off in the auditorium, loud and piercing. They glanced at one another, waited for it to stop or someone to come. No one came. It didn't stop.

Jill raised her voice. "Maybe the janitor's around."

"I'll look," Joey said.

"I'll go with you," said Ingrid. It just popped out, completely on its own. She felt eyes on her back as she and Joey left the auditorium. The alarm followed them down the hall, fainter and fainter.

"How do you like it so far?" Ingrid said.

"This play stuff?" said Joey.

"Yeah."

"I don't know," Joey said. "Do you think Dave Chappelle, Adam Sandler, all those guys were like Brucie when they were kids?"

"That's a scary thought," Ingrid said. The backs of their hands brushed as they went down to the basement.

Echo Falls High was old, much older than Ferrand Middle. The basement corridor, dimly lit, had a brick floor and damp stone walls.

"Janitor's office must be down here somewhere," Joey said. "I'll try this way."

Ingrid went the other, past a couple of locked doors and a bank of rusty lockers, the doors gone, all empty inside. Next came a half-open door, the sign on it reading CUSTODIAN: MR. KRAKEN.

Mr. Kraken? Of course, Carl Kraken Junior. She got the Carls straight in her mind. Carls one and three worked for the Ferrands. Carl Senior had done that horrible thing to Grampy, long ago; Carl the third had climbed into Sean Rubino's Firebird on the gravel road behind the Ferrands' house.

Ingrid glanced in. A man sat behind a desk. He looked a lot like Carl Senior, beaky nose (although his was straight) and pointy chin, but was younger and bigger, with thinning brown hair arranged in a comb-over. Carl Junior, for sure. The office was a mess, but a few details stood out: a cigarette burning in an ashtray, a glass of some light-brown liquid on the desk, the wad of bills Carl Junior was counting.

Ingrid drew back out of sight, knocked on the door.

"Huh?" said Carl Junior. "Who's there?"

Ingrid stepped into view. Cigarette, drink, money—all gone.

"What the hell are you doing here?" he said. "School's closed."

"We—we're rehearsing in the auditorium."

"For Chrissake," he said, rising. He was very tall, with long arms and huge bony hands. "No one tells me nothin'."

From behind Ingrid, Joey said, "The alarm went on. We need it turned off."

Carl Junior gazed at him. "Do I know you?" he said.

"Joey Strade," said Joey.

"Chief's son?"

"Yeah."

Carl Junior went over to a panel on the wall. "Goddamn building's falling apart." He flicked a circuit breaker. "Alarm off," he said. "Happy now?"

"Thanks," said Joey.

"Yeah," said Ingrid, "thanks." Hers was meant for Joey.

TEN

ngrid lay on her bed, reading from *The Complete Sherlock Holmes*. "The Adventure of the Copper Beeches," one of her favorites. She was deep in the story, totally swallowed up as usual, when she came to Holmes saying this: "I have frequently gained my first real insight into the character of parents by studying their children."

It stopped her, threw her out of the story, like off a horse. She thought of Chloe and her parents, the Rubinos, the three Carls. And what about her own family? What would Holmes say if he—

"Hey." Ty stuck his head in the door.

"What's up?" Ingrid said.

"Need a spotter."

"Where's Dad?"

"Went back to the office."

"How about taking the day off?"

"Day off? Next game's West Hill."

Ingrid got up with a sigh. If the Red Raiders went down to defeat, it wasn't going to be on her.

Ty loaded plates on the bar: one eighty-five. Ingrid took her place, watched the bar go down to his chest, back up. Three sets of ten, clank clank, no breakdown in form, no help needed getting the bar back on the cradle. He added the two tens, just like last time. Except now Ingrid said nothing—this was one of those controlled experiments.

Ty lay down on the bench. He wriggled his feet around, wriggled his body, got his hands on the bar, went still. She looked into his eyes. He didn't even see her. His concentration filled the room. He took a deep breath, lifted the bar out of the cradle, let it down to his chest, breathed out. And then raised the bar. Got it right up there, lowered it, raised it again, form still good. Breathed in, lowered it, breathed out, lifted. Now his arms started to shake, form breaking down, but when Ingrid made a little movement forward, he barked, "No!" And got it up into the cradle, three successful lifts at two-oh-five, unlike last time, and no help necessary. No human help.

Ty lay there, breathing heavily, chest rising and falling, face flushed, partly with effort, partly with pride.

"We need to talk," Ingrid said.

He sat up, wiped his face with a towel. "'Bout what?" he said. "See that? I did two-oh-five."

"Yeah," said Ingrid. "I saw." No human help. Ingrid began to understand what this was all about. It wasn't the acne, the tantrums, the liver damage, the cancer, all Mr. Porterhouse's mumbling stuff in health class. Bad, yes. But the worst thing was the nagging wonder: Who was lifting the weight, winning the race, scoring the touch-down, getting the glory—you or some supernerd in a chemistry lab? And if it was the supernerd, why bother playing the games at all?

"Why're you looking at me like that?" Ty said.

"I know you like football."

"Duh."

"But you wouldn't do anything stupid, would you?"

"What the hell are you talking about?"

"For example," said Ingrid, "where's your DVD player?"

"Huh?" said Ty. But as he said it, his eyes shifted as though he were checking his rearview mirror, just like Dad.

"The DVD player that's normally on the shelf in your room," Ingrid said.

"What's your point?"

"It's not there."

"It's not?"

"You didn't know?" she said.

They looked at each other. Her own brother, who she'd known all her life, and she had no idea what he would say next. Was it possible he really didn't know, that maybe Sean had stolen the DVD player and she had mis-read everything?

"Oh yeah," said Ty. "I lent it to someone."

"Like who?"

Ty's chin tilted up and his eyes narrowed. "What's it to you?"

"Just tell me."

Ty got up off the bench. He'd always been bigger than she was, but the difference had never been like this.

"You're a pain," he said.

"Why is it a big secret?"

Ty came very close. He'd pushed her around once or twice in the past, but weren't they beyond that now? Ingrid stood her ground.

Ty took a deep breath. "I can't believe I'm related to you," he said. "You're the nosiest person I ever met."

"That's not a crime," Ingrid said. A good word to fall silent on. It hung there between them. Ty's eyes did that rearview mirror shift again.

"No goddamn business of yours," he said. "But I lent the stupid thing to Sean."

"Sean Rubino?"

"Yeah. Sean Rubino. I can get it back anytime I want."

"Why'd you lend it to him?"

"Ever heard of being friendly?"

"You're not friends with Sean Rubino."

His voice rose. "Now you're telling me who my friends are?"

"He's a loser."

"Takes one to know one."

"You're a moron."

"Get out of my way."

"No."

He pushed her out of the way, so easily, headed for the stairs. The lights shone on his bare back. He was a liar.

"Look at those zits on your back," she said. "What's going on?"

He whirled around and mimicked her. "Look at those braces on your teeth."

She ignored him. "I won't tell anyone."

"There's nothing to tell." Ty yanked on his shirt. "Know your problem?"

"My problem?"

ABRAHAMSPETER ABRAHAMS

"Yeah, yours, you stuck-up little bitch. Ever since that whole Cracked-Up Katie thing you've been living in a fantasy world."

Her face got red-hot. "That's not true."

He smirked at her, a look she'd never seen on his face before, although she had on Sean Rubino's. Then he turned and went up the stairs.

"THAT'S NOT TRUE!"

Ingrid awoke in the night, a sudden awakening as though some loud noise had startled her. She listened, heard nothing but rain on the roof and Nigel softly snoring. Was it possible she'd got it wrong? Zits on the back might be just zits on the back. Maybe weight lifting alone could make you strong quickly if you happened to hit a growth spurt or something. Maybe Ty actually thought Sean was cool, or maybe it was simply that he was older and had his own car. That didn't explain the $1,649 in Sean's drawer. Couldn't there be lots of explanations for that, mostly bad but not necessarily rubbing off on Ty? And therefore all the rest of it, all that connecting the dots, might be her imagination and nothing more. And if so, could it be that Ty was right and she was living in a fantasy world?

She sat up. Was it true? Was that her? If it was, she'd

have to change her whole personality. Could that even be done?

The rain fell on the roof, not as hard as drumming, not as soft as pitter-pattering. Her imagination and nothing more. Except. Except what? Something was bothering her.

Ingrid got up, started getting dressed. She was lacing up her shoes when she remembered: the medicine bottle from Mexico, up in the tree house. All that Spanish writing on the back, and the only words she'd understood— *anabolic steroids*—halfway down. But what about that Spanish writing? Did it say, "Do not mix with anabolic steroids," or "Sale and consumption of anabolic steroids are illegal" or some other innocent thing?

"Stay," she said to Nigel, very softly. He whimpered once but slept on. Ingrid went down the hall. Ty's door was closed and so was Mom and Dad's. The house was quiet and dark, no lights on. Ingrid didn't need them, could have gone anywhere in the house with her eyes shut. She went to the kitchen for the flashlight kept in the drawer by the sink, then continued down to the basement, where she opened the slider and stepped outside.

Cold rain fell invisibly from a sky the color of charcoal. Ingrid crossed the lawn, entered the town woods. The trees were a little darker than charcoal, the path darker than that. She turned off the path, came to the huge dark form of the oak with the double trunk, felt for Dad's footholds.

Flashlight between her teeth, Ingrid climbed to the tree house, pulled herself through. She switched on the flashlight, shone it on the leaf pile in the corner. Only there was no leaf pile in the corner. It was swept clean.

She panned the light around, saw the two stools, red for Ingrid, blue for Ty; and the sign: THE TREEHOUS. OWNR TY. ASISTENT INGRID. Even the Ping-Pong ball was still there, lying against the wall, in case of any surviving Meany Cats. But that Fabricado en México bottle was gone. Ingrid got down on her hands and knees, covered every inch. Gone.

She switched off the flashlight, gazed out the window. The woods spread out in the distance, dark and spiky.

Back in the mudroom, Ty's sneakers were wet.

"I'll protect you," he'd said. Only a game, yes, and even then Ingrid had been ninety-nine percent sure that Meany Cats didn't exist, but still, she'd felt safe.

"I hate when the days get so short," Stacy said. The next day, in Stacy's bedroom after school, homework scattered all over the place.

"What's the Continental Congress?" Ingrid said.

"Is that the tea thing?" said Stacy.

"This packet is huge," Ingrid said.

Shadows were already falling outside.

"This country has way too much history," Stacy said. "If we lived in 1770, we wouldn't have to study the Continental Congress."

"How about 1491?" Ingrid said. "No history homework at all." She closed her packet.

"Did any women go with Columbus?" Stacy said.

"I don't know," Ingrid said. "There were women pirates."

"Yeah?"

"Bonnie somebody."

"Cool." Darker and darker outside, real fast, like someone was turning a dial. "My mom made brownies," Stacy said.

"Those almond ones?"

"Yeah."

"Sounds good."

"I'll get them."

Stacy left the room, went downstairs. The Rubinos' house was quiet, Mr. and Mrs. Rubino at work, Sean God knows where.

Sean, one of those dots, possibly unconnected.

The next thing Ingrid knew, she was down the hall, slipping into Sean's room, quick and silent. No defense for this, the kind of invasion of privacy she would have hated if it had happened to her. But she couldn't stop herself, didn't even really try. Ingrid had to know what was fantasy, what was real.

Sean's room: squalor as before, maybe worse. Plus those bare walls with bits of masking tape where posters had once hung. For some reason that bothered her. She stepped over a pile of dirty clothes and opened the bottom drawer of Sean's desk. Still crammed—wrinkled homework, car magazines, and down at the bottom, the baseball glove. She took it out, opened it. Nothing inside. The $1,649—gone.

Ingrid replaced the glove, closed the drawer, straightened. Her gaze fell on Sean's TV. Something else wrong—Ty's DVD player was gone.

Reality or fantasy? You needed data, Holmes said, but what if the data kept disappearing before you could fit things together? Had Holmes ever—

Sean walked into the room eating a brownie, his hair gelled up in spikes.

"Hey," he said. "What are you doing here?"

Ingrid's heart started beating fast, like she'd been caught doing something terrible; which was kind of true.

"Um," she said.

The expression on Sean's face was in transition from puzzlement to something nastier. Ingrid glanced around, hoping for an idea and quick.

"I was looking for a book."

"A book?"

There didn't seem to be a single one in evidence.

"About—" The name, please. It came to her, thank God. "The Continental Congress."

"What the hell's that?" Sean said.

"This history thing. Sorry. Didn't know you were home."

"I wasn't," he said. The expression on his face was changing again, maybe getting ready to settle on mild annoyance when another kid—no, a man—walked in, three brownies in his hand. He saw Ingrid.

"Who's this?" he said.

"Just a friend of my sister's," said Sean.

The man looked down at her. In his twenties prob-ably, not particularly tall, not as tall as Sean, for example, but he did have that beaky nose. Plus long stringy hair and eyes a little too close together. If Ingrid had seen him before, it had been from a distance. She had to be sure.

"Hi," she said, sticking out her hand. "Ingrid Levin-Hill."

He gazed at her hand as if he'd never done this before. Then he remembered his manners and shook it, grinding a few brownie crumbs into her palm. Also he forgot to say his name.

"And you are?" Ingrid said.

"Carl," he said. "Carl Kraken."

Carl the third, assistant caretaker at the Ferrands'. He let go of her hand, then did something that no one had ever done before to Ingrid, something that made her feel weird. He looked her up and down, real fast, but she caught it. What had Grampy said about the Krakens? *A rotten family from way back.*

"Ingrid," Stacy called from downstairs. "Your mom's here."

Mom drove her home.

"Something wrong, Ingrid?"

"Nope."

She went up to her room, peeking into Ty's on the way by. His DVD player was back on the shelf. Like nothing was wrong.

ELEVEN

ngrid awoke in the night. She wasn't used to all this waking in the night, had always been a good sleeper, dreaming the nights away in her seaworthy little boat.

Voices came from down the hall. Mom and Dad. Dad said something that ended with "Chicago." Mom said, "What about the kids?" followed by fainter words, but Ingrid's hearing was sharp: "Their roots are here."

Dad's voice rose. "Means nothing without a job," he said. "They're squeezing me out."

"Maybe you're blowing it out of proportion," Mom said.

His voice rose some more. "That's you, every time—no help."

"I'm trying," Mom said. A long pause. "There may be an offer on Blueberry Lane."

"Whoopee."

After that came Dad's footsteps, into the hall, downstairs. Then silence.

Ingrid felt around for Mister Happy, found him in his usual place, jammed against the wall. She held him close. Beside her, Nigel sniffed the air. He was awake too.

"Have you been wearing the appliance?" asked Dr. Binkerman. He loomed up close like a figure in a nightmare, but Ingrid, although tired from her restless night, was wide awake. If, in some universe gone totally crazy, she ended up as an orthodontist, wouldn't she make sure she didn't have long nose hairs poking out her nostrils? Damn sure.

"The appliance?" Ingrid said. She was supposed to wear the appliance, a Spanish Inquisition kind of device, every night to make her teeth unjumble faster. *"Sí, señor."*

Dr. Binkerman got a funny look in his eye. "What was that?"

"Yes to the appliance," Ingrid said. Not a lie: She *had* worn it since her last visit, three or even four times.

"Doing your best?" said Dr. Binkerman.

"Yes." True as well, especially if he'd known how

crowded it could get in her bed—Nigel, Mister Happy, appliance, Ingrid. She was doing her best under the circumstances, which is what he'd meant to say.

"Keep it up," said Dr. Binkerman.

Mom paid on the way out.

They drove to soccer practice. Warm in the MPV—Mom had the heat way up, as usual—but cold outside, with a line of low clouds scudding across the silvery-blue sky.

"How much do these appointments cost?" Ingrid said.

"There's a contract for the whole treatment," Mom said. "We pay in installments."

"How much is the whole thing?"

"I forget the exact figure," Mom said. "It's reasonable."

"What's reasonable mean?"

"A lot less than if we lived in a big city somewhere."

Chicago. Big city, essence of.

Ingrid pulled down the visor, flipped open the mirror, bared her teeth. "This is good enough," she said.

"What is?"

"My teeth."

"Don't start, Ingrid."

"Start?"

"We've been through this a million times," Mom said. "The braces come off when Dr. Binkerman says so."

"God almighty," Ingrid said. She snapped the mirror shut.

"What's your problem?" Mom said.

The answer: It was about saving money, not getting the braces off. But Ingrid, pissed now, let her glare do the talking.

They drove up hospital hill in silence. Ingrid got off at soccer field one, closing the door harder than she had to. Eyes on the girls over by the bench, gathering around Coach Ringer, she didn't really notice the Boxster until Julia LeCaine stepped out.

"Hello, Ingrid," she said, adjusting the whistle around her neck. "That your mom?" The MPV turned out of the parking lot, headed back down the hill.

"Yeah."

A little smile flickered across Julia LeCaine's face, like maybe she'd caught Ingrid's temperamental exit. "Haven't met her yet," said Julia, "but I hear she's very nice." They walked across the field. "Has your father mentioned we work together?"

"Yeah."

"I hear you and Chloe are friends."

"We—I've known her for a long time."

That little smile came to life again; Ingrid had never seen one quite like it. It almost made her believe there was a third party to the conversation, smarter than the others.

"Maybe we can get together sometime," Julia said.

"Get together?"

"You, Chloe, and I," said Julia. "Lunch in West Hartford, say. There's supposed to be a halfway acceptable oyster place."

"Well—"

"Or a trip to the mall—maybe that would be more your style."

"Uh, thanks."

Julia's cell phone rang. "Yes?" she said.

Ingrid recognized the voice on the other end—Dad. After ten or fifteen seconds, Julia interrupted him.

"I thought we agreed on three and a quarter," she said.

Dad started saying something. Julia cut him off again.

"Three eighths?" she said. "You can't be serious."

Dad was silent. Julia clicked off, glanced down at Ingrid. Julia was vice president of long-range planning. Dad was vice president of making the numbers work. But they'd been arguing about numbers and Julia had won. So what did that mean? Ingrid tried to make her face a blank, but did it wear that defiant look she saw on Ty's from time to time? Probably. Julia smiled her little smile.

"Gonna work on shooting today," said Coach Ringer. "Our shooting's been pis—been not too good. You don't put the ball in the net, you don't score." He paused to let that sink in. Rain began to fall, light but icy. "Guarantee you one thing, ladies—don't score, you won't win." He let that sink in too. We could still tie, Ingrid thought. Lots of times she might have said it out loud. Today she wasn't in the mood.

"I know a good shooting drill," Julia said.

"We already got one," said Coach Ringer. "All right, ladies, shooting drill, hustle up."

Ingrid, running to her shooting drill position, happened to see Julia's face. It had gone white.

In shooting drill, the two goalies defended one goal at the same time and everyone else took turns blasting away, supposedly from the top of the box but soon the taking turns part got messed up and balls flew from all over the place. Coach Ringer stood by one of the posts and yelled mysterious instructions, like, "Eyes, eyes, for Chrissake," or "vicy-versy, vicy-versy." Ingrid's mood improved. She didn't know whether Coach Ringer's shooting drill actually helped, but it sure was fun.

"Hey, Coach LeCaine," Coach Ringer called. "Mind sending those balls back in?"

A few balls had rolled out near midfield. Julia trotted after them. She moved well, not gliding along effortlessly like Coach Trimble, but powerful. Ingrid drove the last ball in her area toward the top right corner of the net, missed by a mile.

"Come on now, funny feet," said Coach Ringer. "How many times I got to tell you?"

Ingrid turned to midfield, waiting for the balls to come in. He could tell her funny feet till the end of time and she still wouldn't have a clue what he meant.

Julia kicked the balls in, long high kicks that carried and carried. Ingrid jumped up, settled the first one off her chest. The second ball sailed over her head and into the net on one bounce. And the last ball: the boom of Julia's kick was louder than any Ingrid had heard on a soccer field. Ingrid watched its flight, a thing of beauty, not high, but whizzing through the air on a line, an actual whiz you could hear, a gray blur headed right for the far post, where—

Oh my God. Where at that moment Coach Ringer was huddled sideways against the wind, lighting a cigarette.

"Coach!" Ingrid shouted.

But too late. The ball struck him right on the ear with a sickening whack. His head banged against the post, making another sickening sound, metallic this time. Coach Ringer slumped to the ground and lay still.

For a moment, everyone froze. Then some of the girls dropped to one knee, which is what they'd been taught to do for injuries on the soccer field. A few of them, including Ingrid, moved toward Coach Ringer, but not running, more confused. The only one running was Julia LeCaine. She blew by all the girls, knelt over Coach Ringer.

"What happened here?" she asked.

"Did a ball hit him?" said one girl.

"I think it was me," said another. She started crying. "I kicked it."

"Calm down," Julia said. "It was an accident. And in all that chaos, there's no way of knowing who did what." She flipped open her cell phone and called 911.

The girls crept closer. Coach Ringer lay on his back, eyes closed, his Towne Hardware jacket riding up and his flabby white belly sticking out, rising and falling.

"He's breathing, obviously," said Julia.

Ingrid came forward, tugged down the hem of the jacket.

Julia's eyes darted toward her, too quick to read. "Give him some room, please, Ingrid," Julia said. She rose, squishing out Coach Ringer's cigarette butt with the ball of her foot.

An ambulance came rolling onto the field in less than a minute, lights flashing. As the EMTs raised Coach Ringer on a stretcher, his eyelids fluttered open. "Shoot the frickin' ball," he said. They got him inside the ambulance and drove off to the hospital, only a few hundred yards down the hill.

Julia checked her watch. "The field is ours till five fif-teen, I believe?" she said. "Let's try another shooting drill, slightly more organized."

The parents—except for Ingrid's, who were often late—came at five fifteen. Lots of buzzing conversations started up. Julia raised her hand for silence. "He was conscious when they took him away," she said. "I'm sure he'll be all right. See you on Saturday."

Everyone drove off. Ingrid sat on the bench, waiting. Mom and Dad had busy lives. The sky darkened, the wind picked up, the rain fell harder. After a while, she took off down the road; only one way up, so there was no chance of Mom or Dad missing her.

Ingrid came to the turn-off to the hospital, stopped. Still no Mom or Dad. The emergency entrance, an ambulance parked in front, was just a few steps away. A moment or two later, pretty much without thinking, Ingrid was in the emergency waiting room.

No one there but a nurse at her station, writing on a clipboard. She looked up: Mrs. Rubino.

"Ingrid."

"Hi, Mrs. Rubino. Is Coach Ringer okay?"

"They took him up to the ward," said Mrs. Rubino. She put down the clipboard. "Tell you what—I'll go take a peek, be right back."

"Thanks."

Mrs. Rubino went through a door marked INPATIENT. Ingrid sat by the window, picked up a magazine. Usually she could lose herself in just about any written material, but now she couldn't get past the first few words. Could it have been on purpose? Was anyone that good with a soccer ball? Was Julia LeCaine really unaware of whose ball had actually done the damage? And was she, Ingrid, one hundred percent sure about that herself? Those questions were twisting around in her mind when Carl Kraken the third came in from the street entrance.

He glanced at the empty nurse's station, crossed the room, and went through a door marked AUTHORIZED PERSONNEL ONLY. Ingrid rose. That was kind of strange, since Carl the third worked for the Ferrands, not the hospital. Ingrid walked over to the AUTHORIZED PERSONNEL ONLY door and opened it, just to see what was on the other side.

A long corridor, harsh white lighting, no one in sight. Ingrid looked back into the emergency waiting room. No one there either. She stepped into the corridor. The door closed behind her with a compressed-air hiss.

Ingrid moved down the corridor. Just to see. She passed an empty lounge, came to a door marked STOR-AGE, open an inch or two. She listened, heard nothing, gave the door a little push. A little tiny push, but for some reason it swung wide open, and with a bang.

The noise startled the two men in the room. One, dressed in green scrubs, dropped a bottle that smashed on the floor, spilling green pills all over the place. The other one, Carl the third, whirled toward her and said, "What the hell?"

"Oops," Ingrid said. "I must be lost."

"What you lookin' for?" asked the man in green scrubs. He had a gold tooth, first time Ingrid had seen one outside the movies.

"The ward," said Ingrid, reading his name tag: Rey Vasquez, Orderly.

"This ain't it," he said, pointing the way she'd come.

"Thanks," said Ingrid, backing out, but as she did, Carl the third's eyes narrowed with recognition and his mouth opened. Ingrid walked quickly down the corridor, through the door, into the emergency waiting room.

Mrs. Rubino came in a second later. "He's resting comfortably," she said.

"So he's all right?" Ingrid said.

"Guess what he said to me."

"What?"

"He wants Stacy back on the team."

"Wow," said Ingrid. Stacy was a great player, but she'd

gotten into a battle of wills with Coach Ringer and ended up on the Bs. "The ball must have knocked some sense into him."

Mrs. Rubino laughed. She had a loud laugh, kind of tough sounding. "Too bad about the skull fracture," she said.

"Skull fracture?"

"Very slight," said Mrs. Rubino. "No surgery necessary. He'll just have to take it easy for a while."

TWELVE

Sometime late Friday night or early Saturday morning, Ingrid dreamed of St. Joseph. At first he was just the white plastic real estate freebie, long-haired, vacant-eyed, expressionless. Then a bunch of dead leaves blew by and St. Joseph's eyes slowly opened. He looked right at her. "If the numbers don't work, we'll have to make a noose," he said. Right after that, she was soaring through a blue sky, high above the treetops.

When she awoke, her room was filled with milky light, the dream gone, totally forgotten except for the dead leaves part and a vague sense of unease. Ingrid glanced at the clock. Five minutes after eight. Ridiculously early on a Saturday morning, just about a sin to be up. She closed her eyes, tried to drift back down into foggy sleep. But the uneasy feeling stayed with her, got all mixed up with the word *sin*, started to grow. And then it hit her—MathFest. She'd forgotten it again.

MathFest! Oh my God. She sprang out of bed. What time was MathFest? 8:30. And the clock now read 8:08. That left her—what? For a moment, Ingrid couldn't do this simple subtraction. Irony, essence of.

She ran down the hall, throwing off pajamas, pulling on clothes. It came to her: twenty-two minutes. "Mom!"

No answer.

"Mom! Dad!"

Silence.

She zoomed down the stairs, practically airborne. Nigel, lying by the front door, got one eye open.

"Hey, where is everybody?"

A note on the kitchen table explained.

> *Morning, Ingrid. Hope you had a good*
> *sleep. Dad's out with the Sandblasters,*
> *I'm taking a course on the new software*
> *in Hartford and Ty slept over at Greg's.*
> *I'll be back in time to take you to your*
> *game.*
>
> > *Love, Mom*
>
> *PS—Nigel could use a walk.*

Ingrid came close to pounding her fist on the table. MathFest was trying to kill her. She ran to the mudroom, grabbed her jacket, ran upstairs—pencils and Scotch tape, ran back down. Scotch tape? She tossed it away, somehow losing her grip on the pencils too.

The high school. What was the route? Mom went right by it on her way to work. Left on Avondale, right on High—

The phone rang. She snatched it up.

"Hi kid," said Grampy. "Good news—just the threat of pigs was enough to make them back off."

"Great, Grampy." Should she ask him for a ride? 8:12, and the farm was twenty minutes away, maybe more. "I'll call you later—I've got MathFest."

"Is it a school day?" said Grampy, or something like that; she was already hanging up.

—right on High, past Nippon Garden—and then what? And how far was it, how long would it take on her bike?

Those questions bubbled in her mind. Clock on the kitchen wall: 8:13. Oh my God. Jacket half on, half off, Ingrid raced through the kitchen door into the garage. Two plus fifteen minutes, seventeen, whatever. Breakneck speed was the only answer.

Ninety-nine Maple Lane was one of the oldest houses on the street, but when Dad got promoted to vice president they'd renovated the whole thing except for the garage. It was dusty, shadowy, cluttered with all sorts of junk.

Plus fresh spiderwebs every morning. Ingrid stepped around one, kind of beautiful, shimmering as though in a slight breeze, as she crossed to her bike, leaning against the far wall.

Breakneck speed. That was her last coherent thought. Then came a jumble—the scrape of a hard heel on the cement floor behind her, cold hand wrapping over her face, the smell of something like swimming pools, but much stronger.

Ingrid returned to a horrible world. It was almost no world at all, completely black. Was that because her eyes were closed? She tried to open them, could not. Something held them shut. Fear bloomed inside her like some awful flower taking over. She tried to scream but couldn't even open her mouth. Something held it shut too. Everything taped up. She couldn't breathe. No air, no air at all. Ingrid thrashed around. She was going to die. Die? She was thirteen years old. *Please don't let me die.*

After seconds, minutes, she didn't know, Ingrid realized she was still breathing, breathing through her uncovered nose. She took a deep, deep breath, then another, calmed herself slightly.

Could she move? Yes, because she'd thrashed around: that proved it. Ingrid shifted a little, hit her head on something hard. Her arms? Held tight together at the wrists, bound in front of her. Her feet? Free. She felt around, panicky quick, discovered she was in some small space. The only sound was rumble rumble, the only feelings the awful flower growing inside her, plus motion. Memory bits came back—MathFest, garage, a cold hand over her face.

She was in the trunk of a car.

That realization, bad as it was, settled her down a little, connected to things she'd learned. Like you were never supposed to get in the car of a stranger, not ever. Nothing good happens after you do that, so avoid at all costs. And if you were already in the car, locked in the trunk? No one had taken it that far, but the answer was obvious: You had to get out.

Or else you were going to die.

She breathed. The car rumbled. Now she could also hear the whine of rubber on the road. Plus music. Music? She even recognized the tune, one of those stupid oldies, "I Guess That's Why They Call It the Blues." Whoever was driving, whoever had done this, had the nerve to listen to music at the same time. A little piece of her fear chipped off and turned to hate.

Pop the trunk. That was the expression. People said it

all the time. You could pop the trunk with the key from the outside, or with some gizmo up front, near the driver. She didn't have the key, wasn't outside. Neither was she up front with the gizmo. But the gizmo must unlock the lock from inside the trunk, and she was inside. Eyes taped, mouth taped, hands taped, but inside with that locking mechanism.

Ingrid rolled onto her stomach, bound arms stretched out in front of her, and felt around with her fingertips. She touched one of the interior walls. But which? She ran her fingertips along it, some carpety material, and then—what was that? Hard rubber. Hard rubber with grooves—the spare tire. Where would that be? Usually at one side, right? So this next interior wall—she twisted around—would be either the front or the back. If it was the back, and she kept running her fingertips over it, halfway along she'd encounter—

The locking mechanism.

Was this it? A square plastic-feeling thing, sticking out a little bit? That was all? How could that unlock anything? She got up on her knees and elbows, tried pushing and pulling at the square plastic thing with her fingertips. Nothing happened. The panicky flower started sprouting inside her again.

Please don't let me die.

Ingrid tore wildly at that plastic thing. And all at

once, by accident, she got a fingernail under one of its corners and it snapped off.

What was underneath? Ingrid explored with her fingertips, trying to slow down and understand everything they were telling her, fit the details together. Details like this little hooked thing; and a long horizontal rod that felt like coat-hanger wire. Yes, a locking mechanism. Ingrid had seen one like it on Grampy's shed. Maybe if she tugged on the rod like so, the little hooked thing might—

Pop. The trunk sprang open.

Still total darkness, but now she felt the rush of cold fresh air on her skin. Ingrid knelt blindly in the open trunk. Was she in traffic somewhere? If so, someone would see her right away and start honking or calling the police. But she heard no other cars. Was this some lonely road? How long before the driver noticed the trunk lid bobbing up and down—or heard that squeak of hinges? And then?

She would die, no question.

Ingrid knelt in the open trunk, facing the inevitable choice. She thought of Jamaica, that all-inclusive vacation, the best week of her life. They had a cliff where you could jump into this cool blue lagoon. She and Dad went up. It was so high, the lagoon far far down there, but other people were jumping off, everyone screaming all the way.

The car leaned to her left, slowed down a little, then some more, like it was going around a sharp curve.

Dad said: "The longer we stand here, the harder it gets," and holding hands, they'd jumped off, screaming like all the others.

Ingrid got her feet under her. She rose, standing straight up in the trunk. The longer she stood, the harder it would get.

She leaped. Not a Jamaican-style screaming leap, impossible because her mouth was taped. She just jumped out of the trunk, silent and blind.

Then came a moment, a long, long moment, of free fall, so long she had time to think: *Am I dead already?*

She hit the ground, left shoulder first, but not hard. Soft, grassy ground, and slanting. Ingrid rolled and rolled, down, down, and finally came to a stop. She lay on her back, listened, heard nothing—no squeal of brakes, no shouts, no quick footsteps. The only sound was her own panting. Panting? It took her a moment to realize the tape over her mouth was gone.

Ingrid sat up. Any pain? None at all. She raised her taped wrists to her mouth. Ingrid's teeth might have been a hideous mess from Dr. Binkerman's point of view, but they were sharp. She bit and sawed at the tape with her teeth. Rip, rip. A split opened up, freeing her hands a little. She tried to pull them apart, at the same time working even harder with her teeth. Rip, rip, rip—and suddenly her hands were free. A moment later, she'd yanked the tape from her eyes. Free!

Free, alive, unhurt. She was sitting in a gully: gray sky overhead, woods on one side, a steep hill on the other, torn-up duct tape at her feet. She must have rolled down that hill. That meant the road was up there, and the driver might have pulled over already, might have gotten out of the car and sprinted around to look in the empty trunk, might appear at the crest of the hill any second.

Ingrid rose. She had to get out of this gully, and fast, and going back up that hill was out. The only other way was into the woods. Ingrid walked into the woods, looking back once at the steep hill. No one there. She hurried on.

Dead leaves covered the ground, brown and damp, silent under her feet. Ingrid went up a rise, down another, glanced back once more. Now there was nothing to see but bare trees all around. And nothing to hear, not the sound of someone coming after her or anything else. It was silent in the woods.

Where was she? Ingrid had no idea. How long had she been in the car? She had no idea of that either. What time was it? She didn't know, had forgotten her watch in the mad dash to get to MathFest. She checked the sky: low and gray, could be any time of day at all. These woods could be anywhere. Ingrid had read that moss grew on the north side of trees, but she didn't see any moss, and what good would knowing north do? She kept going.

Lots of kids—Ty, to take one obvious example—had their own cell phones. Not Ingrid, due to this weird family rule forbidding personal cell phones till ninth grade. Like a lot of family rules, it turned out to be pretty damn—

Ingrid stopped. There, just ahead at the base of a tree, lay a pile of empty beer cans. And on the trunk of the tree, in red spray paint: RED RAIDERS RULE!

She was in Echo Falls, had to be. Ingrid started running, first up a slope, then across a long flat stretch, and suddenly she burst out of the woods and—could it be? Yes! She was in the end zone, the end zone with the scoreboard, at Echo Falls High.

Ingrid ran across the field, through the parking lot, around to the main door. The main door to Echo Falls High stood at the top of ten or twelve stone steps, framed by two columns. As Ingrid flew up the steps, the door opened and a person came out, the first human being Ingrid had laid eyes on since she'd been kidnapped.

Ms. Groome.

Even though this first human being turned out to be

Ms. Groome, Ingrid wanted to embrace her, was raising her arms to do it.

"Oh, Ms. Groome," she began, and started to cry.

"Save your breath," said Ms. Groome, gazing at Ingrid with distaste. "MathFest finished ten minutes ago. This is going to cost you."

THIRTEEN

"This child," said Ms. Groome, "has a rather wild story I suppose you should hear."

"Hello, Ingrid," said Chief Strade.

"You know her?" said Ms. Groome. They stood by the chief's patrol car at the bottom of the high school steps.

"From way back," said Chief Strade. He was a big man with a big rough face and watchful eyes.

"Has she been in trouble before?" said Ms. Groome.

Chief Strade ignored her. "What happened, Ingrid?" he said.

"I got kidnapped, Mr. Strade," Ingrid said. Her voice wobbled a little; she fought to keep it steady. "I jumped out of a car."

"On the morning of MathFest, by happy coincidence," said Ms. Groome. "I've heard a lot of excuses in my time, but this one really takes the cake. You would not believe the lengths some kids will go to these days to get out of—"

Chief Strade held up his hand, a powerful hand with fingers like sausages. Ms. Groome fell silent.

"First of all," said Chief Strade, "are you hurt?"

"No."

"Nowhere at all?"

"No."

He gazed down at her. "Tell me the whole story."

"It . . . it was horrible," Ingrid said. And then the tears came—she couldn't help it. "I thought I was going to die."

"You may not know," said Ms. Groome, "but Ingrid has a lot of acting ability. A leading light of the Prescott Players, I'm told."

Chief Strade turned to her. "Ms. Groome, is it?"

"Correct."

"Thanks for your input, Ms. Groome. If I need more, I'll be in touch."

Ms. Groome's head snapped back. "I'm sure you know your business," she said, "but it's just common sense that jumping out of cars leaves a mark, and there's not one on her." She walked back up the stairs and disappeared inside the school.

Ingrid wiped her eyes on the back of her sleeve. "That's because I rolled down the hill," she said.

"What hill?" said the chief.

"I don't know, exactly," said Ingrid. "Where I jumped out."

"Why don't we start at the beginning?" said Chief Strade.

Ingrid started at the beginning, tried to tell a sensible story: garage, bike, shimmering spiderweb, swimming pool smell, duct tape, lock mechanism. It all got totally messed up. She could see that in Chief Strade's eyes. And when she got to the part about jumping from the car—

"A moving car, Ingrid?"

"Yes."

"About how fast?"

"I don't know."

—his eyes went quickly to her face and hands. She checked her hands too: not a mark, as Ms. Groome had pointed out.

"You rolled down a hill?" Chief Strade said.

"Yes."

"Then walked through some woods?"

"Yes."

"And came out at the football field?"

"Yes."

"Scoreboard end?"

"Yes."

The chief nodded, as though something added up. "You went into the garage at eight thirteen."

"Or maybe a minute later."

"And got to the high school ten minutes after this math thing, which ended at nine thirty."

"Yes. Now I want to go home."

"All right," he said, just for a moment laying his hand on her shoulder.

They got into the cruiser, Ingrid sitting up front with Chief Strade. "Seat belt, please," he said.

Ingrid buckled her seat belt. They sat there for a moment. The chief's car smelled of coffee and pine trees. She took a long, slow breath.

"Handle a quick detour first?" the chief said. "See if we can't find this hill of yours?"

"Okay."

A light rain began to fall as he pulled away from the high school. Ingrid shivered.

"Heat?" said the chief.

"Thanks."

He turned on the blower, drove a few blocks. "Didn't know you were a math whiz," he said.

"I'm not," Ingrid said.

"No?"

"I hate math."

"Then how come you're in this MathFest competition?"

Was it a competition? A math competition with a fun name: of course. So slow sometimes to clue in. "It was a punishment," Ingrid said.

The chief's eyes shifted toward her, real quick. "For what?"

"Fooling around in class."

"What kind of fooling around?"

"Passing a note."

"What was in the note?"

"I was just asking the word for something."

"What?"

"For contradictions in terms—like giant midget."

"They've got a word for that?"

"Oxymoron," Ingrid said.

He glanced at her again. "Teachers must see worse notes than that," he said.

Ingrid shrugged. He turned onto Benedict Drive, a road she didn't know. A curvy road with not many houses, and a sign saying TOWN DUMP, pointing straight ahead.

"How do you and Ms. Groome get along?" the chief said.

"All right."

"Who's Joe got for math again?" the chief said. "I forgot."

"Mr. Proctor." Joey was in Pre-Algebra. That was where Ingrid belonged too. Then none of this would have happened.

"One thing's for sure," Chief Strade said. "Joe's no math whiz."

Up ahead, Benedict Drive curved sharply to the left. Chief Strade pulled over. They got out of the car, walked to the side of the road. A thin strip of dirt bordered the pavement. Beyond that, the ground sloped steeply away to a gully below. Beyond the gully lay the woods.

"This it?" said the chief.

"I think so."

"Pretty sure?"

"I think so."

The chief peered down the slope. Rain fell steadily. A drop trickled off the brim of his hat.

"Help me out on a few things," he said. "You were still taped up when you popped the trunk?"

"Yes."

"And jumped."

"Yes."

"Duct tape, the silver stuff?"

"Yes."

"But you ended up getting it off somewhere."

Ingrid pointed down the slope.

"So you didn't see a thing—not the car, not the driver, nothing."

"Nothing," said Ingrid.

The chief put on a pair of white plastic gloves, like investigators on TV. "How about we go after those pieces of duct tape?"

"Okay."

"Only if you're up to it," the chief said. "I could drop you off, come back."

"I'm up to it," Ingrid said.

They started down the hill, the scrubby grass matted and slick now with rain. There wasn't much grass in the gully at the bottom, mostly stones, stunted brown weeds, patches of dirt. Not much cover at all: It only took a minute or two to establish that the duct tape pieces weren't there.

"Sure this is the spot?" the chief said.

Ingrid gazed into the woods. Trees like any others, a thick carpet of damp leaves on the ground, no landmark. And it had all happened so fast.

"I think so," Ingrid said.

The chief walked to the edge of the woods, lifted some leaves with the toe of his big black shoe. No duct tape.

"Thing with these woods," he said, "is they're the

only ones that back onto the high school." He faced the hill, peered up at the crest. "And this is the only slope into them off Benedict Drive."

"So the duct tape has to be here," Ingrid said.

"Got to be," said the chief.

Ingrid wandered around in the gully, the rain falling harder now, flattening her hair. No duct tape. Was it possible an animal had dragged off the pieces or a bird had flown away with them?

"Something on your mind?" said the chief, behind her, his voice quiet.

She turned to him. "Don't you see?" she said.

"See what?"

"Whoever did this must have come back and picked up all the duct tape. There's no other explanation."

"For what reason, Ingrid?"

"To get rid of the evidence," she said. "Maybe his fingerprints were on the tape."

"Why do you say *his*?" said the chief.

"It just came out."

"Did you hear any voices?"

"Just on the radio."

"The radio?"

"Or CD player. I heard that song 'I Guess That's Why They Call It the Blues.'"

The chief nodded. "Elton John. I've got all his stuff."

"You do?"

"Big fan," said the chief. He lifted up a fallen branch Ingrid had seen him lift already, tossed it aside. No duct tape.

"Maybe whoever it was left footprints," Ingrid said.

Down in the gully, water was collecting in puddles. Little rivulets trickled down the slope.

"Not a good day for footprints," the chief said. "Let's get you home."

But he stopped at the hospital on the way.

"I don't want to go to the hospital."

"Got to," said the chief.

A quick checkup: not a mark on her. Totally unharmed.

"Oh, sweetheart!" Mom said, her eyes filling with tears. She held on to Ingrid.

They were in the kitchen at 99 Maple Lane—Chief Strade, Mom, Ingrid; Dad still out with the Sandblasters, Ty still at Greg's. The chief told Mom the whole story. Mom squeezed Ingrid tighter and tighter until it got to be too much and Ingrid backed away.

"But who would do something like this?" Mom said.

"Can't know for sure because Ingrid ruined the plan so fast," said the chief. "But it usually comes down to two types—someone after ransom money or a sicko."

"But we're not rich," Mom said. "And we don't know any sickos."

That last remark was pure Mom. Ingrid had never loved her more than she did at that moment.

"Can I check the garage?" the chief said.

"Of course," said Mom.

The chief went into the garage.

Mom turned to Ingrid, her eyes wetting up again.

"I'm all right, Mom."

"You're sure you're not hurt?"

"Sure."

"Not . . . hurt in any way?"

"Don't worry, Mom. It's over."

The chief came back in the kitchen.

"Anything?" Mom said.

He shook his head. "There's only one other possibility I can think of," he said.

"What's that?" said Mom.

Chief Strade turned to Ingrid. "Do you have any enemies?" he said.

"Enemies?" said Mom. "She's thirteen years old."

"Other than Ms. Groome," said the chief.

"The math teacher?" Mom said. "You think she had something to do with this?"

"It's a joke, Mom," said Ingrid.

"Sorry," said the chief. He actually blushed a little. It looked very weird on that craggy face.

"But I don't understand," Mom said.

"Mom, forget it," said Ingrid. "No enemies," she told Chief Strade.

"See?" said Mom. "No enemies. So where are we?"

"I don't know," said the chief. He turned to Ingrid. "Remember *The Sign of Four*?"

"What's that?" said Mom.

"Sherlock Holmes," Ingrid said; the chief was a Holmes reader too.

"One of my favorites," the chief said. "That's where Holmes says, 'When you have eliminated the impossible, whatever remains, however improbable, must be the truth.'"

"And therefore?" said Mom.

The chief unfolded three fingers, one at a time. "Ransom—no note, no call. Sicko—no evidence. Enemies—don't exist." He unfolded a fourth, his ring finger, although the chief, divorced, wore no ring. He gazed at that finger, glanced at Ingrid, lowered it without saying anything.

"What does that mean," said Mom, "if it's none of them?"

"Not necessarily anything," said the chief. "We'll just have to forget motive for now, get busy with some old-fashioned grunt work."

"Like what?" said Mom.

"Fingerprints first," said the chief. "State crime lab'll be here Monday. Meantime, don't touch anything in the garage. And for now, Ingrid better not go anywhere alone."

"Oh, God," said Mom. "Is she still in danger?"

"My gut says no," said the chief. "But we can't rule it out." He moved toward the door, stopped. "Anything you've left out, Ingrid? Anything else you want to say?"

"No."

He gave her a long look, then nodded. "That was an incredible thing you did."

"Thanks."

It was only after Chief Strade had gone that Ingrid thought about the word *incredible*, a word that no one took literally but in fact did have a literal meaning. The literal meaning was *not believable*.

FOURTEEN

"She wants to go to soccer," Mom said.

"She does?" said Dad.

They sat around the kitchen table—Mom, Dad, Ty, Ingrid. Ty's eyes were open wide.

"It's the play-offs," Ingrid said.

Ty nodded. That made sense to him.

"Play-offs?" said Mom. "What difference does—"

"If she feels up to it, she should go," Dad said.

"I feel up to it," Ingrid said. In fact, she really wanted to get out there, to run around, to play.

"How does she know what she feels?" Mom said. "This all just happened. She could be in shock."

"She looks kind of the same as always," Ty said,

peering at her from across the table.

"Hey," said Ingrid. "I'm right here. Stop talking about me in the third person."

"She's right," said Dad.

The whole family went to the soccer game, excluding Nigel. Dogs had to be leashed at the soccer fields, and Nigel didn't do well on a leash. Mom, Dad, and Ty crossed the field to the aluminum stands on the far side. Ingrid walked toward the bench, where the girls were huddling around Julia LeCaine, a few of them bouncing up and down with pregame jitters. Ingrid usually had pregame jitters too, but not today. Kind of a strange interval, no one else knowing yet what had happened that morning. Correction: She had jitters, all right, just nothing to do with soccer.

Stacy—yes, Stacy, now back on the As where she belonged—saw Ingrid and said, "Hey, Ingrid—got any gum?"

Julia LeCaine spun around. She saw Ingrid too, at the same time possibly stepping in a hole, because she staggered a little. "Ingrid?" she said.

"Hi," said Ingrid. "Sorry I'm late."

Julia looked at her watch, stared at it in a funny way, like maybe it wasn't working.

The ref blew his whistle.

"This is when Coach Ringer gives the pep talk," said one of the girls.

They all looked at Julia, standing motionless, mouth slightly open but not saying anything. Did she have pregame jitters too? The whistle sounded again. Coach Ringer's pep talks were usually pretty confusing, but Ingrid didn't like the idea of going out on the field without a pep talk, and she could see on the faces of her teammates that none of them did either.

"What was that thing you said the last time?" asked another girl.

"Last time?" said Julia, licking her lips. She looked a little pale, pregame jitters or maybe coming down with something.

"'Whatever it takes,'" said Ingrid. "Wasn't that it?"

The girls nodded, but not enthusiastically. Ingrid thought she knew why: It was a game, right? That made "whatever it takes" a little over the top.

"How about—let's win it for Coach Ringer?" said Stacy, which was pretty cool considering her history with him.

"Yeah!"

They clustered tight together, raised their hands high, making a kind of cone in the sky.

"Coach Ringer!"

"That's as loud as you can do?" said Stacy. "Come on now, so he can hear it down at the hospital."

"COACH RINGER!"

Then they went out on a cold, rainy afternoon and beat up on Torrington, four to one. Glad to win, glad that Stacy was back on the team, glad to be muddy, they went through the handshake line—"good game, good game, good game," no spitting on their palms first, or any of that other boy stuff—and returned to the bench for the coach's postmortem. Julia was already gone.

"Different style of coaching," said one of the parents, coming across the field.

"Works for me," said another. "How are the girls going to relate to an old coot like him?"

One thing about Ingrid: She never took naps during the day. But after the game, rain falling hard now and the wind really blowing, she went down to the TV room. That old couch, the one that used to be in the living room before Mom upgraded at Pottery Barn—so comfy. She pulled up Mom's mohair blanket, clicked through the channels. Wall-to-wall college football. Ingrid didn't care about college football. She cared about Echo Falls football, specifically how Ty was doing. A disk was in the DVD player. She hit Play to see what it was.

An impossibly beautiful black-and-white face appeared on the screen. Were any faces in the whole history of the human race ever really as beautiful as that?

The face spoke. The voice was beautiful too: "Oh, Rick."

No, not *Casablanca*.

But it was. Mom's favorite movie—Ingrid had tried to sit through it once, a sappy tale about always having Paris or something like that, with a song about do or die that had made Mom cry tears in buckets. None of that was important, except for the fact that Mom and Dad had actually named Ingrid after Ingrid Bergman, the star of the picture. In the whole history of Hollywood there must have been thousands of female movie stars to pick from, including Daisy Duck. Mom and Dad could have done way better.

Rick told the piano player never to play that song again, or possibly to keep playing it, as a sort of punishment, although who was being punished wasn't clear. Cigarette smoke curled upward. A ceiling fan spun. Ingrid's eyes closed.

Whiz. Thump.

"Phone."

Ingrid awoke, dim light in the room, blue screen on the TV, portable phone lying in a curl of the mohair blanket.

Ingrid picked it up. "Hi."

"Hi," said Joey.

"Hi."

"You, um," said Joey, "all right?"

For a moment, she'd forgotten the whole thing. Now it all came back: shadowy garage, swimming pool smell, darkness. "Yeah," she said.

"Like what happened?" Joey said.

"Didn't your dad tell you?"

"Yeah."

"Well that's what happened."

"You got kidnapped."

"Yeah."

"And escaped out of a car trunk?"

"Yeah."

"And all this, um, duct tape, was gone?"

"That's right."

"Um. Are you okay?"

"I played soccer this afternoon."

"Yeah?"

"Yeah."

"You win?"

"Four one over Torrington."

"Cool. Score any goals?"

"No."

Silence.

"So," said Joey.

"So?"

"Like, why?"

"Why what?"

"Why would someone do that to you?"

Ransom—no note. Sickos—no evidence. Enemies—none. What other possibilities were there? "I don't know," Ingrid said.

Silence.

"What's up, Joey?"

"Thing is," said Joey, "guess who came over here."

"Just tell me."

"Ms. Groome."

"Ms. Groome came over to your house?"

"She just left." Joey paused. "She was talking to my dad. In the kitchen. You know the front hall at our place?"

"Yeah."

"You can hear what goes on in the kitchen from the hall. I snuck down there."

"And?"

"She was saying all these bad things about you."

Did that really surprise Ingrid? Maybe not. But it made her sick for a moment, just the same.

"Like what?" she said.

"Stupid stuff."

"Tell me."

"Really dumb."

"Joey—are you going to tell me or not?"

"She thinks you made it all up."

"Why would I do that?"

"That's what my dad said. And she told him it was all to get her back for making you go to MathFest."

"That's so wacked."

"Yeah."

"Did he tell her she was out of her mind?"

Pause. "He didn't say much, just kind of listened. She, uh, thinks you're, um, what's that word?"

"What word?"

"Means, like . . ." Joey lapsed into silence.

"Like what?"

"Like when you, uh . . ."

"Manipulative?"

"Yeah, that's it—she thinks you're manipulative. You've got everybody fooled."

"She said that?"

"Uh-huh."

"Your dad knows me."

"Yeah."

"So there's no way he's going to believe her."

Silence.

"He believes me, right?"

More silence. At last Joey said, "I believe you, Ingrid."

* * *

Ingrid went upstairs. "Anybody home?"

No answer, even though she knew Ty had to be around somewhere. She glanced in the driveway. No cars. But Chief Strade's cruiser was parked across the street. For a moment, Ingrid thought maybe he was standing guard. Then she noticed he wasn't actually in the car but at the Grunellos' front door, talking to Mrs. Grunello.

Mrs. Grunello wore a pink housecoat and had pink curlers in her hair. She pointed at the birdbath on the front lawn. Chief Strade went over, walked around it, said something. Mrs. Grunello shook her head. The chief said something else. Mrs. Grunello looked across the street at 99 Maple Lane and shook her head again. She closed her door. The chief got in the cruiser and drove away.

Ingrid stood in the hall for a long time, gazing out at the Grunellos' house. It seemed to get closer and closer, as though she were crossing the street. The next thing she knew, Ingrid *was* crossing the street. She had to know.

She knocked on the Grunellos' door. Mrs. Grunello opened up. She still had the curlers in but now she wore a wine-colored pantsuit instead of the housecoat, and held a lipstick in her hand. Her eyes: surprised for a second; then a shift to some quick thought; and back to their normal expression, warm and friendly.

"Hello, Ingrid," she said.

"Hi, Mrs. Grunello," said Ingrid.

"Are you all right?"

"Sure," said Ingrid and saw an opening. "Why wouldn't I be?"

"I don't really know," said Mrs. Grunello. "That is, Mr., uh . . ."

"Mr. Strade?"

Mrs. Grunello laughed, a laugh that somehow told Ingrid that Mrs. Grunello realized she'd been watching from across the street. "He didn't exactly tell me the reason for his questions," Mrs. Grunello said.

"What kind of questions?" asked Ingrid.

Mrs. Grunello paused. "He didn't say I couldn't discuss it, either."

Ingrid waited.

"I got the idea that maybe there'd been a stalker or something in the neighborhood this morning," Mrs. Grunello said.

"Yeah?" said Ingrid.

Mrs. Grunello nodded. "Mr. Strade asked if I'd seen a car parked outside your house between eight and eight thirty."

"And?"

"I didn't. And it just so happens I was out on the front lawn the whole time."

"You were?"

"Working on the birdbath."

"The birdbath?"

Mrs. Grunello pointed. "Prepping the base for this new protective coating stuff I got from Towne Hardware. The stone's starting to dissolve, like it's getting eaten away by acid."

"Oh," said Ingrid.

"I hope it's not pollution," said Mrs. Grunello. "That would be scary."

"Very," said Ingrid. All of a sudden she heard Nigel barking, no doubt right behind the door at 99 Maple Lane.

"But the point was I didn't see any cars parked on the street," Mrs. Grunello said. "None even drove by the whole time I was there."

From inside the house, Mr. Grunello called, "Where the hell are my tassel loafers?"

"Where they always are, in the closet," Mrs. Grunello called over her shoulder. She lowered her voice back to normal and added, "You dope." And then to Ingrid: "So what's this all about?"

"I wish I knew," said Ingrid.

FIFTEEN

IM-ing, Sunday night.

Powerup77: i'm hearing weird stuff

NYgrrrl979: i-girl—is it true????

Gridster22: what are u hearing?

NYgrrrl979: u made up some story to ditch mathfest

Gridster22: NOT TRUE

Powerup77: thats what I thought

Gridster22: mia—u think its true?

NYgrrrl979: no no no no no

Gridster22: because it happened

NYgrrrl979: so you were really????

Gridster22: yeah

NYgrrrl979: but who would do it????

Powerup77: if we knew who this would be o-ver

Gridster22: yeah

NYgrrrl979: or why????

Powerup77: same answer—u not getting it girl

Gridster22: stace—who told u?

Powerup77: sean—but lots of people seem to know

Gridster22: lots?

NYgrrrl979: it must have been so scary

Powerup77: you ok?

They got on the phone. Ingrid told them the whole story.

"Morning, petunia," said Mr. Sidney as Ingrid stepped on the bus.

"Morning, Mr. Sidney."

A normal Monday start, but after that things changed.

At first it was just an uneasy feeling. Ingrid sat down beside Mia. The uneasy feeling didn't come from Mia, who said, "Hey," and held out half a blueberry muffin. It came when Ingrid, taking a bite, glanced around and saw kids looking at her. Not all the kids, just some here and there. None of them met her glance; all eyes quickly averted. The muffin turned dry in her mouth, and Ingrid handed the rest back to Mia.

"What?" said Mia. "You love blueberry muffins."

After that, a kind of prologue, things went bad in three acts.

Act One: Math class. Ingrid sat in her place at the back, the best seat in the house, but her mind no longer wandered pleasantly. She kept her eyes on Ms. Groome the whole time. Ms. Groome never looked at her once. She taught a lesson about if Miguel is three years older than Faraz and Faraz is two years younger than some other kid, and on and on, completely incomprehensible. At the end of the class, with Miguel and all the others ranked in order of age on the blackboard and everyone nodding falsely that they understood why, Ms. Groome said, "And now it's my pleasure to present the MathFest awards. Mia McGreevy, would you step forward?"

Mia walked up to Ms. Groome's desk.

"For coming second in the entire MathFest celebration, Mia wins a twenty-five-dollar Blockbuster gift certificate. Congratulations, Mia." She handed Mia an envelope. Mia turned pink and went back to her seat.

"Bruce Berman?"

Brucie was already halfway there.

"For participating in MathFest, Bruce wins a coupon good for one medium-size ice cream, cone or dish, at Moo Cow. Congratulations, Bruce."

"Math rules," said Brucie, pumping his fist.

Someone spoke in a low voice. "He gets a prize for just showing up?"

A low voice, but Ms. Groome heard everything. "Precisely," she said.

As though Ingrid were some kind of magnet, eyes shifted toward her from all over the room. The lunch bell rang.

"Dismissed," said Ms. Groome.

Act Two: Lunchtime. Ingrid hung out with Stacy at one of the picnic tables near the swings. She took out her lunch—PB&J on whole wheat, milk, a Macoun apple, her favorite—found she wasn't hungry. On the far side of the swings, some boys were playing touch football. The ball spiraled up into the sky. A blue sky: That surprised Ingrid because of how dark everything seemed.

"Letting that sandwich go to waste?" Stacy said.

"It's all yours."

Stacy bit into Ingrid's sandwich. "I love the way your mom puts in those banana slices," she said, or something like that, her mouth practically glued together with peanut butter.

Mia came over, laid the Blockbuster gift certificate in front of Ingrid. "Here," she said.

"No thanks."

"Take it."

"No."

"I don't want it," said Mia.

"If no one else wants it," said Stacy, sweeping it up.

Mia shot her an angry look. They sat quietly for a minute or two, the only sounds Stacy's chewing and the thump of the football.

"Stop looking at me like that," Ingrid said.

"I wasn't looking at you," Stacy said.

"Me either," said Mia.

"Just stop," said Ingrid.

"But—"

A shout rose from over by the football game, then another. The boys didn't seem to be playing football anymore. Instead they'd gathered in a ragged circle. In the middle of the circle, raising clouds of dust, two—no, three—boys were scrambling around in a funny way. Was it possible they were—? Yes. Fighting.

Ingrid, Stacy, and Mia were on their feet. Something about fighting made you do that. They moved closer, past the swings, to the edge of the circle of boys.

Three boys, two against one. The two were the Dratch twins, Dustin and Dwayne, the biggest kids at Ferrand Middle, partly because even though the Echo Falls School Board mandated social promotion, they'd both been held back twice and were now fifteen years old.

The kid they were ganging up on was pretty big for thirteen but nothing like the Dratch twins: Joey Strade.

Dustin Dratch threw a punch at Joey, hit him in the chest. Joey punched him right back, caught him on the nose. That got Dustin all fired up, and he took a wild swing that missed completely, but meanwhile Dwayne snuck around behind Joey and kicked him in the back of the knee.

Joey's leg buckled and he slumped to the ground. Dwayne crouched, wound up, hit Joey in the mouth as hard as he could. Then Dwayne and Dustin jumped on him. They rolled around, Joey getting an arm free and pounding on a beefy Dratch back. One of the Dratches growled like a savage animal. Ingrid took a step forward.

But before she could take another one, a man rushed into the circle, pushing boys aside. A man with a whistle around his neck—Mr. Porterhouse. He reached down into the pile, jerked the Dratch twins up by the scruffs of their necks. Joey got up too, dusting himself off. His mouth was all bloody.

"What the hell is going on here?" said Mr. Porterhouse.

The Dratch twins gave him a look, sullen and challenging. Joey glared at them, his hands balled into fists.

"I asked a question," said Mr. Porterhouse.

Silence.

"I'm going to ask once more," said Mr. Porterhouse. "What the hell is going on?"

Then something weird happened. The Dratch twins turned and looked right at Ingrid. Mr. Porterhouse followed their gaze. His mouth opened, but Joey spoke first.

"We were just playing football," he said. "It got a little out of hand."

Mr. Porterhouse's eyes went from Joey to the Dratch twins, back to Joey. And then very quickly to Ingrid, so quickly she almost missed it.

Mr. Porterhouse nodded. "It happens," he said. "Don't let it happen again."

The Dratch twins started to smile. Identical ugly smiles—they were getting off scot-free.

"Would, say, a week of detention help you remember?" said Mr. Porterhouse.

The Dratch twins looked confused. Ingrid knew why: The question was a little too complicated; they knew that either yes or no got them out of detention but couldn't figure out which.

"A week of detention it is, then," said Mr. Porterhouse.

Dwayne pointed at Joey. No problem telling the Dratch twins apart—the cauliflower ear was Dustin. "What about him?" he said.

"Him too," said Mr. Porterhouse. "Now everyone inside. Stop by the nurse's office first, Joey."

Brucie Berman didn't actually play touch football, but he liked to stand on the sidelines and make comments. On the bus ride home he told Ingrid what had happened.

"It was about you," he whispered, bobbing up and down with excitement on the next seat over.

"Me?"

"Dustin said you made up that whole story. Joey was like 'say it again.' Dustin said it again. 'She made up the whole thing.' Joey popped him."

"Zip it, guy," said Mr. Sidney from the front of the bus. He'd said that a million times but never angry like this.

Act Three: At home. No one there, the house a little cold, Nigel sleeping by his empty food bowl in the kitchen.

Ingrid called Joey right away.

"Hello?" Not Joey, but his father, Chief Strade.

Ingrid almost hung up, remembering at the last moment that her number probably showed up on his screen. "Is Joey there?" she said.

"No," said the chief. "That you, Ingrid?"

"Yes," said Ingrid.

"How are you doing?"

"All right."

"Crime lab boys dusted your garage this morning," he said. "No prints."

"Oh."

"Manage to think of anything else in the meantime?" the chief asked.

"Anything else?"

"About the whole incident. Something you might have forgotten to tell me, for example."

"I told you everything," Ingrid said.

Silence. What was he thinking? That she hadn't told him much?

"I couldn't see, remember?" Ingrid said.

"Because of the duct tape," the chief said.

"Yeah."

Another silence. Then the chief said, "I'll tell Joe you called. He should have been home by now."

But wasn't, Ingrid realized, because the week of detention must have started right away. "Thanks," she said, and hung up.

The duct tape. If only those scraps had remained in the gully off Benedict Drive, no one would be doubting her. Ingrid thought back. She remembered rolling down the hill, coming to a stop, panting. Then she'd bitten through the duct tape around her wrists and ripped the blindfold tape from her eyes.

Panting: whoa. She'd been able to pant because somehow that tumble down the hill had torn off the third strip of tape, covering her mouth. She and the chief hadn't found any tape at all, but wasn't it likely that this third strip had been smaller than the others, that it might have gotten twisted up and maybe bounced or rolled or slid beyond their search area?

How small would that strip of tape have been, exactly? Ingrid opened the junk drawer, found duct tape, cut off a small piece. She covered her mouth with it, checked her reflection on a pot hanging on the wall. A small piece, but more than enough.

Nigel opened an eye, saw her, and barked. Ingrid took off the duct tape. He stopped barking. His eye closed.

Bzzz. A little spark went off in Ingrid's mind. She'd felt that kind of spark before. It always accompanied a stroke of inspiration, like lightning with thunder. A minute later Ingrid was checking MapQuest for the directions to Benedict Drive. Two minutes after that she was on her bike, rounding the corner of Maple Lane and Avondale, several strips of duct tape in her pocket. Only later, as she came to the curve on Benedict Drive bordering the gully, did she remember that advice or whatever you wanted to call it about not going out alone.

Ingrid laid her bike at the edge of the slope, peered

down. Everything the same—steep hill, a little clearing at the bottom, woods on the other side. And no glint of duct tape. That didn't discourage her. She was approaching this scientifically now, conducting an experiment in the manner of Sherlock Holmes. What was that line from "Silver Blaze"? "We imagined what might have happened, acted upon the supposition, and find ourselves justified."

This was the acting upon the supposition part. The tape over her mouth got ripped off in the long tumbling fall. Whoever had come back and picked up the other scraps down at the bottom might have missed it. But what exactly would she be looking for?

To find out, Ingrid took the strips of duct tape from her pocket. Suppose, for example, that the strip over her mouth had got twisted up like so? She tossed a twisted strip down the hill. Wow. Completely invisible in the scrubby grass the moment it landed, even though she'd watched it the whole way. And it hadn't come close to reaching the bottom, where she and the chief had concentrated their search.

Or what about if the tape hadn't got so twisted up, just folded over like this? Or maybe balled up? She threw more duct tape down the hill, all of it invisible in the undergrowth except for the folded-over one, which landed on a little bush. One thing was clear: She was going to have to search the whole hillside on her hands and knees.

And here was another thought. Supposing the tape had got torn in two, two pieces, even smaller, even harder to find, like so? She twisted them up as well, flung the scraps in different directions, exploring every possibility like a conscientious scientist.

From down at the bottom came a sudden movement. Chief Strade stepped out from behind a tree.

"What are you doing, Ingrid?"

SIXTEEN

"You must be Ingrid," said Dr. Josef Vishevsky.

Ingrid toyed with the idea of denying it.

"Please sit down."

Ingrid sat down on the visitor's side of Dr. Vishevsky's desk. Dr. Vishevsky was a middle-aged guy with a graying beard and a slight accent that reminded her of Count Dracula. Lots of framed certificates hung on his walls. The closest one said that Dr. Vishevsky was a distinguished fellow of the New England Adolescent Psychological Society.

"Comfortable?" said Dr. Vishevsky.

Comfortable? Ingrid almost laughed in his face. That would have felt great. She'd never been so pissed off in her entire life. Maybe Ms. Groome not believing her shouldn't have been such a big surprise, but now lots of people had jumped on the stupid bandwagon, including Chief Strade. Had he bought her scientific experiment explanation? Not even for a second. The worst part was this angled look in his eyes: He was seeing her in a brand-new way. And after that he'd driven her home from Benedict Drive and told Mom and Dad that he was afraid—that was the way he'd put it—that she'd been planting evidence to back up her story.

That was the moment, there in the front hall at 99 Maple Lane, when Mom and Dad should have gone ballistic and told Chief Strade that he was out of his mind. Had that happened? No. Instead of going ballistic, Mom and Dad looked kind of sick, like they'd both been punched in the stomach.

"Mom? Dad? You don't believe me?"

"Of course we believe you," Mom said. But nothing in the tone of her voice backed up those words.

"Maybe we could have a few minutes alone," the chief said to Mom and Dad.

Ingrid went up to her room. Ten or fifteen minutes later, she heard the cruiser driving off. Then came a knock on her door.

"Yeah?"

Mom and Dad came in.

"It's not that we don't believe you," Mom said.

"Good. Because that's what happened."

"I'm sure it was," Mom began. "Still, we can't help wondering."

"Wondering what?"

"About the goddamn duct tape," Dad said. "What the hell were you—"

"Mark," Mom said.

Dad shut his mouth.

"It might help if you explained about the duct tape," Mom said.

"I already did."

"Tell us again, if you don't mind," said Mom. "Sweetheart."

"I mind."

Mom sat on the edge of the bed. Ingrid shifted away, toward the wall.

"Sometimes," Mom said, "people can convince themselves that something really happened so completely that it's no longer a matter of lying. And no one would treat it that way or get mad. Do you see what I'm saying?"

"No."

Dad, standing in the doorway, said, "If this is some screwed-up plan of yours to stick it to that stupid Ms. Grundy—"

"Ms. Groome," Mom corrected.

"—then cough it up now."

"Go away," Ingrid said.

Dad banged the doorjamb with the back of his hand, stalked off down the hall.

Mom put her hand on Ingrid's shoulder. "Were you more . . . upset about the whole Cracked-Up Katie thing than you let on?"

Ingrid shrugged her shoulder free. "Go away."

"The chief is worried about you," Mom said. "He thinks, and we agree, that it might be good for you to talk to a sympathetic professional."

"You're sending me to a shrink?"

"I wouldn't put it that way," Mom said. "He's supposed to be very nice—his office is in the same building with Dr. Binkerman."

"Is that supposed to be a recommendation?" Ingrid said. "You can forget it."

"You can go kicking and screaming," Mom said, "or just go." Ingrid just went.

"I understand," said Dr. Vishevsky, "that you're into acting."

Ingrid gazed at him. He had soft brown eyes, like a puppy. Ingrid wouldn't have dreamed of kicking a puppy, but kicking Dr. Vishevsky came to mind immediately.

"Yeah," she said, "I like acting."

"Are you in a play now?"

"We're rehearsing a scene from *The Wizard of Oz* for The Xmas Revue."

"And your role?"

"Dorothy."

"Ah." Dr. Vishevsky jotted something on a notepad. "The main character, if I'm not mistaken."

"I guess."

"Meaning you're not sure?"

"The Tin Man and the Cowardly Lion and the Scarecrow are important too."

"Would you prefer to be playing one of them?" asked Dr. Vishevsky.

Ingrid thought about that. All those parts probably started with body movement—stiff for the Tin Man, floppy for the Scarecrow, catlike but in a timid way for the Cowardly Lion—and she wasn't too good with that. "No," she said.

Dr. Vishevsky made another note. "What do you like most about acting?" he said.

Ingrid shrugged. "It's fun."

"What makes it fun for you?"

"I don't know," Ingrid said. And she didn't really want to know. Was it a rule you had to understand what made something fun?

"Could it be the make-believe aspect?" said Dr. Vishevsky.

How could it not be? Acting in a play was make-believe, for God's sake. It was like saying does the chocolate aspect have anything to do with why you're downing that pack of M&M's? "I guess that's part of it," Ingrid said.

Dr. Vishevsky nodded. "And what attracts you about make-believe?"

"I don't know."

Dr. Vishevsky looked at her for a moment, rubbed his beard. Did something fall out of it, some little food particle? Was that possible? "Think about it for a minute or two," said Dr. Vishevsky. He rose. "A soda, perhaps? I have Fresca."

Fresca, Ingrid's favorite, no doubt about that, but was it the brand of soda most people had lying around or offered first? No. They offered Coke or Pepsi or maybe Seven-Up. So Dr. Vishevsky was in the know about her, meaning that people, including her parents, were doing all this plotting behind her back. Ingrid felt a chill.

"I'm not thirsty," she said, although her mouth was suddenly dry. "And I can't answer your question about make-believe."

"Can't?" said Dr. Vishevsky. "Or won't?"

Ingrid didn't reply. She just sat there, staring ahead,

and came close to crossing her arms over her chest.

Dr. Vishevsky surprised her with a smile. It even looked friendly. "Do you know why you're here, Ingrid?"

"My parents," Ingrid said.

Dr. Vishevsky nodded. "How would you say you get along with your parents?"

"Fine."

"How do you feel about them arranging this meeting?"

"I don't know," Ingrid said.

"Angry, perhaps?" said Dr. Vishevsky. "Resentful?"

Ingrid shrugged.

Dr. Vishevsky leaned back in his chair. She saw that his beard grew right down his neck and under the collar of his shirt. She'd seen enough of Dr. Vishevsky.

"How do you feel about expressing your feelings in general, Ingrid?" he said. "Comfortable or uncomfortable?"

Ingrid looked him in the eye for the first time.

"It depends," she said.

"On what?"

On what? How about who she was talking to and what the feelings were for starters? But wasn't that obvious? Wouldn't an experienced shrink like Dr. Vishevsky already know the answer?

"Stuff," she said. "You know."

Dr. Vishevsky made another note. "Do you like to read, Ingrid?"

"Yes."

"Do you have a favorite book?"

"Uh-huh."

"What is it?"

"The Complete Sherlock Holmes."

"Ah," said Dr. Vishevsky, writing it down. "And what do you like about Sherlock Holmes?"

"Lots of things."

"Such as?"

"They're good stories," Ingrid said.

"What makes them good?"

"I just like them."

Dr. Vishevsky sighed; a tiny little sigh, but Ingrid caught it.

"Moving to the character of Sherlock Holmes specifically," he said, "what do you like about him?"

"I don't know. He's interesting."

"In what way?"

At that moment, Ingrid actually figured out what she liked best about Sherlock Holmes: He thought for himself and didn't care what anyone thought about him.

"It's hard to say," she told Dr. Vishevsky.

"I understand," he said. There was a long pause. He seemed to be lost in thought. Then he said, "Do you ever imagine yourself doing the kinds of things Sherlock Holmes does?"

"No."

"Investigating cases, for example? Solving crimes?"

"No."

"Or being the center of attention like him, admired by everybody?"

"No."

"Allowing your powers of make-believe to carry you over to another—"

"No."

Dr. Vishevsky wrote on his notepad, turned the page, wrote some more. "Do you know what a biography is?"

Of course she did. What a question! She gave a little nod.

"Have you read any?"

Ingrid thought. "There was one about Sacajawea."

Dr. Vishevsky blinked. Was it possible he was unaware of Sacajawea? "How about—given your dramatic interests—biographies of actors and actresses?"

She shook her head, at the same time making a mental note to go on the Internet and see what actress bios were out there.

"I've read a few," said Dr. Vishevsky.

"Oh?" said Ingrid. "About who?"

Dr. Vishevsky looked surprised. "I don't recall the

names offhand," he said.

"Maybe the books weren't very good," Ingrid said.

Dr. Vishevsky blinked again. Then his face, a pretty soft one, hardened slightly, as though . . . as though he'd decided he didn't like her. "But I did find a common element in all these life stories," he said. "Any idea what that might be?"

Multiple divorces? Drug and alcohol problems? Nose jobs? Ingrid kept all that to herself. "No," she said.

"They all," said Dr. Vishevsky, "all these actresses and actors, had difficulty expressing their feelings in real life. It was only in the world of make-believe that their feelings came out."

Silence. Ingrid heard a man laughing on the other side of the wall. Dr. Binkerman. She wished she were over there instead, even getting her braces tightened extra tight, a really wacked-out thought.

Dr. Vishevsky leaned forward. "Which brings us," he said, "to this whole episode with your math teacher, Ms. Groome."

Ingrid's chin tilted up in an aggressive sort of way, a motion that seemed to happen all on its own. "Does it?" she said.

Dr. Vishevsky's face hardened a little more.

SEVENTEEN

"Coffee?" Mom said.

"Sounds good," said Chief Strade. He sat down, laid some papers on the kitchen table. Ingrid, from her place on the other side, could make out the name on the letterhead: Dr. Josef Vishevsky. She got up and stood by the wall.

Mom poured coffee. Dad came in, knotting his tie.

"Morning," said the chief.

Dad nodded. "Will this take long? I've got an eight-o'clock meeting."

Mom flashed Dad a quick annoyed glance—a glance that Dad missed but the chief caught.

"I'll try to make it quick," the chief said.

"That's all right," Mom said. "Mark and I know this is important."

"Did I say it wasn't?" Dad asked, spooning sugar into his coffee; he liked lots.

The chief bowed his head slightly to take a sip of coffee, his eyes darting to Mom and Dad. "Real good coffee," he said. "Thanks." Then he turned to Ingrid. "How are you doing, Ingrid?"

"Fine."

He adjusted his body in the chair, trying to get comfortable. Chief Strade was a little too big for the breakfast nook. "I hear a lot of lies in my job," he said. "And I deal with a lot of liars. You don't seem like a liar to me."

"So you believe me?" Ingrid said.

The chief took a deep breath. "I can't see my way clear to do that."

"But you just said she's not a liar," Mom said.

"Yeah," said Dad. "What kind of game are you playing?"

"If anyone's playing games," said the chief, "it's not me."

"What's that supposed to mean?" Dad said.

The chief turned away from Dad, almost as if he had no time for him. "Ingrid?" he said. "Is there anything you want to tell me? This would be the time."

Ingrid had something to tell him all right, but it

wasn't the kind of language you used on a chief of police, not even one who treated her father with contempt, who didn't believe the truth. She just said, "No."

"'Kay," said Chief Strade. He handed Dad the papers from Dr. Vishevsky. "Just read the first paragraph."

Dad read the first paragraph. His eyes went back and forth, fast at the beginning, then slower and slower, almost like they were refusing to go on. Mom came closer, read over his shoulder. Her face got pale. They finished at the same time and looked up at Ingrid.

"On the other hand," said the chief, "you can get a little carried away with this kind of thing."

"What kind of thing?" said Dad.

"Psychology," said the chief, taking the report from him.

"But you just said you don't believe her," said Mom.

"She's given me no facts to back herself up," said the chief. "The opposite. But"—he tore the report in two, then tore up the pieces and stuffed them in his pocket—"I don't believe this either."

"So where are we?" Dad said, glancing at his watch. Ingrid realized he had no idea about the impression he was making on the chief, or maybe didn't care.

"That's the problem," the chief said. "Nowhere. I can only work off facts."

"And therefore?" said Dad.

"Therefore the investigation is officially closed." The chief went over to Ingrid, gazed down at her. "But—are you listening, Ingrid?"

"Yeah."

"Then remember this—officially closed means my mind is still open." His voice got gentler. "In case you've got anything new to tell me."

"Please, Ingrid," said Mom.

Meaning even Mom didn't believe her. Lying put you on a tightrope. Ingrid understood that. But now telling the truth was putting her on the tightrope too. Her chin tilted up in that new aggressive way. She said nothing.

Mom wrote Ingrid a note—*Please excuse my daughter Ingrid's tardiness—she was home with my permission*—and dropped her off at school. She walked up to the wide glass doors. On the other side, Mr. Porterhouse was standing by the drinks machine, a volleyball under his arm. Ingrid paused. One more step and the doors would slide open and Mr. Porterhouse would glance over to see who was coming in.

Ingrid couldn't take that step. This wasn't about Mr. Porterhouse. Mr. Porterhouse was okay. In fact, despite his mumbling, that class about steroids had been pretty helpful, had got her thinking about—

Bzzz. Inspiration, coming out of nowhere. What

were those kidnapping motives again? Ransom, sickos, enemies—none of them right in this case, a big reason why no one believed her. But what about steroids? Could there be a connection between the kidnapping and steroids? How would that work, exactly?

A soda can banged down into the slot. Mr. Porterhouse took it and walked off. Ingrid started backing away from the school.

Suppose the kidnapper had something to do with steroids. Why kidnap her? Was she a threat, an enemy after all, category three? Steroids were an illegal drug, meaning that someone was making money, probably lots of it, from selling them. That would turn anyone who knew what was going on into a threat. But what did she know? Nothing, really. It was all suspicion.

Ingrid crossed the parking lot, passing all the teachers' cars, modest cars with positive bumper-sticker messages, no HELL ON WHEELS stuff here. She remembered about not going places alone. Did that still apply? No way. The case was closed. She was on her own. Ingrid kept going, walking speed normal, mind revving.

All she had was suspicion, but maybe whoever kidnapped her didn't know that. Maybe whoever kidnapped her thought she really knew something, something threatening. But why her in the first place? She hadn't told anyone.

Ingrid turned onto High Street. Home was miles away—3.4 to be precise, measured by the odometer in the TT—and she'd never gone on foot before, but all she had to do was follow the bus route. High, Spring, Bridge, Avondale, Maple Lane, nothing to it. The stores, houses, gas stations went by in a blur. She had a motive!

Plus what about this? She'd told no one about her suspicions, but what was stopping her now? Not a damn thing. The moment she got home, she'd call Chief Strade. How was that going to feel? Great. Chief Strade was smart. He'd get to work right away, probably starting with—

Uh-oh. Ty.

Oh my God.

The chief would want to talk to Ty. Not just talk, but question. Ingrid could picture two forks leading from that conversation. One, maybe the most likely, started with Ty denying everything and ended with him never speaking to her again. The other had the chief breaking Ty down, ended with Ty getting kicked off the team, maybe even going to trial and getting sent to some kind of youth prison, life over.

Sometimes Dad talked about win-win situations. This was lose-lose. And maybe even worse than that— what if the chief didn't buy her story, right from the get-go? Was it possible he'd think this was just another scheme of hers, like tossing duct tape down the hill off Benedict Drive? Oh, yeah, real possible. This was lose-lose-lose.

Where did that leave her? Ingrid had no clue. She came to a stop, looked around, her surroundings slowly unblurring. Hey. What was this? She was standing right in front of Moo Cow. How had that happened? Moo Cow was on Main Street, way off the bus route. But now that she was here . . .

Ingrid shrugged off her backpack, felt inside the Velcro pocket. Sometimes Mom packed her a lunch. Other times she sent cash. Today? Cash. Cafeteria lunch cost $1.50, but Mom usually made it $2. And could there even be some loose change down there? Yes. Ingrid counted the money—$3.11. More than enough. She opened the door and went inside; tinkle-tinkle of a little bell.

Moo Cow looked like an old-fashioned country store. Candy and chocolate counter on the left, ice cream on the right, everything made on the premises, big ceiling fan spinning slowly, the place empty now except for a guy with a gray ponytail halfway down his skinny back. He stood behind the counter, stirring up a cauldron of chocolate, the rising smells heavenly.

"Hi," he said. "What'll it be?"

"Peanut almond mocha swirl," said Ingrid.

"Small, medium, or large?"

"Small."

"Cup or cone?"

"Cup."

"Toppings?"

"Jimmies."

"Two ninety-five."

Sixteen cents to spare. Ingrid knew Moo Cow.

She sat at a little round table at the back. The ponytail guy came over with her ice cream, plus a napkin and a glass of ice water. Moo Cow had class.

"Enjoy," he said, and returned to the front of the shop, trailing a little chocolate breeze.

Peanut almond mocha swirl—a Moo Cow exclusive. Ingrid took that first bite, a perfect cross section with jimmies on the top and swirl on the bottom. Ah. She glanced over at the ponytail guy, back at the chocolate cauldron. How did you get a job like that, anyway? Imagine a life that revolved around Moo Cow instead of school—inventing new ice cream combos, dickering with the jimmies salesman, sampling jujubes from around the globe.

But that wasn't her life. Her life was about somehow turning lose-lose-lose into win-win. Ingrid took a pen from her backpack, smoothed out the napkin, wrote a big ? at the top.

Suspicions, all she had. Could she tell Chief Strade about them? Not without landing Ty in a big mess. Ratting out her own brother was unthinkable. If the situation were reversed, he'd . . .

Actually, Ingrid didn't know what Ty would do, but he'd never rat her out and anyway it didn't bear thinking about because the situation could never be reversed. Anything that put zits on your back was obviously off the table. It was like a sign from above. How much warning did you need?

Ingrid wrote *telling chief S* and drew a line through it. Telling the chief was out. Unless . . .

Unless . . . Was a fresh idea hovering somewhere in her mind? Ingrid felt it, like a pressure behind her forehead. Would another spoonful of ice cream help her think? She took one. And yes, right away, like magic, a thought took shape.

If there were some kind of steroid network in Echo Falls, then Ty was only one little part down at the bottom, a consumer. Her suspicions had begun with Ty, but was there any reason you had to begin there? No. You could begin anywhere, put the pieces together, end up diagramming the whole thing. And then you could go to the chief and say *Look what I found, chief! This is why they came after me.* Ty would be safe, out of the picture.

Did this sound like a plan? You bet. Ingrid wrote

suspicions and drew a line through that too. Suspicions were no good to her. *I can only work off facts,* the chief had said. That meant she had to move beyond suspicions to real facts. She wrote *facts*.

What were the facts? Fact one: back zits plus rapidly increasing strength. Fact two: the medicine bottle from Mexico, in the tree house and then not. Fact three: Ty's DVD player, first in Sean Rubino's room, then back in Ty's. Fact four: the $1,649, first in Sean's baseball glove, then not. Fact five: Carl Kraken the third, seen with Sean . . . and later seen at the hospital. Ingrid pictured the door to the storage room banging open, Carl the third and that other guy, the orderly with the gold tooth, turning toward her—*and a bunch of pills spilling on the floor.* And then— that look of recognition dawning on Carl's face.

Fact five, Carl the third and the orderly had nothing to do with Ty. Wasn't that the place to start?

At that moment Ingrid remembered "The Five Orange Pips" and maybe the most important thing Holmes ever told Watson: *the observer who has thoroughly understood one link in a series of incidents should be able to accurately state all the other ones, both before and after.*

Now Ingrid knew she was on the right track. She started scribbling all the facts on the napkin, the words getting tiny as she crammed them in. She didn't really register the bell tinkling as the door opened, was only half aware of a customer ordering chocolate, kept writing until a shadow passed over the table.

"Ingrid? Is that you?"

Ingrid looked up: Julia LeCaine, wearing those cool European shades, a white Moo Cow bag in her hand.

"Um," said Ingrid. "Hi."

That little smile, so intelligent, flickered across Julia's face. "Playing hooky?" she said. She took off her shades, exposing those green eyes, so green they were almost like shades themselves.

"Not, um, really," Ingrid said.

Julia laughed. "Your secret's safe with me," she said, her glance going quickly to Ingrid's napkin. "Mind if I join you?"

EIGHTEEN

"I played hooky all the time," said Julia LeCaine.

"You did?" Ingrid said.

"Oh, I was terrible." Julia raised her hand, ordered a glass of milk. "This place is a real find. I'm going to miss it."

"You're leaving?"

The ponytail guy came over with a tall glass of milk. Julia took a long sip. "Ah, milk," she said, "so wholesome, just as they say. I can never get enough."

Ingrid drank milk only under duress. "You're leaving?" she asked again.

"Correction: If I ever do," Julia said. "I misspoke. The fact is I'm loving this little town." She drank more milk, looked at Ingrid. "Although I gather it may not be quite as idyllic as it seems."

"What do you mean?" said Ingrid.

"I've heard rumors," said Julia.

Ingrid said nothing.

"Excuse me if I'm being too personal," Julia said. She smiled her little smile. "The fact is you remind me of how I was at your age."

"I do?"

"Very much. That's why I sympathize with what you're going through."

"I'm fine," Ingrid said.

"Really?" said Julia. "I got in a similar situation once, where no one believed me. I remember being terribly upset."

"What happened?"

"Just one of those hackneyed high school stories," Julia said. "I was accused of cheating on a test."

"And you were innocent?"

"Of course," said Julia, looking very surprised. "Why would I cheat on a test?"

Ingrid had never actually cheated—unless you counted happening to notice completely by accident the words *Fort Ticonderoga* on a recent history test of Mia's, an answer she herself would have come up with sooner or later—but she could think of reasons for doing it, such as getting a good grade or just plain passing.

"There was that pep talk you gave us," she said. "'Whatever it takes.'"

Julia's voice sharpened. "I had no reason to cheat," she said. "I was always the smartest kid in the class."

"Oh," said Ingrid.

"I assume you are too."

"Not exactly."

"No?" Julia took a sip of milk, and when she spoke again, her voice was softer. "The point is I know the feeling of no one believing you when you're telling the truth."

"Thanks." It seemed like the polite thing to say.

"If you feel up to it," Julia said, "I'd like to hear what really happened."

"Yeah?" said Ingrid. "How come?"

Julia smiled. "If not the smartest, then you're close," she said. "Let's put it this way." She pointed to the big *?* at the top of Ingrid's napkin. "Finding answers to tough questions is what I do."

Ingrid felt Julia's eyes on her. Green eyes, plus that love of milk—easy to think of Julia as a kind of cat. Ingrid was a dog person herself. She folded the napkin and slipped it in her pocket.

A dog person, not a cat person. Plus there was the whole vice presidential rivalry thing with Dad. And the weird way that long kick of Julia's hit Coach Ringer in the—

"One thing I've been feeling bad about, by the way," Julia said, interrupting her thoughts, "is Coach Ringer."

"Yeah?"

"In all that chaos, I can't be sure, but it might have been my ball that hit him."

Hey! So close to the last thought in her own mind.

"He's all right, thank God—safely back home," Julia said. "I called him last night to say how sorry I was."

"You did?"

"Guess what he said," said Julia. "'That's the way the cookie bounces.'"

Ingrid laughed. That was Coach Ringer. Julia was laughing too. She was smart, no doubt about that. Bringing up the whole steroid thing, out of the question, of course, because of Ty, but what harm could there be in going over the kidnapping? Maybe, solver of tough problems like she was, Julia would see something everyone else had missed.

Ingrid told Julia the kidnapping story—garage, car trunk, escape—and the aftermath—no duct tape, no sighting by Mrs. Grunello of a car outside 99 Maple Lane, no credibility.

"This kidnapper," Julia said, "did you get any impression of him at all?"

"No," said Ingrid. "I can't even say for sure it was a him."

Julia gazed at her glass of milk, almost as though it were a crystal ball. Ingrid could feel her thinking, the pressure wave crossing the table and touching her own brain. When Julia spoke at last, her question took Ingrid by surprise.

"How is the famous Grampy taking all this?" she said.

"Huh?"

"Your grandfather," said Julia, looking up. "Aylmer Hill."

"What did you mean, the famous Grampy?"

"No disrespect intended," said Julia. "The opposite, in fact—isn't he one of Echo Falls's leading movers and shakers?"

"Oh, no," said Ingrid. "Mover and shaker? That's not Grampy."

"I'm sure you see another side of him," Julia said, picking up the glass. "In his reaction to all this, for example."

"I don't think he even knows about it," Ingrid said.

"He—" The glass somehow slipped from Julia's hand. It seemed to hang in the air, then shot down to the floor and smashed, spraying milk and glass bits all over the place.

Julia peered down at the mess as though unsure of

how it had happened, her skin going pale. Then she gave herself a little shake and said, "How clumsy." Her eyes, now on Ingrid, widened slightly. "Don't move," she said. "There's glass in your hair."

Ingrid didn't move. Julia reached across the table, plucked a shard of glass from Ingrid's hair. She held it so Ingrid could see—a really sharp shard, one edge all jagged.

"Ouch," said Julia, dropping it on the floor. "God damn it." A drop of blood appeared on the ball of her thumb, a round, quivering drop. She licked it off.

By then, the ponytail guy was hurrying over with mop and broom. "Not to worry," he said. "Happens all the time." He had it cleaned up in seconds. "More milk?" he said.

Julia checked her watch. "Some other time."

He returned to his chocolate cauldron.

Julia laid some money on the table and rose. "Glad we could have this chat," she said. "Hang in there, Ingrid."

Ingrid gazed up at her. *Hang in there.* "Does that mean you believe me?" she said.

Julia met her gaze. She smiled that little smile. "I've got your back," she said.

"Thanks," said Ingrid.

Julia walked out, sat in the Boxster, drove away.

Ingrid went back to her ice cream, kind of runny now.
But still, so perfectly deli—

Something crunched between her teeth, something
much harder than a jimmy. Oh my God. Glass. Ingrid
spat the whole mouthful into her cup. Whew. A close
call.

To thoroughly understand one link in the chain:

Ingrid bicycled up the hill to the hospital. Actually,
she biked until it got too steep and then walked the rest
of the way. Bike racks stood near the emergency entrance.
Ingrid locked her bike and went inside.

The emergency waiting room was deserted except for
a nurse—not Mrs. Rubino—at the desk. She was busy at
her computer and didn't even look up. Ingrid crossed the
room without making a sound and went through the
door marked AUTHORIZED PERSONNEL ONLY.

She entered the long corridor with its harsh white
light. No one around. She passed the lounge—a nurse sat
in a chair with a paper cup in her hand, staring into
space—and came to the door marked STORAGE. Last time
it had hung open an inch or two; now it was closed.

Ingrid stood there for a moment, unsure. She reached
into her pocket to consult that napkin. Fact five: Carl the
third, the orderly with the gold tooth, pills spilling on the
floor. Ingrid had remembered fact five, of course, but

somehow seeing it in writing—even though it was her own writing, nothing official—gave her strength. If there was a chain, fact five had to be a link. She turned the knob and opened the door.

Nobody there. Ingrid went in, the door closing behind her with that compressed-air hiss. The storage room had open shelves from floor to ceiling on both sides, plus a cabinet with steel drawers at the end. What was she looking for? Evidence. Evidence that would prove there was a steroid network in Echo Falls, a network that knew she was onto them.

But what kind of evidence? Best would be a signed confession from all the perpetrators. *What a wacked-out thought, of no use at all. Get it together, Griddie. Think of those pills spilling on the floor.*

Yes. What were those pills? Data. Holmes was very clear about data. In "A Scandal in Bohemia," he said it was a capital mistake to theorize without data, because you ended up twisting facts to suit theories instead of the other way around. But she had those pills for data, so maybe it was okay to come up with a little theory. Such as the steroids got stored inside the hospital.

And why not? Ingrid headed toward those steel drawers at the other end of the storage room. If you wanted to hide a tree, plant it in a forest. Hospitals were full of pills, right? She tugged at one of the drawers. Locked. Little keyholes in the middle of all the drawers: all locked.

What about the open shelves? Ingrid saw lots of stuff you'd expect: boxes of gauze bandages, stacks of folded sheets and blankets, big brown bottles of disinfectant. No keys, of course; the keys to the drawers would be—

She heard footsteps outside the door. Oh my God. She tried to make up some cover story, got no further than *I, uh.* The door started to open. Ingrid scrambled onto the nearest shelf, wriggled behind a row of those brown bottles.

Big brown bottles with round shoulders. Ingrid peered over one of those shoulders and saw a man in green scrubs come in. He paused for a moment, turned right toward her. She ducked her head, but not before recognizing him: Rey Vasquez, the orderly with the gold tooth.

He sniffed the air, then continued on to the steel drawers and unlocked one. Ingrid knew all that from the sound. She didn't dare raise her head.

More sounds: the drawer sliding open, clinking things being lifted out, drawer closing, keys jingling. Then, through the bottles, brown, distorted, miniature, she saw Ray Vasquez walking back toward the door, shoving something into his pocket. A cell phone rang. He unclipped it from his belt and said, "Yo."

Ingrid heard a tinny voice on the other end, tinny

and angry. Rey Vasquez answered in Spanish. Ingrid didn't know any Spanish, except for *caramba* and *cucaracha* and a few words like that. The foreign-language option in Echo Falls didn't kick in until high school.

The tinny voice on the other end got angrier. Rey Vasquez went quiet. A few seconds later, he said, "Okay, okay, Cesar," and clicked off. "Gimme a break," he said to himself, then left the storage room, the door hissing closed.

Ingrid counted silently to sixty, then shifted the bottles aside and climbed off the shelf. Ear to the door: silence. She opened up and stepped into the corridor.

Uh-oh. Rey Vasquez was leaning against the door leading to the emergency waiting room, on his cell phone again. The storage room door started into that hissing noise. Rey Vasquez's head came up, like he was about to look her way. Ingrid turned her back and went down the corridor, walking at what she thought was a businesslike, every-right-to-be-here speed.

No voice rising behind her, no footsteps. Ingrid came to the end of the corridor. Signs pointed right to ICU, left to Radiology. Ingrid, not clear on the meaning of ICU, chose left.

She walked down another corridor, which broadened into a sitting area with chairs and little tables with magazines on both sides. Straight ahead stood a door marked

MRI. It opened and out walked Grampy, buttoning his shirtsleeve.

"Grampy?" Ingrid said.

He stopped, looked at her. His face got real angry. "What the hell are you doing here?" he said. "They sent you to spy on me?"

NINETEEN

"Spying on you, Grampy?" Ingrid said. "I don't understand."

"That's one thing I won't tolerate," Grampy said. "Spying."

"I would never do that," Ingrid said. "I didn't even know you were here."

"You didn't?" Grampy said.

"No," Ingrid said. "But what *are* you doing here, Grampy?"

"Nothing," Grampy said. He clamped his mouth shut, almost like a little kid. A nurse came by, pushing one of those rolling beds. The man on it, hooked up to an IV, wore one of those horrible johnny outfits, bony white legs sticking out. His eyes were closed.

"Let's get out of here," Grampy said.

Ingrid followed Grampy down the hall, left turn, right turn, another left. He seemed to know his way around. They came to the main door. As it slid open, Grampy paused.

"Is this a school day?" he said.

"Kind of."

"Then I can ask you that same question," he said. "What are you doing here?"

Ingrid paused.

"You're not sick or anything?" He peered at her. "Don't look sick."

"I'm fine," Ingrid said.

"Well, then," said Grampy. "Spit it out."

"It's complicated, Grampy."

"Do I look dumb?"

"Of course not."

"Then try me."

Ingrid lowered her voice. "It's about steroids," she said.

"What the hell's that?" said Grampy.

"Steroids?"

"Never heard of it."

"Them, Grampy." Ingrid started to explain, soon got the feeling she wasn't being even as clear as Mr. Porterhouse.

Grampy looked confused and said, "You take some medicine to get pimples on your back?"

"That's more of a side effect," said Ingrid. "Getting strong is the main thing, and calling it medicine is maybe—"

Grampy held up his hand like a traffic cop. "You get strong from an honest day's work," Grampy said. "Everybody knows that."

They did? What about all those millions of workers tapping away like crazy on their keyboards? Were they bulking up? "This is more the kind of—"

"I'm hungry," Grampy said. "You hungry?"

"Not re—"

"We'll talk about this stereo thing over lunch," he said. "Up at the farm." He got a funny look in his eye. "Bacon sound all right? How about ham or pork chops or pork ribs?"

"Grampy!" Ingrid said. "You didn't hurt that little pig?"

Grampy lifted Ingrid's bike into the back of the pickup— tossed it in, really, with an easy motion like a young man. They crossed the bridge, the river flowing fast beneath, black and ripply.

"Anyone ever warn you about falling in a pigpen?" Grampy said.

"No."

"And you're how old again?"

"Thirteen."

Grampy shook his head. "Stereo medicine to give you pimples and not knowing about falling in a pigpen. This country's in big trouble."

"What happens if you fall in a pigpen?" Ingrid said.

Grampy turned onto 392, followed the river north. "Pigs are smart and always hungry, just like us. Only difference is they're short."

"You're just trying to scare me," Ingrid said.

"Wouldn't do that, kid," said Grampy. "Run that stereo thing by me one more time."

Ingrid tried to think of the right place to begin. The answer came all by itself. "I got kidnapped, Grampy. But no one believes me." The next moment she was crying, really sobbing like a little kid, out of control. Grampy looked over in total alarm.

Ingrid got it together.

"Uh," said Grampy, "might find a rag in back you could wipe your face with."

"I'm fine," Ingrid said, and she wiped her face on her sleeve. Then, in a voice that sounded lower than her real voice, she told Grampy the whole story, leaving out nothing except the Ty part. Of course, the story didn't really make sense without the Ty part, but maybe it wasn't making sense to Grampy anyway. His face didn't change from beginning to end, except for darkening when the name Kraken came up. Was he keeping up with the story? Did he believe her?

"That's it?" he said, turning up the long drive to the farm.

Ingrid nodded.

"One thing I don't get," he said.

"What's that?"

"How come you didn't tell the cops about this motive?"

"The steroids?"

"Yeah."

She glanced at him. Face still expressionless, but he'd followed the whole story. And his not getting just that one thing had to mean he believed her. She loved Grampy.

But what could she say? Ingrid made a tough decision, a decision that meant breaking her code, the code of kids in Echo Falls and maybe everywhere. "Promise not to tell?" she said.

Grampy shook his head. "That's not a real question," he said.

"What do you mean?"

"Because you'll never get a real answer," he said.

That rang like a bell in Ingrid's head, completely true.

"It's about Ty," she said, and gave up the rest of it. "So that's why I can't tell Chief Strade. Ty'd have to go to court. He'd be kicked off the team and maybe worse than that."

"The law of the land comes first," Grampy said. He drove past the barn. The little pig was in its pen, head poking out one of those round windows Grampy had cut, looking cute and harmless. "Except for stupid laws, of course," Grampy added. "Goes without saying that family comes before stupid laws, and Ty getting in law trouble for these pimple pills would be stupid."

"He just wants to be stronger for football," Ingrid said.

"Football's not his game," said Grampy.

That pissed Ingrid off. "You've never seen him play," she said. "He's the only freshman on the varsity."

"Doesn't matter," said Grampy. "If football's going to be your game, you got to love to hit. Really love it, like the rest of the game is just an excuse. And that's not your brother."

Ingrid thought back to Ty's games. Grampy was right. Ty was very brave about the hitting, but he didn't love it.

"Wasn't your father, either," said Grampy, parking by the house.

"Huh?" said Ingrid. "Dad was the star of the team."

"Because he was a real good athlete," Grampy said.

"Lots of athlete genes in this family, kid. But he wasn't a hitter."

"Did you tell him that?"

"Course not," said Grampy. "What good would that do? Can't make someone a hitter."

"Did you play football, Grampy?"

Grampy, reaching for the door handle, got a faraway look in his eye. He nodded slightly.

"For Echo Falls High?"

"And after," Grampy said.

"After?"

"In college."

"But you didn't go to college, Grampy."

"Hmmm," said Grampy.

"What do you mean, hmmm?"

Long pause. "This is one of those things not too many people know about," Grampy said. "Most likely none."

"So I have to promise not to tell?" said Ingrid.

Grampy gave her a long look. "Too bad there's not football for girls," he said.

"Are you saying . . . ?"

"You're a hitter, sure as shootin'," said Grampy. "Takes one to know one. Come on in the house. I'll show you something."

* * *

They walked up to the house. Grampy always used the back door, a barn-red door with white trim and window-panes in the upper half. Now he'd left it open for some reason. And . . . what was this? One of those window-panes had a big jagged hole in it, fist size.

Grampy stood before his back door, a puzzled look on his face. "I don't . . ." His voice trailed away.

"I think someone broke in, Grampy," Ingrid said.

Pink patches appeared on Grampy's cheeks. A growl came from deep in his throat and then he strode inside. "Say your prayers, you son of a bitch," Grampy called out in a voice so scary, it would have given Ingrid the chills if she hadn't had them already.

The back door opened right into the kitchen. It was a mess. The piles and piles of mail that usually lay on the table were now scattered all over the place. Every cupboard door stood open, and some of the drawers had been yanked right out and dumped on the floor. The broom closet was open too. That was where Grampy kept his guns—the .22 rifle that Ingrid had learned on, the .357 handgun she was too young to use, and the twelve-gauge shotgun, a beautiful old Purdy side-by-side with a wooden stock that glowed like it was alive.

Grampy grabbed the shotgun. He fumbled around on a shelf at the back for a box of shells, broke the gun open, loaded both barrels.

"Right behind me, now," Grampy said.

"Shouldn't we call the police?"

"Can't trust a cop," Grampy said. "How many times I have to say it?"

Shotgun half raised, index finger resting on the trigger guard, Grampy went through every room in the house, Ingrid right behind him.

"Goddamn it," Grampy said.

Every room in the house was turned upside down. The front door, like the back, hung open, but none of its panes were broken. Meaning—someone had opened it from the inside, probably on the way out.

"Maybe whoever it was heard us coming," Ingrid said. "Or saw the pickup on three ninety-two."

Grampy nodded. He gazed through the doorway, past the barn, the brown fields, the highway and the tree line on the far side, smoke rising from one of those distant cottages on the old Prescott farm. And no one in sight. He lowered the shotgun.

"Is anything missing, Grampy?" Ingrid said.

"Better check," said Grampy, his voice quiet and dull, like there wasn't enough air in his lungs all of a sudden for making lots of sound. Ingrid stepped in front of him and closed the door, locking every lock.

They went back through all the rooms, reshelving things, putting them back in drawers, righting a tipped-over lamp or two.

"Nothing missing," Grampy said, his voice still not normal.

The kitchen, messiest room by far, they tackled last. Grampy took care of the cupboards and drawers; Ingrid handled the mail.

"Nothing missing," Grampy said again.

"So what was the point of the break-in?" said Ingrid.

No answer from Grampy.

So much mail, almost all unopened, some of it going back months, as Ingrid could see from the postmarks.

"Don't you ever open your mail, Grampy?" she said.

"All junk," said Grampy, putting the shotgun back in the broom closet.

Some of it didn't look like junk to Ingrid. She sorted it into three huge mounds—definite junk, possible junk, other. Sorting away at the table, she felt a draft on her ankles, glanced down and saw one of those heat-duct grates in the floor. No heat on yet, of course, not Grampy's style, meaning cold air was snaking around down there. And what was that? A little white glimmer in the darkness under the grate. One more letter.

Ingrid knelt, stuck her hand through the bars of the grate, couldn't quite reach.

"Looks a little better," Grampy said, his voice not

quite so weak. "How about something to drink?"

Ingrid rose, leaving the letter down there. "I'll make tea."

Their eyes met. "You're a good girl," Grampy said.

That was nice.

"Someone tried to kidnap you?" he said.

"Yes."

"Their life is over," said Grampy, his voice back at full strength.

Grampy built a roaring fire. Ingrid made tea. They drank it from big mugs at the kitchen table. Grampy poured some VO into his.

"Is that a kind of whiskey?" Ingrid said.

"Canadian," said Grampy. "Had a Canadian buddy."

"Was that during the war?" Grampy never talked about the war.

He nodded.

"On Corregidor?" Ingrid said. Corregidor was some horrible thing. Mr. Sidney had been there with Grampy, although Ingrid had never heard any of the details.

"No point discussing that," Grampy said. "Tell me again why the kidnapping's connected to these pills."

"What else could it be?" Ingrid said.

They went over the whole story a few more times. They drank more tea, Ingrid's with milk and sugar,

Grampy's with VO. Grampy started repeating some of the same questions. Smudges darkened the hollows under his eyes, turned a little purple. He was getting tired.

"So you think this orderly's involved with one of the Krakens?" he said for the third time.

"The youngest one."

"Krakens are scum of the earth."

They'd gotten to that point already. The sky darkened outside and the wind came up. Ingrid rose and taped cardboard in the broken windowpane.

"What should I do, Grampy?" she asked.

"No I," said Grampy. "We."

That felt nice too, especially if it had practical results. They sat in silence for a while. Then Grampy startled her by smacking his hand on the table.

"Got an idea," he said. "I'll lend you the three fifty-seven."

"I don't—"

"You could carry it around in that backpack of yours."

"—think that's a good idea."

"Oh, right," said Grampy. "I haven't taken you out with the three fifty-seven yet." He glanced outside. "Maybe a little too dark now. How about tomorrow? There's an old scarecrow in the barn. We could pin a heart on his chest and—"

"The gun won't help us solve anything," Ingrid said.

"Studied any history yet?" said Grampy.

He thought some more. No other suggestions followed. Maybe Grampy just couldn't get his head around the whole steroid thing, the way the clock on his VCR was always flashing twelve. He drove her home, mostly in silence, except for a bit of coughing on Grampy's part. Ingrid could feel his mind drifting somewhere else.

"What was it you were going to show me in the house, Grampy?" she said.

"Nothing important," said Grampy.

TWENTY

No one home: Ty still at practice, Mom and Dad at work. No one home and very quiet, the sound of Grampy's pickup driving away still audible. The house was full of shadows, the edges of everything all fuzzy, but Ingrid didn't turn on any lights. She went upstairs and lay on her bed, not like her at all on a late afternoon.

She spoke out loud. "What the hell am I going to do?"

Ingrid had read somewhere that sleep was a time when the brain got busy on its own, knitting together this and that, making sense of things. Right now would be good for a sleep like that. But just as Ingrid was about to close her eyes, her gaze fell on the statue of St. Joseph, standing on the shelf over her computer.

A plastic man, bearded and long-haired, not much taller than the soccer trophy beside him. Ingrid didn't know exactly who St. Joseph was. Somebody's father, maybe? All she knew was that Mom's clients liked to bury him upside down in their yards to make their houses sell quickly.

What if you buried him right side up?

I guess your house would never sell.

Ingrid got up. She felt funny, not quite herself, more of a virtual self, a figure in a dream. Maybe her brain was doing some knitting after all. She took St. Joseph off the shelf, carried him downstairs, entered the garage.

Gardening tools hung on wall hooks. Ingrid selected a little hand spade, six or seven inches long. She went out to the front yard.

Where was the best spot for this? Maybe by the dogwood bush, her favorite landscape feature at 99 Maple Lane. Ingrid knelt, cut out a circle of grass, careful not to damage it—Dad was fussy about the lawn, sprinkled all kinds of stuff around every spring. Then she dug a hole, narrow and a little more than a foot deep. No frost yet, the earth still pretty soft—digging was fast and easy.

Ingrid buried St. Joseph right side up in her front yard.

* * *

Her mood lifted before she even got back inside, no longer tired or fuzzy. She switched on lights, sat at the kitchen table with a cold Fresca and a minibag of Fritos, a great combo. Yes, her mood was lifting, like something good was on the way. She thought of Grampy's .357. Sherlock Holmes didn't go in for a lot of gunplay—his favorite weapon was a hunting crop. Watson had a pistol. It appeared in "The Adventure of the Speckled Band," for example, one of the scariest of the Holmes stories because of that swamp adder, *deadliest snake in India.* But in the climactic scene, the pistol plays no role; in fact, the snake doesn't even get killed.

For some reason, Ingrid's mind wanted to stay with that last scene. By then, Holmes had figured out how Dr. Roylott killed Miss Stoner's sister, but he had no proof. For proof, he had to be inside the mansion when Dr. Roylott went after Miss Stoner herself. Holmes kept Miss Stoner safe from the swamp adder, of course, secretly moving her to another room and hiding out with Watson in her bedroom while Dr. Roylott got that whole diabolical snake plan going. It was really a kind of . . .

Sting.

Bzzz.

Ingrid felt an idea, a huge one, struggling to be born. The sting was one of the strongest weapons of law enforcement. How did it work, exactly? You set up the bad guy, made sure you were there when he committed the crime, caught him red-handed. For example, say you knew a guy was selling stolen cars. What do you do? Buy one from him, maybe saying at the same time, "This sure is a great price, buddy."

And he'd snicker, guilty as sin. Tucking the cash into his greasy pocket.

"What's that little laugh all about?" you'd say.

And he'd say, "You don't wanna know."

"Oh, but I do," you'd say, as you snapped on the cuffs.

The door opened and Mom came in from the garage. Ingrid looked up, startled. She hadn't heard a thing.

"Hi, Ingrid," Mom said, giving her a close look. "How was school?"

"School?" said Ingrid. "Oh, fine. You know."

"Much homework?" said Mom, kicking off her shoes and sliding on her sheepskin slippers.

"Um," said Ingrid.

"What does that mean?" said Mom. "I know things may be . . . difficult now, but it won't help to let your schoolwork slip."

"No chance of that," Ingrid said.

Mom did a quick double take. "You're in a good mood today," she said.

"Pretty good." True, and kind of amazing, what with

everything she'd been going through. But Ingrid knew why: Now she had a plan. She was going to sting them like they'd never been stung.

"I'm glad," said Mom.

All very well, Ingrid thought while Dad drove her to the high school for the *Wizard of Oz* rehearsal, to talk tough about stinging, but exactly how was a sting organized, anyway? It had to start with putting out the word that you were in the market for something—in this case, steroids. Putting the word out meant she'd have to have a target, someone on the receiving end of the word. Who was that going to—

Dad's cell phone rang. He answered it. "Hi, Tim."

Ingrid couldn't hear what Mr. Ferrand was saying, but she caught the tone, not nice.

"But that wasn't what she—"

Mr. Ferrand's voice rose.

"I'll be there in a few minutes," Dad said, and clicked off.

Dad sped up, shifted gears, grinding them slightly, which never happened. He was a great driver and loved the TT, treating it like a baby.

"Going back in to work, Dad?"

He nodded. A passing streetlight turned his face into all bones and shadows. Had he lost some weight?

"It's kind of busy these days, huh?" Ingrid said.

"Can't be afraid of hard work, Ingrid. Haven't we been through this?"

"You mean all that globalization stuff?"

Dad's hands tightened on the wheel. "Try to express yourself a little more maturely," he said.

That hurt. Ingrid sat back in the seat. Had she been grating on him, grating on her own father? She folded her arms across her chest and didn't utter another word.

"It might help," said Jill Monteiro, sitting on the auditorium stage at Echo Falls High, feet dangling over the edge, "if we shared an understanding of what this scene's all about."

Silence from the cast—Stacy, Mia, Brucie, Joey, Ingrid—all of them sitting with their feet dangling too. Somehow Brucie's sneaker fell off, landing with a loud smack. Brucie had big feet for his size.

"Brucie?" said Ms. Monteiro.

"Yeah?"

"Any ideas?"

"Sure," said Brucie. "How about a car that washes itself?"

Stacy jabbed him in the arm, hard.

"Ow," said Brucie.

"Retard," said Stacy.

He batted his eyes at her, like he was in love.

"Joey?" Jill said.

Joey, sitting next to Ingrid, gazed down at his script. "Scene?" he said, like it was a foreign word or something.

"This little episode," said Jill. "When the four travelers finally meet the wizard they've been seeking. What ends up happening?"

Joey's eyes stayed on the script, but he couldn't have been getting any help from that, because it was turned to the title page and just said *Wizard.* "Ends up happening," he mumbled to himself.

"Pay no attention to the man behind the curtain, dudes," said Brucie.

"Joey?" Jill said.

Joey took a deep breath. "They find out he's a con man."

Jill clapped her hands together. "Exactly."

Joey looked up, a surprised and slightly pleased expression on his face. A great expression, in Ingrid's view.

"The wizard is a con man, as Joey says," said Jill. "This is where we get to see what's behind the curtain, the way things really are. And when we do, there's another surprise."

"What was the first one again?" said Brucie.

They all ignored him, including Jill, a fast learner. "Anyone?" she said.

Blank looks, except for Mia. "Even though the wizard's a fake," she said, "he ends up giving them what they want anyway."

Wow. Mia was so smart.

Then Ingrid got a little idea of her own. "Except for Dorothy," she said.

Jill smiled. "Now we're ready," she said. "Let's put on a play."

Was there anything like the theater? Not even close.

"Can we pause right there for a sec?" said Jill, not long after. "In my script, Brucie, that line doesn't read, 'I am Oz, the great and terrible and oh so cool.' It just says 'the great and terrible.'"

"That's called ad-libbing," said Brucie.

"Let's stick to the script for now," said Jill.

"Jawohl," said Brucie.

Stacy whacked him again, actually hard enough to hurt. Brucie didn't bat his eyes this time. Things went smoothly after that.

Just before the end of the rehearsal, Ingrid saw a little old man coming down one of the side aisles. Hey, Mr. Samuels.

"Ms. Monteiro?" he said.

"Hi, Mr. Samuels," said Jill.

"I'm going to be doing a piece on The Xmas Revue

this year," he said. "Any chance I could snap a few rehearsal photos?"

"Free ink?" said Jill. "Fire away."

"You showbiz types," said Mr. Samuels, taking a camera from his coat pocket.

He came close to the stage, took pictures as they rehearsed. Ingrid made sure to block out his presence completely, although she did allow a dazzling yet somehow mysterious smile to play across her face from time to time. Yes, she was a showbiz type.

Only when Jill said, "That's all for today," did Ingrid remember the braces and clamp her mouth shut. Too late.

They filed out to the lobby. Parents were parked outside, all except Ingrid's. Jill and the kids drove off, leaving Ingrid plus Mr. Samuels, squinting into the viewer of his camera, checking his photos.

"Got some good ones here, Ingrid," he said. "Who's the wizard?"

"Brucie Berman."

"Is his father the rabbi?"

"Yeah."

"Oh, boy," said Mr. Samuels, putting the camera away. "How's that grandfather of yours these days?"

"Good."

"I ran into a few snags trying to nail down the own-ers of those cottages where the complaint got filed," Mr. Samuels said.

"It doesn't matter," Ingrid said. "The pig thing worked."

"Happy to hear it," said Mr. Samuels. "But I'm going to keep digging anyway. This one's got my curiosity up."

"How come?" said Ingrid.

"Turns out that Delaware outfit, DRF Development, is just a shell."

"A shell?"

"Like one of those Russian dolls," said Mr. Samuels. "Eggs within eggs. The innermost one I can find so far is Black Coral Investments, based on one of those Caribbean islands. Which of course is why I got curious."

Ingrid wasn't following this too closely. What did it matter, now that the pig thing had worked?

"Those Caribbean islands," Mr. Samuels went on, "where anonymous companies hide out when they don't want scrutiny from Uncle Sam. This particular island's one I hadn't heard of. Anguilla, I think is how you say it."

Ong Willa. Hey. That rang a bell, but before Ingrid could figure out why, Mr. Samuels changed the subject.

"Not particularly interesting to a civilian, I guess," he said. He came a little closer. "And how are you yourself doing these days, Ingrid?"

"Fine," said Ingrid.

He gazed down at her; not too far down, because Mr. Samuels was just a little guy. A curious little guy, with still and watchful eyes that didn't miss much. He knew something. Oh my God. Could all this get in the paper? SCHOOLGIRL CAUGHT IN ELABORATE RUSE. Unbearable.

"Sure about that?" said Mr. Samuels.

"Yeah," said Ingrid. "Very."

He backed off a step or two. "The press can be your friend," he said. "I hope you know that."

He waited for her to say something. "Give us a good review," she said.

Mr. Samuels was silent for a moment. Then he said, "I call 'em like I see 'em. No integrity, otherwise."

"I didn't mean—"

"No problem," he said. He glanced outside. "Someone coming to get you?"

"They're just a little late."

"I could drop you off."

"Thanks, Mr. Samuels," Ingrid said. "But I'll be okay."

The door had barely closed behind him before Ingrid realized something very important: Time was a factor. There were going to be headlines, and soon, all about her. A permanent record and completely false. She couldn't afford a lot of musing about the fine points of organizing a sting. That kind of dithering was what had got Hamlet in trouble. Ingrid had never actually read or seen *Hamlet*, but Jill had told everyone the whole story during a rehearsal break two or three productions ago. And, hey! What was that whole play-within-a-play scene if not a sting?

She had to hurry.

And . . . and here she was, alone in the deserted high school. The high school where Ty and Sean and God knew how many other steroid customers spent their day. Also the high school where Carl Kraken the third's father, Carl Junior, worked out of that basement office. The observer who truly understands one link understands the whole chain.

Ingrid looked outside. No headlights approaching, no Mom or Dad about to pull up to the front door. Ingrid headed back into the school, passed a big pep rally poster—Red Raiders Rule—and took the stairs leading down.

TWENTY-ONE

Ingrid walked along the basement corridor in Echo Falls High. This was the oldest part of the school, the walls stone, the brick floor worn smooth. Grampy had gone here long ago, maybe strolled right down this corridor when these bricks were new. She'd known about Grampy going to the high school but never really thought about it. Now it turned out that Grampy had played for the Red Raiders too, a ferocious hitter on the football field, probably a big star like Dad. She tried to picture a teenage Grampy and couldn't. Hard enough to picture a teenage Dad.

Those rows of unused rusted-out lockers went by.

Somewhere nearby a furnace rumbled. The floor vibrated under Ingrid's feet. She came to the door marked CUSTODIAN: MR. KRAKEN. Closed. Ingrid put her ear to it, heard nothing.

No sound at all, except for the furnace. Getting late now, the school emptied out, Carl Junior probably long gone. Long gone, so he'd have locked the door behind him. Ingrid tried it. Unlocked. Were things starting to go her way? She opened the door—it squeaked on its hinges, the custodian's own door, which had to say something about him—and stepped inside.

No one there. The office was dark except for the desk lamp, spreading a narrow cone of light. Ingrid went over to the desk.

A messy desk, all kinds of bills and memos scattered on it, a few glass jars filled with nuts and bolts, an ashtray overflowing with butts. But what caught Ingrid's attention the most were some little waxy crescents: fingernail cuttings. Really gross. Of course, if you snuck into someone's personal space, you were bound to—

Whoa. Fingernail cuttings. Something Holmes had said was coming back to her, something about—yes, that was it: *the suggestiveness of thumbnails.* From "A Case of Identity," right? One of her favorites, but she'd never really understood what the suggestiveness of thumbnails meant, beyond Holmes's usual thing about observing closely. Now she wondered whether Holmes was somehow ahead of his time. When was DNA discovered, anyway? Ingrid didn't know, but she was pretty sure it was after Holmes.

She tore off the top page of Carl Junior's desk calendar—the day was practically over anyway—and blew two fingernail cuttings onto it. No way was she going to actually touch them. Holmes wouldn't have either. She folded the page into a square and pocketed it. Kraken DNA: might come in handy.

On a roll now? Ingrid got the feeling she was. She pawed through all the papers on the desk, found a pen, kind of greasy. Now to compose a note. Why was putting something in writing, even a sentence or two, always so hard?

Ingrid pulled the desk calendar closer and wrote on the new top page.

> *Echo Falls athlete looking to get stronger.*
> *Meet me Sunday at noon at*

Ingrid paused. Where would be good? Maybe after you'd set up three or four stings you'd know the perfect location right off the top of your head, but this was her first one. She mulled over a few possibilities—the swings at Ferrand Middle, the parking lot at Blockbuster, the

Punch Bowl pond in the town woods—saw pros and cons for each. She was still mulling, pen poised over Carl Kraken Junior's desk calendar, when she heard hard footsteps coming down the corridor.

Her heart pounded in her chest, going into a panic that spread instantly to the rest of her. What was her story going to be? *Quick, quick, like now.* But no story came. Ingrid whirled around, noticed a closet at the back of the room. The hard footsteps got louder. She ran to the closet door, threw it open.

A big closet, dark and shadowy. A glimpse of file cabinets, cardboard boxes, clothes hanging from a rail, junk all over the floor, and then she ducked inside, closing the door softly behind her. At the same moment, the office door opened with its little squeak.

Almost total blackness inside the closet, just a band of dull yellow light, almost brown, leaking in at the bottom. Ingrid scrambled back into the closet till she could go no farther, wedging herself between two filing cabinets. Her heart—she could actually hear it.

Footsteps sounded on the office floor. Ingrid heard a little *hmmm*, quiet and thoughtful. Made by a man, no doubt about it. Then came shuffling sounds—he was going through the papers on the desk. Too late, Ingrid remembered her *Wizard* script. She'd had it in her hand when she'd entered the office, and didn't have it now.

Could she have laid it on the desk, say when she was writing her sting note? Very possible. And had she written her name on the title page the day Jill had handed them out? Sure, that was one of Jill's rules, and Ingrid, maybe not a great follower of rules in general, always followed Jill's. *Ingrid L-H*—she could picture it, just below *Wizard*.

A drawer opened and closed. Then another. Ingrid heard a clink of glass, remembered Carl Junior boozing at his desk. She didn't hear any unscrewing or pouring sounds, though, just another clink, maybe a bottle going back in the drawer. She also remembered that Carl Junior had been counting money at his desk. Money: a link in the chain? Ingrid thought of the $1,649 in Sean's baseball glove, $1,649 not there the second time she looked. Where had it gone? What was that expression? Follow the money. Good idea, if she ever got out of here.

Silence. What was going on? Could he—

Suddenly Ingrid heard voices. Faint voices, not in the office but from the corridor outside. The man in the office must have heard them too. The next moment, he was on the move, his footsteps almost silent now, very quick. And headed her way. Was he going to—

The closet door opened. Light rushed in. Crouched between the file cabinets at the back, Ingrid looked up. Her view was mostly blocked by clothes hanging on the rail—overalls, flannel shirt, yellow slicker. A man came in, but all Ingrid caught were a few slices of him: thick upper arm clad in a dark shirt, dark pant leg, big black shoes. Not his face. Did that mean he couldn't have seen her? The door closed and the closet went black again, except for the ribbon of light under the door.

Ingrid heard the man brush against the hanging clothes. Then came tiny little pats, like he was feeling around.

The outer door opened, making that squeak again. The man in the closet went still. So close, but he wasn't aware of her at all—those little pats had proved it. Ingrid was aware of almost nothing else but him. She could hear him breathing, slow, even breaths, perfectly calm.

Ingrid tried to make herself small, to breathe like some tiny little creature no one would ever notice. She recalled a scene like this in a movie. They'd played it for laughs.

More footsteps, moving in the office. A voice spoke, low and quiet.

"Coast is clear."

Only three words, but enough. Ingrid knew that voice: Sean Rubino.

Someone else spoke, farther away, in the doorway or still out in the corridor.

"Maybe this isn't a good idea."

Ingrid knew that voice, too. There wasn't a voice she knew better.

Ty.

Sean made a clucking noise, like a chicken.

"I mean it," Ty said. But he sounded closer, now in the room. And Ingrid knew him: He only half meant it.

"Wimpin' out on me?" said Sean.

"Yeah, right," said Ty. "It's just like, you know."

"I don't know," Sean said. He sounded like a man when he said that, a full-grown man, and not a nice one.

"Well," said Ty, "what makes you think he keeps any around?"

"'Cause he's a dumbass Kraken," said Sean. "Retards, all of them. Everyone knows that."

"Yeah?" said Ty. "I thought they were kind of . . ."

"Kind of what?"

"Dangerous."

"Ooooh, dangerous," said Sean in a gay voice.

"Go to hell," said Ty, lowering his voice, making it sound tougher.

"Hey, just jerkin' your chain," Sean said. "I know Carl the third personally. Take it from me—he's harmless."

A drawer opened.

"Get a load of this," Sean said.

"What is it?"

"Duh, bourbon," said Sean. "Want a hit?"

"Now?" Ty said. "We should probably . . ."

Gurgle of liquid, followed by lip smack. "Piss," said Sean. "Jim Beam's way better. You tasted JB?"

"Oh, yeah, sure," said Ty, from which Ingrid knew he'd never even heard of it.

"When?" said Sean.

"Lots of times," said Ty. "In the woods."

"You talking about the tree house?" said Sean.

"Yeah."

"Cool spot," said Sean. A pause. And then: "That sister of yours."

"What about her?"

"I don't trust her."

"My sister?"

"Caught her snooping in my room."

"I don't—"

"Think she knows anything?" Sean said.

A split-second pause. "How could she?" Ty said. "Anyway, she'd never rat anyone out."

"What makes you so sure?"

"She's my little sister, for God's sake."

"I don't like the way she looks at me. If she wasn't a girl, I'd—"

"Sisters are a pain. You know that."

"I'm not talking about that normal stuff—I'm talking about this look she has," said Sean.

Ty's voice rose a little. "Leave my sister out of this,"

he said. "You don't know her."

Silence. Then Sean said, "You still owe me."

"Where'd that come from?" Ty said.

"Just in case you think I forgot," said Sean. "DVD player or cash equivalent."

"Don't have to remind me," Ty said. "I'm gonna—"

The desk phone rang. Seven rings—Ingrid counted them—before the caller gave up.

Silence.

"Maybe he's coming back," Ty said.

"Who?" said Sean.

"Mr. Kraken," said Ty. "That's his phone, right? Someone expects him to be here."

"Um," said Sean. More silence. "You could be right."

"Better split," said Ty.

"Yeah," said Sean.

Squeak of their sneakers on the floor, squeak of the office door opening and closing. They were gone.

A few seconds passed. Ingrid grew aware of the smell the man in the closet had. She'd been smelling it the whole time: a piney kind of aftershave. He blew a quick burst of air through his lips, making a contemptuous sound.

The man opened the closet door and went out. Ingrid saw nothing but his broad back before the door closed. Then came the sound of retreating footsteps, squeak of the outer door, and he was gone too.

Ingrid stayed where she was, scrunched between the filing cabinets, her legs aching. Was Carl Junior on his way back, as Ty had said? Or—an even scarier thought— had he been the guy with her in the closet? Why would he do that? Ingrid didn't know.

She got to her feet, went to the closet door, heard no sound from the other side. She pushed the door open. The office looked exactly the same as before.

Ingrid went to the desk. There, on top: her copy of the script, just as she'd thought. She grabbed it and turned to go. Her gaze fell on the desk calendar, tomorrow's page, where she'd started to set up her sting:

> *Echo Falls athlete looking to get stronger.*
> *Meet me Sunday at noon at*

That was where she'd paused to think of a good place, just before things in the office got so busy. But that second sentence no longer ended with *at*. Someone had added three more words: *the tree house.*

Ingrid got an icy feeling. *Be calm.* She forced herself to leave slowly, closing the door quietly behind her, walking down the corridor like an everyday school kid

249

doing everyday things. But that didn't last. Ingrid's feet took over. They wanted out of the building.

Down the corridor, up the stairs, into the lobby, racing speed now.

Deserted, thank—

Except for Carl Junior, who stepped out of a classroom, mop in hand. His eyes narrowed. His mouth opened. But before he could speak, Dad came through the front door, his long leather coat flapping behind him.

"Where have you been?" he said. "Didn't you hear me honking?"

"Sorry," Ingrid said. "Bathroom."

"School's officially closed," said Carl Junior.

Dad ignored him completely, was already on his way back out. Ingrid crossed the lobby, taking a route that passed fairly close to Carl Junior.

He looked at her in surprise. Too close maybe, but Ingrid had to know. She took two quick sniffs and hurried out the door.

Carl Junior had a smell, a strong one, but it was all stale sweat and cigarettes. Nothing piney about him. One hundred percent pineless.

So who was the man in the closet? Who had written the end of the sting note on tomorrow's calendar page?

A note that Carl Junior would be laying his eyes on pretty soon.

Uh-oh. Should she go back inside, try to get it?

The window of the TT slid down. "Would you stop dawdling?" Dad said, really irritated. "Hustle for once."

TWENTY-TWO

"How was rehearsal?" Mom said, looking up from a set of house plans.

"Good," said Ingrid. "Where's Ty?"

"Not home yet," said Mom. "He went right from practice to Greg's, some project for science they're doing together."

Ingrid knew the part about going to Greg's right from practice had to be a lie. She stood there for a moment, across the kitchen table from Mom.

"Ingrid?" Mom said. "Something on your mind?"

Telling Mom: impossible, of course. But the funny thing was that if the phone hadn't rung at that moment, Ingrid might have blurted out the whole story. Mom had the kind of love for her that you could feel, like it was part of the atmosphere, meaning that blurting was always an option.

"Hello?" Mom said, picking up. "Push back the closing?" She reached for a notepad. "What about the rate lock?" Her pen started moving. Ingrid heard Dad opening the liquor cabinet. She went upstairs.

"Nigel!"

Nigel turned. He tried to look innocent, but that was hard to do with Mister Happy in his mouth.

"PUT HIM DOWN!"

Nigel wagged his tail, kind of like everything was normal and Mister Happy was invisible. Or maybe Nigel had somehow forgotten all about him.

"I'm not going to say it again."

Nigel's ears and tail drooped at once. Mister Happy fell to the floor. Ingrid was taking him, all tattered and drooly, to her bedroom, when she heard Dad on his way up. He came to the top, drink in one hand, briefcase in the other, dark shadows around his eyes.

"Homework all done?" he said.

"Just taking care of it," Ingrid said, remembering that she didn't even know what the homework was.

"Don't fall behind," Dad said. He went into the office.

Ingrid followed him. He was already at the computer, staring at a screen full of numbers.

"Dad?"

"What is it?"

"Can I borrow the digital recorder?"

"Huh?" said Dad, tapping at the keys. "Borrow what?"

"The digital recorder."

Dad took a deep breath, rubbed his eyes. "In the briefcase," he said.

"Thanks," Ingrid said. She rummaged through the briefcase, found the digital recorder in a side compartment. At the same time she couldn't help noticing a bunch of files with a Post-it stuck on top, a Post-it with a note Dad had written to himself.

1. Think

2. Anticipate

3. Work harder

She glanced at him. His finger came down hard on the delete key. "Maybe this globalization stuff isn't such a good idea," she said.

He turned to her. "That's like saying the tide's not a good idea," he said.

"Oh." Right. Ingrid had forgotten the forces, those forces out there making the future grim.

She started from the room, paused at the door. "Love you, Dad."

Silence, except for tapping at the keys. He hadn't heard. Ingrid went to her room.

She practiced with the recorder. It was pretty simple. You pressed the green button and spoke. "Ms. Groome? I'm afraid it's bad news." Then you pressed the red button and listened. The only problem was hearing your own voice. She sounded about six years old and immature for her age. Ingrid tried out some changes—making it older, deeper, huskier, and was working on adding a menacing undertone, when Mom called up.

"Ingrid? You've got a visitor."

"Who?"

"Let's not shout from room to room," Mom shouted. "Just come down."

Ingrid went downstairs. Joey stood in the front hall. Mom lingered in the kitchen doorway, trying to look like she was in the middle of doing something.

"Hi," Ingrid said.

"Hey," said Joey.

Silence. Ingrid paused, two steps from the bottom. Joey shuffled his feet, took an envelope from his pocket, put it back.

"Maybe Joey would like something to drink," Mom said.

"I'm good," said Joey.

"Or something to eat," Mom said.

"He just ate," Ingrid said.

Mom backed into the kitchen.

Ingrid stepped down into the hall.

"Hi," she said.

"Hey," said Joey. "You sick?"

"Huh?"

"'Cause you weren't in school today."

Ingrid put a finger to her lips, maybe shooting him an angry glare at the same time.

"Oops," Joey said, glancing toward the kitchen. No sign of Mom. Joey started inching the other way, in the direction of the living room.

"Come on in the living room," Ingrid said.

"Thanks," said Joey.

They went into the living room. Joey looked out the big south windows. "Hey," he said. "The woods."

"Correct," said Ingrid.

"Like, the view," Joey said. "Nice."

"Uh-huh," Ingrid said. "What's in the envelope?"

Joey put a hand to his pocket. "If you weren't sick . . ." he said.

Ingrid tilted up her chin. "Continue," she said.

"If you weren't"—lowering his voice—"sick, then is it because you're scared—not scared, I mean like, um, you know . . . about not wanting to be around people who don't believe you. And stuff."

"No," Ingrid said.

"No, that's not it?" said Joey.

"What I said," said Ingrid.

"Okay," said Joey. "Cool."

"I was kidnapped," Ingrid said. "It doesn't matter who believes me." She felt tears coming, strange, hot ones, even powerful, if that made any sense.

Joey looked alarmed. "I believe you," he said.

"You said that before."

"'Cause, like, I meant it," Joey said. "Mean it."

The tears didn't come, although the hot, powerful feeling didn't quite go away. "I'm going to prove it," Ingrid said.

"How?" said Joey. "Maybe I can help."

She gazed at Joey. Was there any harm in telling him? Maybe. Ty getting pulled in, for example. Chief Strade was smart. If there was something he wanted out of Joey, Ingrid was pretty sure he could get it. Plus she remembered Grampy, when he told her the story of Carl Kraken Senior and the noose: *No one can protect you. Got to protect yourself.* That was kind of scary, maybe even flat wrong. But it felt right to Ingrid, like she and Grampy shared some gene, a prickly, independent one.

"What's in the envelope?" Ingrid said.

"Oh, yeah," said Joey, taking it out. "Why I came

over." He opened up the envelope, took out two tickets. "Monster trucks at the Hartford Civic Center," he said. "Some guy gave them to my dad."

"Wow," said Ingrid.

"You wanna go? There's a bus from the Rec Center."

Ingrid had only a vague idea of what monster trucks were all about, but just the name sounded great. "When is it?"

"Sunday at noon," said Joey.

"This Sunday?"

"Yeah."

"Oh," said Ingrid.

"Oh what?" said Joey.

"Sunday's no good."

"How come?"

"I'm busy on Sunday."

"Soccer?" said Joey. "I thought that was Saturday."

"Not soccer," Ingrid said. "It's more like . . . this family thing." She couldn't look him in the eye when she said that.

Joey went a little pink. He put the tickets back in his pocket.

"Some other time?" Ingrid said.

"Sure," said Joey, already moving toward the door.

He didn't believe her, knew she'd invented an excuse. So was he taking the next obvious step, thinking she didn't want to go with him? How could she let that happen?

"Joey? I—"

Mom came into the room, phone in hand, puzzlement on her face. "Has Sean been around?" she said.

"Sean Rubino?" said Ingrid.

"His mom called. He's late getting home."

"Why's she calling here?" Ingrid said.

"She said he's out with Ty. They were going to the mall."

"With Greg?"

"I called Greg's. Ty never went there. Greg had to do the whole project on his own."

Uh-oh.

The front door closed. Through the window, Ingrid saw Joey hopping on his bike. The spokes of his wheels flashed under the driveway lamp. Then he was gone.

Ty came home an hour later, walking in through the garage door, backpack over his shoulder, pencil tucked behind his ear. A great touch, that pencil, Ingrid thought. The return of the hard-working schoolboy. She put away her English packet, e-mailed over by Mia—only two more weeks of adverbs to go!—and waited for the ambush to begin.

"Hey," he said. "How's it goin'?"

"Not bad," said Ingrid, downing the last of her Fresca. "So far."

"Cool," said Ty.

Mom and Dad came in from the dining room.

"Hi, everybody," Ty said. "The whole fam, to quote Bill Murray."

Ingrid laughed. Ty wasn't usually this funny. Then she caught a whiff of alcohol on his breath. Yikes.

"Ingrid," said Mom, "would you give us a few moments, please?"

"Sure," said Ingrid. "Take as long as you like."

"Meaning go to your room," said Dad.

"Huh?"

"Now," said Dad.

"Do I have to?"

"You heard me."

"What did she do?" said Ty.

Ingrid went upstairs, lay on her bed. Voices rose from the kitchen. She couldn't make out the words. That made it more like music, a strange and noisy trio playing three different tunes—Mom's part high and anxious, Dad's low and grinding, Ty's all over the place. Not the kind of music you'd want to listen to.

Everything was so screwed up, just a big mess with tentacles everywhere, wriggling out all over the town, into the high school, the hospital, her friends' families, her own family. What was that knot story from mythology? Some knot so complicated—the Gordian knot?—

that no one could untie it. Then along comes this guy, name escaping her at the moment, and he slices through it with one stroke of his sword. That was what her sting operation would do, slice right through the mess, restoring order.

How bad was it that someone else—most likely the stranger in the closet—had picked the tree house? Maybe not bad at all: the tree house was home territory, Mom and Dad practically right there.

Ingrid put in some more practice on the voice recorder, working it from her pocket by touch alone.

"You're all under arrest. Hands where I can see them."

She still sounded so young.

"And don't try any tricks. I can shoot a Coke bottle off a fence from a hundred yards."

That sounded a little better.

Downstairs the angry trio came to a ragged conclusion. Ty stomped up, went into his room, slammed the door hard enough to shake Ingrid's walls. Ingrid waited a few minutes, then crossed the hall.

"Knock knock," she said.

"What the hell do you want?"

She opened the door.

Ty sat at his desk, playing a video game. He was just as good at video games as he was at football and baseball, blowing three hideous creatures to smithereens in a flash.

"So," she said, "what was that all about?"

"They're such jerks," Ty said, eyes on the screen. *Blam. Kapow.*

"Who?"

"Dad and Mom, who do you think?"

"Because they caught you in a lie?" Ingrid said.

Ty turned to her. A muscle twitched in his shoulder. On the screen, monsters multiplied quickly, devouring all the soft and fuzzy beings in sight.

"Caught in a lie?" Ty said. "Look who's talking."

"What's that supposed to mean?"

"Kidnapped," said Ty. "What a crock. Mom and Dad's little pet, and they don't even believe you."

Ingrid was so angry, she didn't know where to start. "I'm nobody's goddamn pet."

"Whatever."

"And you're the jerk," Ingrid said. "You don't even know how big."

He threw something at her, the nearest thing at hand, an eraser. It bounced off the wall above her head and rebounded across the room, landing softly at his feet. Ingrid laughed, a taunting kind of laugh she hadn't known herself capable of.

"Ever stop to think what that temper's all about?" she asked.

Ty's face started getting all bloated and purple. At that moment, Dad yelled up the stairs. "What's going on up there?"

Ty lowered his voice, low but still plenty mean. "You better get out of here."

Ingrid's voice stayed nice and loud. "And you better watch who you're hanging out with."

"You threatening me?" Ty said.

Dad again: "Don't make me come up there."

"It's a warning, bro," Ingrid said. "You don't want to get swept up in this."

"Swept up?" said Ty. "What the hell are you talking about?"

Dad: "Damn you kids."

"Think about it," Ingrid said.

She was back in her room before Dad reached the top of the stairs. Silence while he paused there, and then heavy treads back down. Outside Ingrid's window, the moon shone on the town woods, silvering the treetops and leaving dark shadows below. No wind at all; everything very still except for Ingrid, shaking a little.

TWENTY-THREE

A real big storm, but Ingrid's snug little boat was riding it out beautifully. Ingrid sat in the cabin, warm and dry in front of a roaring fire, the kind Grampy made, reading a book and sipping hot chocolate. Her little boat steered itself no problem, never needed any—

"Ingrid! Wake up!"

Ingrid opened her eyes, peered out through a gummy veil. Mom stood over her, toothbrush in hand and mouth a bit foamy.

"It's five after seven, Ingrid. Don't make me come in again."

"Sure thing."

"Ingrid! Your eyes are closing!"

Because they were so heavy—wasn't that obvious?

"I'm not leaving till you sit up."

Whatever makes you happy. Just keep the noise level down.

"Do I have to pull the covers off?"

Was there anything worse than having the covers pulled off, especially on a cold late-fall morning in a house with a dad who kept the heat down? Close to child abuse. Ingrid sat up.

And once up realized she felt pretty good, had had her best night's sleep since all this started. Why? Must have been because now she had a plan. Foolproof, the very best kind.

"You up for good?" Mom said.

"Yeah."

Mom took a quick look around the room. She was always doing things like that. "Where's St. Joseph?" she said. "Wasn't he on your shelf?"

"Um," said Ingrid. "Must have fallen down behind." The fact that he was out in the front yard, right side up and one foot under, ensuring that the house would never sell: Weren't people entitled to the odd little secret about themselves?

Mom had a thought of some kind. "Everything all right at school?" she said.

"Never better," said Ingrid; pathetically, that was almost true.

"Good," said Mom, a little surprised. "See you tonight."

She left the room, then poked her head back in. "Maybe you can do me a favor when you get home—I need a sign stuck in."

"Where?"

"One thirteen."

"One thirteen Maple Lane?"

Mom nodded. "I got the listing."

One thirteen Maple Lane, four houses down, was a shabby house unlived in since Mrs. Flenser—a terrifying old woman, like out of the brothers Grimm—had finally been dragged off to a nursing home a year or so before; but being the listing broker was never bad.

"Nice job," said Ingrid.

"I hate estate sales," Mom said.

"Does that mean Mrs. Flenser's a goner?" Ingrid said.

"I wouldn't put it that way, but yes," said Mom. "And the inspection's going to be a disaster." Mom was starting to fret.

"Don't worry, Mom," said Ingrid. "All it takes is one stupid buyer."

"I wouldn't put it that way," said Mom.

* * *

"Morning, petunia."

"Hi, Mr. Sidney."

"Planning to see that grandfather of yours sometime soon?"

"Yeah. Probably."

"You could tell him about the reunion. I'm on the committee. We sent letters, but he don't answer."

No surprise. Ingrid pictured those piles of mail all over Grampy's kitchen. "What reunion?" she said.

"Corregidor vets," said Mr. Sidney.

"Oh." Ingrid knew Grampy and Mr. Sidney had fought on Corregidor together, but whatever happened there wasn't something Grampy talked about. This reunion thing wasn't going to fly with Grampy. "How about calling him?" she said.

"He never answers," said Mr. Sidney. He glanced up at her from under the bill of his BATTLE OF THE CORAL SEA cap. "Any chance he's got hold of that caller ID?"

Grampy? What a thought. "No way," said Ingrid. "He must've been out in the barn or something."

She moved toward the back of the bus. Maybe a few kids looked at her funny, maybe not. She didn't care. This was all going to be over real soon.

Ingrid sat next to Stacy. "Yo," said Ingrid.

"Hi."

Just a soft little *hi* from Stacy, not her at all.

Ingrid lowered her voice. "What's up?"

"Yeah," said Brucie, leaning forward from the seat behind. "I'm all ears."

Stacy turned quickly. Brucie shrank back, did a Dracula-in-sudden-daylight thing with his arms.

Stacy pulled her history notebook out of her backpack and wrote: *Sean and my dad had a fight.*

Ingrid took the pencil. *physical?*

Stacy took it back. *last nite.*

"Ai haf cahm," said Brucie, "to sock your blahd."

The bus pulled up to the door at Ferrand Middle.

"Got a note?" said Mr. Porterhouse in homeroom.

"Note?" said Ingrid.

He checked his sheet. "You're down as missing in action yesterday."

"I forgot it," Ingrid said, coming very close to patting her pockets, a pantomime that would only make her less believable.

"But you'll remember tomorrow."

"Yeah."

"Or else it's level two."

Level two already? That was where detentions started, and it was only November. At this rate, she'd hit level five—death row—by April.

* * *

"He'd been drinking, no question," said Stacy, on the bench by the swings at lunchtime. "Slurring and everything. Then my dad was, like, give me the keys to the Firebird, and Sean said no."

"So your dad tried to get them off him?" said Ingrid.

"Yeah."

"And that's when the fight started?"

"My mom had to break it up."

"God."

"My dad was crying."

"'Cause he got hurt?"

"I don't think so." Stacy looked like she might start crying too, and Stacy was not a crier. "Just that it was all so . . . gross."

Ingrid handed Stacy half her peanut butter sandwich.

"Marshmallow Fluff in it?" Stacy said.

"Yeah."

Stacy ate in silence for a while. Then she said, "You ever think about having kids?"

"Nope," said Ingrid. "I plan to be a kid all my life."

"Makes sense."

"Total."

The bell rang. They got up, walked back toward the school.

"After it was over," Stacy said, "Sean took off."

"In the Firebird?"

Stacy shook her head. "On foot. My dad ended up getting the keys."

"Did he come back?"

"Sometime in the night. Mom found him zonked out in the truck. Kind of funny—he was the only one who got any sleep." Stacy's face, always glowing with health, looked patchy and washed-out.

"Everything's going to turn out all right," Ingrid said.

"What makes you so sure?"

"A feeling," said Ingrid.

"Great," said Stacy, brushing the corner of her eye. A sharp wind was rising.

After school, Ingrid carried Mom's for-sale sign—RIVER-BEND PROPERTIES, CALL CAROL LEVIN-HILL—down the block to 113 Maple Lane. It was really blowing now, twigs getting ripped off the trees, dead leaves making tornadoes in the air, low dark clouds speeding across the sky. Nigel whimpered the whole way.

"Suck it up," Ingrid said.

One thirteen was set back deeper than the other houses on Maple Lane, its shingles aged almost black, the whole front overgrown with bushes and vines. Ingrid found a good spot near the road and stuck the sign in the ground. The metal pole had a sharp end and a little foot-pad for pressing down on. It went in real easy.

She stepped back to check it was straight for traffic coming either way. Nigel picked that moment to cross the lawn and lift his leg in front of the garage door, making a puddle that spread and spread.

"Nigel. Get over here."

Instead he found a dry place and curled up like a sled dog trying to survive a blizzard.

"It's just a little wind."

But he didn't budge. And then came a particularly strong gust. Nigel closed his eyes as though getting ready to die, like with Scott at the South Pole. Ingrid went after him.

She'd never actually been on this lawn before—Mrs. Flenser had spent a lot of time on the front porch, always with knitting needles in hand. The grass was long, brown, and stringy, clumps of weeds everywhere, the driveway pavement cracked in three or four places. An odd kind of driveway—it seemed to continue around the side of the garage.

Ingrid went around the corner for a look. The pavement soon petered out, but a pair of ruts extended all the way to the woods, twenty or thirty yards away. And what was this? Tire tracks in the ruts? Ingrid knelt and examined them. Not fresh tracks; kind of eroded, maybe by rain. When had it last rained? Ingrid didn't know for sure. The last rain she remembered was on the day she and Chief Strade failed to find any duct tape evidence in the gully off Benedict Drive.

She followed the ruts to the beginning of the woods, the tire tracks sometimes very faint but visible till the end. She looked to the right, toward her own house. Surprise. Ninety-nine Maple Lane couldn't be seen from here, the woods jutting in so sharply that they even blocked most of the house next door. You could park a car here and no one would know. And a car had been here, beyond doubt. Plus: If she was right about the last rain, then the car had parked here before she was kidnapped, maybe just before. *Like maybe around the time Mrs. Grunello was seeing no cars at 99 Maple Lane, one of the biggest holes in Ingrid's story.*

She stepped into the woods. Was there a path that led from the back of one thirteen to the back of ninety-nine? No. But if you could squeeze past this tangle of brambles, the horrible purple kind, so spiky and—

Whoa. What was this? Caught up high in a twist of thorns: a baseball cap. Ingrid reached up, pulled it free. A Yankees cap, not unusual in Echo Falls, right on the border between Red Sox and Yankee territory. Ingrid turned it over, spotted four dark-brown hairs inside, about five inches long. Carl Kraken Junior had hair that color, not a lot, but enough for a comb-over. Wouldn't comb-over hair be pretty long?

Ingrid folded the cap with care and stuck it in her jacket pocket. Hair equaled DNA. Now she had two samples. And that quiet excitement that always overcame Holmes when he was building a case? She felt it in real life.

Something nudged the back of her leg. Ingrid glanced down and there was Nigel, tail wagging, suddenly energized.

"Good boy." He'd overcome his fear, or maybe it had just slipped his mind.

Nigel wagged his tail harder, to the point of ridiculousness, then nimbly made his way around the brambles. Ingrid followed. The going grew easier—no path, but plenty of space between the trees. A minute or two later, she stepped out of the woods and into her own backyard.

She walked up to the garage. There was a little door at the back, never locked, too crooked to even close properly. Ingrid opened it: all shadowy inside, feeble light barely penetrating the dusty windows. For a moment she saw her garage through a predator's eyes. It would do nicely.

What was the expression? Knowledge is power?

Ingrid felt herself getting stronger.

The wind was dying down. Nigel was perking up. He chased a squirrel up a tree and thought he almost caught it. Dogs fooled themselves all the time.

TWENTY-FOUR

Mom and Dad both came home before five, very unusual. Ingrid was at the table, rearranging her homework in different piles. Ty was standing in front of the open fridge drinking OJ from the carton—a no-no. His back stiffened, taken by surprise.

But they didn't call him on it. Instead Dad said, "Mom and I have been talking."

Uh-oh.

"And we've decided we could all use a quick getaway," Mom said.

"To Jamaica?" said Ingrid. That Christmas at the Sands of Negril two years ago: the best week of her life—

splitting coconuts with a machete, the reggae band around the pool, snorkeling at the reef, all those little fishes like jewels that had learned to swim.

"No," said Dad.

"But we can discuss it over dinner," said Mom. "The dinner we're all going to make right now, together." She laid some grocery bags on the counter.

"Ingrid," said Mom, "you can set the dining-room table."

"We're eating in the dining room?"

"Ty," said Dad, "clean the grill."

"The barbecue grill?" said Ty. "Outside?"

"Hasn't been used since Labor Day," said Dad. "Needs cleaning."

"Now we're barbecuing in the winter all of a sudden?" said Ty.

"I got swordfish," Mom said. "I'm making that wonderful barbecue sauce, the one with the balsamic vinegar."

"And by the way, Ty," said Dad, "it's not winter yet. Try to be more optimistic."

Eating in the dining room on a weekday, on any day for that matter, except Thanksgiving, Christmas, and birthdays? Swordfish? That wretched balsamic gunk? What the hell was going on?

* * *

They sat around the dining-room table, Mom and Dad digging into swordfish steaks smothered in balsamic sauce, plus wild rice and mesclun salad, Ingrid and Ty eyeing the food warily.

Dad poured wine for himself and Mom.

"How about a little sip for the kids?" he said.

"I'm not sure that's the direction we want to go," said Mom.

"Oh, right," said Dad.

Mom gave him a quick look. "How was everyone's day?"

"Fine," said Ingrid.

"Yeah," said Ty.

"How's Shakespeare coming along?" Mom said. First semester, ninth grade at Echo Falls High meant *Romeo and Juliet*, no exceptions.

"No complaints," said Ty.

"Good," said Mom. "Where are you in the play?"

"You know, um," said Ty.

Ingrid swirled the Fresca in her glass. Entertainment was on the way.

Ty cut off a big hunk of swordfish, stuffed it in his mouth. "Hey, real tasty," he said, or something like that—hard to tell with his mouth so full.

"Your mom asked where you are in the play," Dad said.

Ty made a big show of chewing, held up his index finger for more time.

"It doesn't really matter," Mom said, "as long as he's enjoying it." She got a faraway look in her eye. Ingrid knew what was coming: poetry. Mom had tons of it in her head. "'What's in a name?'" she said. "'That which we call a rose/By any other name would smell as sweet.'"

"That's from *Romeo and Juliet*?" Dad said.

"Act two," said Mom.

Ty's Adam's apple bobbed as he got the swordfish down. "We're still on act one," he said.

"I'm not sure about that," said Ingrid.

"What the hell?" said Ty.

"Not where you are in the play," Ingrid said, just stopping herself from adding *bozo*, what with this formal dining-room atmosphere and all. "I mean about the rose."

"Huh?" said Ty.

"Smelling as sweet by any other name?" Mom said.

"Yeah," said Ingrid. "Like what if it was called a skunk instead of a rose?"

"Are you making fun of your mother?" said Dad.

"Mark," said Mom, "of course she isn't. She's raising an interesting point."

"What's interesting about it?" said Ty.

"This whole question of names," said Mom. "Would

you be any different if we'd called you something else?"

"Brucie, for example," said Ingrid.

"Like that dork on your bus?" said Ty. "You're saying I'd be a dork?"

Ingrid tried the wild rice. Not bad at all.

"'Cause you're the dork," Ty said.

"Kids," said Mom. "This is a nice family dinner."

"So knock it off right now," said Dad, with a quick glare for each of them.

Ty rose. "I'm done anyway."

"But we haven't discussed the weekend yet," said Mom.

"What about it?" said Ty.

"Please sit down," said Mom.

"I've got homework," said Ty. Ingrid almost laughed out loud. Then she remembered the note she needed for Mr. Porterhouse. She could a) make up some lie to tell Mom, b) forge a note, c) accept getting bumped up to level two. C was actually the easiest. At that moment she knew for sure she wasn't cut out to be a criminal.

"I said sit," said Dad.

Ty sat—on the edge of his chair, feet gathered beneath him for a quick escape, but sitting.

"Tell them, Mark."

"About the getaway plan?" Dad sat back, dabbed his lips with a napkin. Still the handsomest dad in Echo

Falls, although he was so dark around the eyes lately. Now Ingrid was glad to see them light up a little. "Everyone needs a break from time to time," he said, "and this deal happened to fall into my hands."

"What deal?" said Ingrid.

Mom slid a brochure across the table. Elbow Beach Club, Bermuda.

"We're going to Bermuda?" Ty said.

"Saturday afternoon, right after Ingrid's soccer game," Dad said.

"The flight only takes a couple hours," said Mom. "We'll be there in time for a swim."

"And coming back when?" said Ingrid.

"Sunday night," said Mom. "Monday's a school day."

"A weekend getaway," said Dad. "Well, let's have some reaction."

"What about Nigel?" Ingrid said.

They all glanced at Nigel, dozing by his water bowl as he so often did, like a drought might happen at any moment.

"We've already booked the kennel," said Mom.

Nigel stretched his front legs, got a little more comfortable.

"We can swim?" said Ty.

"Pool and ocean," said Dad, "plus golf and tennis and maybe we can check out parasailing too."

"Parasailing," said Ty. "Wow."

Ingrid said nothing. Monster trucks and now Bermuda: why, of all Sundays, this one?

Saturday, eleven sharp, field one: Mid-State League U13 semifinals, Echo Falls versus Glastonbury. Glastonbury, first-place finishers in the regular schedule, had some dynamite players, especially that big red-haired fullback, already being scouted by a few colleges, according to Coach Ringer.

Coach Ringer, out of the hospital but not allowed to come to any games because of the excitement, doctor's orders, had faxed a message to Julia. She read it just before game time, as the team gathered around.

"'Four dimensions. Tell the kids to use 'em all.'"

"That's it?" said Stacy. "The whole message?"

The girls muttered to themselves. "Four dimensions? Like width and stuff?"

"He's back to his normal self," Ingrid said.

The referee blew his whistle. A few of Ingrid's teammates were still laughing as they ran onto the field.

Biggest game of the year, and Ingrid started well, zipping up and down her wing, taking a long looping pass from Stacy and driving one wide by only inches in the very first minute. But not long after that, she caught sight of Mom, Dad, and Ty in the stands. Ty never came to her games, was there only because they were driving to the airport right after. But how could she go? The sting was all set up for Sunday at noon.

Ingrid lost her focus after that. The red-haired sweeper dribbled past her three times, and Ingrid muffed a point-blank scoring chance. Then, just before the half, her corner kick landed on the back of the net, never even reaching the field of play.

Score at the half: 0–0. The girls sat on the bench and sucked on orange slices supplied by Mr. Rubino. Julia stood before them in her fur jacket and cool shades.

"Everybody understands the importance of the first goal in a game like this?" she said.

The girls nodded.

"We've had more chances," she said, as the referee got out of his car where he'd been sitting with the heat on and headed for midfield. "Now we've got to close the deal." Julia licked her lips. "So close the deal. Whatever it takes. On three."

"One two three—Echo Falls!"

The girls ran out. Julia put her hand, a surprisingly strong hand, on Ingrid's shoulder, holding her back.

"Something on your mind today, Ingrid?"

Ingrid saw her face reflected in Julia's sunglasses, a pinched, worried-looking face. "Nope."

"No new developments in what we were talking about at Moo Cow?"

"Everything's fine."

Julia peered down at her for a moment or two longer. "Their goalie jammed her right thumb just before the whistle," she said.

"She did?" said Ingrid.

"Do you understand what I'm telling you?"

"Not exactly." The face in the sunglasses got a little more worried.

"I'm giving you a tip, Ingrid. Shoot high and to the left."

"Oh," said Ingrid. "Thanks."

High left. Sounded good, but first you had to control the ball, and all of a sudden Ingrid couldn't. It kept taking funny bounces, squibbing off the side of her foot, developing a mind of its own. Down at the Echo Falls end, Glastonbury had two good scoring chances—a penalty shot by the red-haired girl that grazed the crossbar, and a dangerous curving corner kick that Stacy headed away at the last instant. The ball went out of bounds off Glastonbury.

"Ref," said Stacy, taking the throw in, "how much time?"

The ref glanced at his watch, held up one finger.

"We have to play overtime if it's tied?"

He nodded.

"Overtime sucks," said Stacy.

"Language," said the ref.

Stacy shot Ingrid a quick glance, then threw the ball in to her. Ingrid kicked it right back to Stacy, then took off down the sideline with all the speed she had left, maybe not much. She didn't even glance back. This was a play she and Stacy had practiced for years, until Coach Ringer broke them up. Stacy's job was to boom one down into the corner. Ingrid's was to catch up before it crossed the end line, then send a pass in front of the net or take it in herself.

The ball came curving down into Ingrid's line of vision, landed ten or fifteen yards away, bounced a few times, then rolled. From the corner of her eye she saw the red-haired sweeper angling across the field, real fast for a girl her size. Ingrid chased the ball down in the corner, looked toward the net. No one to pass to. And then the red-haired girl was on her. Ingrid tried that little left-footed fake Dad had taught her and that had worked so well against this girl earlier in the season. But this time she was ready, went right to the ball and stole it away. She cocked her leg for one of those tremendous kicks upfield. Just in time, Ingrid stuck her toe in, stole the ball back, took off for the net.

The goalie inched out to meet her, cutting off the angle, already sharp. The red-haired girl came up from the side, gave Ingrid an elbow. The stupid ball got away, rolled toward the goalie. The goalie came running to snatch it up. But Ingrid was running too, and so was the red-haired girl. Three girls and the ball all came smacking together and Ingrid, the smallest, went flying.

The ground rose up fast and hit her hard—*boom*— knocking the wind right out of her. But Ingrid's eyes were open, and she saw the red-haired girl and the goalie going down too. And the ball, all by itself now, was still rolling, slower and slower, but rolling. Rolling, rolling toward the far post. Too wide? Not quite. It bumped off the post and wobbled into the net.

The ref blew his whistle. Game over. The Echo Falls girls came racing over. Ingrid got her breath back and was about to jump up when—

Bzzz. She had an idea.

Ingrid stayed where she was.

Everyone was standing over her—ref, players, and soon Mom and Dad.

"Ingrid? Are you all right?"

She groaned, then tried a little fluttering thing with her eyelids.

Mom knelt beside her.

"Hey," said the ref. "Everybody back off."

Everyone but Mom and Dad withdrew a step or two. Ingrid caught a glimpse of Julia, her head cocked at a slight angle, the sun glaring off her sunglasses.

"Ingrid?" Mom said. "Say something."

She made her voice small and weak. "I don't feel so good," she said.

"Where?" said Mom. "Where don't you feel good?"

"All over," said Ingrid. "Not too good." Then came a guilt pang, worrying Mom like this. "Not too bad, but not too good either," she added.

"Huh?" said Dad.

"Anything broken?" said the ref.

Ingrid moved her limbs around experimentally.

"Can you get up?"

Ingrid made a heroic effort to rise, adding a subtle little stagger at the end. Dad reached out to catch her.

She walked slowly off the field, Dad on one side, Mom on the other.

"Should we take her to the hospital?" Mom said.

"Oh, no," said Ingrid. "I'm fine."

"Attaway," said Dad.

"Not too fine, Dad," Ingrid said.

They got to the parking lot. Ty had the side door of

the MPV open, suitcases inside. "In fact," Ingrid said, "I just want to lie down."

"You can lie down all the way to the airport," Dad said.

Ingrid tried a light-headed weavy precollapse type of move.

"Oh my God, Ingrid," said Mom, grabbing her shoulder.

"Clock's ticking," said Ty.

Ingrid faced her parents. "I don't think I can go," she said. The watering up of her eyes just then? Somehow that happened for real. "I'm just too . . . shaken up."

"What's her problem?" said Ty.

Mom gazed down at Ingrid; not really down anymore—they were almost the same height. "I guess we'll have to cancel," she said.

"Cancel the trip?" said Dad. His golf clubs lay on the backseat.

"No, no," said Ingrid. "You guys go. I'll stay home."

"By yourself?" Mom said. "What are you talking about?"

"Ingrid can stay with us," said Stacy, standing by the Rubino Electric truck.

"Sure thing," said Mr. Rubino, coming into view, Tupperware container of orange peels under his arm.

Mom and Dad exchanged a look.

"She'll be fine with us," said Mr. Rubino. "And Ellie's a nurse, don't forget."

"True," said Dad.

"I don't—" said Mom.

"Have a blast," said Mr. Rubino. "*Bon voyage.*"

TWENTY-FIVE

Sunday morning, breakfast at the Rubinos'. Sausages, ham, eggs, pancakes under lakes of butter: piles and piles of food, Mr. and Mrs. Rubino both wearing aprons.

"Don't care for sausages, Ingrid?" said Mr. Rubino.

"I do, but—"

"Here's a couple more," he said. "Make it three. How about you, son?"

Sean grunted something, stayed hunched over his plate at the far end of the table. He had a little cut over one eye. So did Mr. Rubino.

Mr. and Mrs. Rubino exchanged a look. "We've got a surprise for everybody," Mrs. Rubino said.

"Like what?" said Stacy, dipping a forkful of ham in an egg-yolky pool.

"Monster trucks," said Mrs. Rubino.

Mr. Rubino reached into his apron pocket, fanned five tickets on the table. "A customer laid these on me," he said. "Don't forget your earplugs."

"Hey," said Stacy, picking up a ticket. "Front row."

Oh, God, Ingrid thought. The monster trucks—they wouldn't go away, kind of like real monsters. "Thanks," she said. "But I don't know if I'm really feeling . . . up to it."

"I thought you were all better," said Mrs. Rubino.

"I was," said Ingrid. "I mean, I am. Just a slight little headache, that's all. But monster trucks . . ."

Mrs. Rubino nodded. One of those total lies that lucked into making sense.

"We can see them another time," said Mr. Rubino.

"Oh, no," said Ingrid. "You guys go. I'll be fine by myself."

"I'm not sure—" said Mrs. Rubino.

"Really I will," said Ingrid. "I'll just watch movies, lie around, relax. That's what I feel like doing."

Mrs. Rubino thought it over. "I guess it's all right," she said.

Sean looked up. "I'll give it a pass too," he said.

"No way," said Mrs. Rubino.

"Why not?" said Sean.

"You know the arrangement," said Mrs. Rubino. "About being alone in the house."

"I wouldn't be alone," Sean said. He pointed his chin at Ingrid. "I'd be with her."

"She has a name," said Stacy.

Sean glared at his sister.

"Kids," said Mr. Rubino. "Let's not spoil it. This is going to be a real fun day."

The Rubinos left at ten thirty. Stacy said good-bye to Ingrid down in the entertainment center, Ingrid lying under a blanket, *Pretty in Pink* on the big screen.

"Sure you're all right?" said Stacy.

"Yeah."

"You've really got a headache?"

Ingrid hated lying to Stacy. "Just a little one. Tiny."

Stacy gave her a long look. "Okey-doke."

The Rubinos drove off, on their way to Hartford and the monster trucks. Five minutes later, Ingrid was on Stacy's bike, heading home.

She turned into the driveway at 99 Maple Lane. The house looked different in some way. Ingrid ran her gaze over it, saw no changes, but that didn't keep it from having a strange effect on her. Was it because this had never happened before—by herself, house empty, her whole family thousands of miles away, or hundreds at least, and Nigel in the kennel? Was this the feeling you got revisiting a place you'd lived in long ago? Then she glanced over at the spot in the front yard where St. Joseph stood buried right side up, making sure that 99 Maple Lane couldn't be sold. When she looked at the house again, everything was back to normal.

Ingrid unlocked the front door and went inside. The house was cold. Thermostat check: Dad had it all the way down to fifty. She went to her room and got the digital recorder. Time: 11:06.

What else would she need? Money, of course, key part of every sting, and in this one for sure, what with Carl Junior counting a big wad of the stuff, and the $1,649 in Sean's desk drawer. In her own desk drawer she had $102, combined birthday money and Booster Club tips. She took it all. Time: 11:09.

At that moment, Ingrid remembered another police term: not *sting* this time, but *backup*. Then came a crazy thought: How about calling Grampy? She went back and forth on that for a while. Cop-show cops always called for backup, but Holmes never seemed concerned about it. Cops shows came and went. Holmes was forever.

Time: 11:11. Early, but didn't that make tactical sense, the way brilliant generals like George Washington used the element of surprise? She half recalled a packet about the Battle of Trenton, or possibly Tenafly.

Ingrid left by the back door and walked into the woods.

She followed the path, around a bend and up a little rise. There, on the left, stood the thick double-trunked oak with the tree house about twenty feet up. Ingrid went closer, her feet silent on damp leaves. She peered up through the round hole in the tree house's plywood floor, saw nothing but her red stool and the crude roof above. This was where she and Ty had played Dark Forest Spies, where he'd fought off the Meany Cat with Ping-Pong ball grenades. Now she had a real prop, the digital recorder, in her pocket. Ingrid got hold of the wooden rungs nailed to the trunk and started climbing up.

She stuck her head through the hole, boosted herself into the tree house. The first thing she saw was the old sign. THE TREEHOUS. OWNR TY. ASISTENT INGRID. Then she rose and swung around.

And there was a man, his back to her, gazing out the window.

Ingrid's heart went wild, a terrified little creature in her chest. On the inside, she was losing it completely, on the outside, she was frozen in place—except for some remote automatic part of her that remembered about the digital recorder in her pocket and sent the signal to switch it on.

The man turned, in no hurry, and faced her. An old man, bent and creaky, with beaky broken nose, pointy chin, big flat ears with lots of sprouting hairs: Carl Kraken Senior. He held out a piece of paper. Ingrid recognized it: the desktop calendar page from Carl Junior's basement office in the high school. *Echo Falls athlete looking to get stronger.*

"This your handiwork?" he said. His tiny old eyes, sunk way back in his head, looked into hers.

At that moment, Ingrid felt one of those inspiration buzzes. She could just say, "I don't know what you're talking about. I'm here to play in my tree house." Situation resolved, easy as that. But then where would she be? Square one. For the first time in her life, Ingrid overrode that buzz.

"Yeah," she said. "My handiwork."

Her heart calmed down a little. What was there to be afraid of? This was a creaky old guy, not strong like Grampy. Then she remembered two things. One: The story of the noose, when Carl Senior and Grampy were little boys. Two: He was still strong enough to climb up to the tree house.

"What's it supposed to mean?" said Carl Senior.

"Just what it says," said Ingrid.

He put on a pair of glasses and squinted at the writing, holding the page very close. His eyes were bad. Was it possible he hadn't recognized her? He'd only seen her once, that time at Chloe's.

"Who's this athlete?" he said.

"Me," said Ingrid.

"You're a girl."

"So?" said Ingrid. "I've got money."

"Think there's other girls interested in this?" he said.

"Interested in what?" said Ingrid.

A long pause. "Getting stronger," said Carl Senior.

"You haven't sold to any girls?" Ingrid said.

"Not yet."

Wow. As close as you could get to an admission of selling to boys, digitally recorded. She tried to nail it down. "So I'd be the first."

He nodded.

A nod was no good to her.

"The very first," she said.

Another nod, this one barely perceptible.

"And all the rest are boys," she added.

But he wouldn't bite. Instead he peered down at her. "I know you from somewheres?"

"No," said Ingrid. "Did you bring the stuff or not?"

"In a hurry, ain't you?" said Carl Senior. "What's the rush?"

"You don't have it?" Ingrid said.

"I didn't say that."

"It's the"—what was the right kind of sleazy expression?—"good stuff I want," said Ingrid.

"The good stuff?"

"That the boys get," she said. "From Mexico."

"Mexico?" said Carl Senior. "What do you know about Mexico?"

"Nothing," said Ingrid. "I don't even know how it gets here from Mexico."

Carl Senior went still. "What'd you say?"

"Like all the stops along the way," Ingrid said. "Or do you go down there and get it yourself?"

Carl Senior came a little closer. Ingrid stepped back. "You ask a lot of questions," he said.

"Everyone says that," said Ingrid. Breezy, all of a sudden. What was wrong with her? Had she gone insane? "If you'll just sell me the good Mexican stuff, I'll be out of your hair."

Carl Senior gave his head a hard little shake, like some bee was buzzing close by. "What's all this about Mexico?" he said.

"Forget I mentioned it," Ingrid said. "I don't know anything about Mexico." But then another bit of insanity took over. "I don't even know any Mexicans—except maybe that guy at the hospital."

Carl Senior slid one hand inside his coat. "Hospital?"

"And he might not even be Mexican," Ingrid said.

"His name's Rey Vasquez." A quick shift of those sunken eyes. "Know him, by any chance?"

"No."

"Then that's that," Ingrid said. "I've brought a hundred and two dollars. What does that get me?"

"Let's see the money," said Carl Senior.

"First I need to know you brought it."

"I brought it."

"You brought what?"

"The pills, for Chrissake. The steroids. What else are we talking about?"

There. At last, he'd spoken the magic word. She'd done it! Now just a quick exchange, money for—

But at that moment, a third voice spoke. This third voice, metallic and soulless, spoke from her pocket.

"Remaining recording time two minutes and ten seconds."

Carl Senior's gaze dipped to her pocket, then rose back up to her face. His own face went through quick changes—confusion, understanding, rage.

In one motion, without a thought, Ingrid jumped right through the hole in the tree house floor. She clutched at the tree trunk, got a grip on one of those footholds, lost it, and fell. A long fall—hands flailing at the bark, fingernails breaking—that ended with a hard landing in damp leaves, the wind knocked out of her.

Ingrid looked up. Carl Senior's booted feet came through the hole, felt around, found a foothold. He started down.

Ingrid sat up, sucked in air. Carl Senior's boots scraped against the tree. Ingrid got to her feet. His head appeared through the hole. She turned for home, not feeling great, but good enough. No way she couldn't outrun this old man.

She ran. Back onto the path, back up the rise, a minute or two from being in her locked house and dialing 911. Around the bend, running hard now, almost full speed, and—

A man stepped out from behind a tree, cutting her off. Very tall, huge hands, that same beaky nose, comb-over: Carl Junior.

Ingrid spun around. Carl Senior came over the rise, walking stiffly but pretty fast with—oh my God—a noose swinging in his hand.

Ingrid looked left, then right. Left led deeper into the woods, but wouldn't right take her toward the long rutted drive behind 113 Maple Lane? She bounded off the path, heading right. Turning it on now, with hard footsteps fast behind her, Ingrid dodged around a tree, leaped over a boulder, ripped right through a clump of those purple brambles, tripped over a tree root, regained her balance, and charged through a little clearing—straight into the arms of Carl Kraken the third.

His fingers dug deep in her shoulders. "Hey," he called out. "This is her—little snoop I was tellin' you about."

"Hold her right there," Carl Junior called back.

"Don't worry, Pop, I got her." One hand still digging into her shoulder, the other grabbing her hair. That hair grabbing: Ingrid had never hated anything more in her life. Grampy's words came to her: *I kicked him in the place where sometimes you got to kick a guy.*

Ingrid kicked Carl the third right where Grampy said, hard as she could. When it came to kicking, Ingrid wasn't at the level of big girls like Stacy and Glastonbury's red-haired sweeper, a long way down from that.

But good enough. The air went whooshing out of Carl the third, and he let go of her and crumpled down on the forest floor, making agonized noises. Ingrid took off. The problem was, those agonized noises were so loud, she hadn't heard Carl Junior coming. He tackled her before she'd gone two steps.

Ingrid tried to wriggle away. No good. Carl Junior was strong. He flipped her over, locked both her wrists in one of his huge hands, stuck a knee in her back.

Carl Senior came hurrying up, stepping over his writhing grandson without a glance. He was breathing hard, a foamy ring around his mouth. "She's got some kinda tape recorder in her pocket."

"Goddamn," said Carl Junior, pressing harder with his knee.

"I'm gonna kill her," groaned Carl the third.

Ingrid started to scream, but Carl Junior clapped his other hand over her mouth. His hand smelled horrible. Carl Senior leaned down, squinted at her. Recognition dawned.

"By God," he said. "Aylmer Hill's little darlin'." He felt his crooked nose. Then he smiled, a horrible smile, all brown pointy teeth and a strange white-tipped tongue. That scream of fear ballooned inside Ingrid, bottled up by Carl Junior's stinking hand. She was about to bite it when someone shouted, "Freeze!"

Someone Ingrid knew.

They all looked up. Chief Strade stepped into the clearing. He had a gun in his hand, pointed right between Carl Junior's eyes.

"Whether you see another day, Junior," said the chief, "depends on how fast you let go of her."

Carl Junior turned out to be very fast.

"Hands up," said the chief.

The Krakens raised their hands. By now, Carl the third was on his feet. He started backing away toward the trees, his mind easy to read: *How's he going to cover us all?* That was when Sergeant Berry, who played Santa in the

Christmas parade, came huffing and puffing into the clearing from the direction of the tree house, a few other cops behind him. Carl the third froze again. Sergeant Berry clapped the cuffs on him.

"Entrapment, that's what it is," said Carl Senior, giving Ingrid a furious glare.

"Cuff him," said Chief Strade. "Cuff 'em all." The chief looked even more furious than Carl Senior. He came closer, stood beside her. The chief had a piney smell. "Sorry, Ingrid," he said. "You got started a little ahead of schedule."

Things fell into place. "That was you in the closet?" she said.

He nodded.

"You picked the tree house?"

He put his arm around her shoulders. "I've been working on this operation for some time," he said. "Just not with your kind of efficiency."

"Then you know about Rey Vasquez."

"Who's he?" said the chief.

Ingrid explained.

"Sergeant Berry, go pick him up," said the chief.

Sergeant Berry took a hit off his inhaler and headed off.

"What else you got for us, Ingrid?" said the chief.

"Nothing, really," said Ingrid. "Just this recorder. Oh,

yeah, and some DNA."

He smiled down at her, anger draining out of him. "I can see you've got a question," he said.

"Joey's monster truck tickets," said Ingrid.

"Just my dumb attempt at keeping you out of harm's way," Chief Strade said. "Not my only dumb move."

"Meaning you believe me?" Ingrid said.

"Be a fool not to," said the chief. "Let's get 'em locked up."

TWENTY-SIX

From *The Echo*:

> *STEROID RING BUSTED*
>
> *Four local men have been arrested on charges of trafficking in steroids, according to Chief Gilbert L. Strade. More arrests and more charges, including kidnapping, are possible, the chief said.*
>
> *In an exclusive interview with* The Echo, *Chief Strade described a web of deceit that stretched from clandestine labs in Mexico all the way to the athletic locker rooms and gyms of Echo*

Falls. Few details were available at press time, but the chief made a point of emphasizing the assistance rendered by a Ferrand Middle School eighth grader.

Without the help of this student, whose name is being withheld, "the bad guys might still be on the loose," said Chief Strade.

Currently being held without bail are Rey Luis Vasquez, 34, an orderly at Echo Falls Hospital; Carl K. Kraken, Senior, 80, employed as a caretaker in Echo Falls and said to be the ringleader of the group. . . .

And the rest of the Krakens, but not a word about Ty. His name never came up, not in *The Echo* and not with Chief Strade.

"I'm not going to bust anyone for possession," he said, standing in the kitchen at 99 Maple Lane late Sunday night, Ingrid and her stunned and sunburned family gathered around. Ingrid had already shown him where the kidnapper had parked behind 113, and handed over the Yankees cap with the four precious hairs inside, plus the nail clippings from Carl Junior's office.

"Not this time," said the chief. "I don't even want to

know who they are, for now." Impossible to tell if Ty was turning red, he was so red already. "But I am speaking to every single coach in town, and all the players."

"And after that?" Ingrid said.

"All bets are off," said the chief. "Besides being illegal, it's poison and it's not happening on my watch."

He didn't look at Ty when he said that, but Ingrid did. Her brother's eyes met hers. Complete understanding passed both ways.

"We're behind you one hundred percent, chief," Dad said. He went over and put his arm around Ty, patting him on the back. "It's just infuriating to think how hard Ty here works to get in shape and then find out that some kids are doing it the easy way."

"I'm sure it is," said the chief.

That was where the chief stood on possession. Selling was another matter, which left Sean Rubino on the hook. But his name never came up either. Instead, after Chief Strade discovered that Sean was on a job with Mr. Rubino the morning of the kidnapping—easily remembered by everyone involved by how hard it had been to get him out of bed; and after he'd checked the trunk of the Firebird, bare metal so rusted out at the bottom that any human being—even Ingrid's size—would have fallen right through, the chief made a deal with the Rubinos.

Stacy called Ingrid to tell her about it.

"What deal?" Ingrid said.

"Sean has to go to a military prep school."

"Or else?"

"They never got to 'or else,'" Stacy said. "He just handed my parents a list of schools."

"And?"

"Sean leaves for Smoky Mountain Military Academy tomorrow. It's in Kentucky or Oklahoma or some place."

"Oh my God. What did he say?"

"Not a word. Mr. Strade had a private little talk with him first."

"Wow."

"You know the way Sean's so into his hair, gels it up and everything?" said Stacy.

"Yeah."

"They shave the cadets bald the second they get off the bus."

"Does he know?"

"Oh, yeah," said Stacy. "He's been staring at himself in the mirror all day."

A few nice things happened. The Ferrands sent flowers. No one had ever sent Ingrid flowers before. Red roses— two dozen!—and an engraved card with a picture of the

Ferrands' house and a handwritten note: *To Ernst and Alicia—thanks for everything, see you in Anguilla.* A note meant for Ernst and Alicia, whoever they were, who must have got the note meant for her, whatever it said—the kind of mistake that might happen easily to people in the habit of sending lots of flowers, people like the Ferrands. Mom needed two vases to get them properly displayed. Dad wondered aloud who Ernst and Alicia were.

Another nice thing: Ms. Groome stopped Ingrid on the way out of math class and said, "I understand everything worked out."

"Yeah," said Ingrid.

"A cause for celebration, I suppose."

"Thanks, Ms. Groome," said Ingrid.

And one more. She talked Mom into buying her Rollerblades at Sportz and went blading with Joey on the bike path after school. Ingrid could blow Joey away in a footrace, especially a short one, but blades were different. Joey had this effortless technique that somehow got him zooming. Ingrid couldn't keep up with him. Right from the start he jumped out ahead and then kept increasing his lead till he was out of sight, not exactly what she'd had in mind.

Joey was waiting on a bench at the end of the path, not too far beyond the falls. Ingrid sat beside him. The bench was angled so they could look back at the falls, the water so black at this time of year, the foam a muted cream. The falls did their *shhh* thing, but this wasn't one of those spots where you could hear the double *shhh* that had given the town its name.

"How are the Blades?" said Joey.

"Good."

"I could maybe take them down to the shop," he said. The Strades—just Joey and the chief, his mom not around after the divorce—had a whole workshop in their basement. "If you want."

"And do what with them?" Ingrid said.

"Customize," said Joey. "What else?"

"Sounds good," Ingrid said.

Not long after, they were in Joey's basement, Ingrid's Rollerblades on the workbench, separated into all their component parts and maybe a few more. Joey switched on a strong light.

"See these things?" he said.

"Those?" said Ingrid, pointing; their hands touched for a moment.

"Yeah," said Joey. "I'm going to put in better ones."

"Better how?"

"More titanium."

Titanium—one of those words you heard from time to time, but Ingrid didn't know much about it. "What's so special about titanium anyway?" she said.

Joey, working with a tiny screwdriver, the tip of his tongue sticking out, paused. "Strong as steel and half the weight," he said.

"Yeah?"

"Plus it won't corrode."

"How do you know all this?"

Joey shrugged and went back to work. At that moment, maybe because of the bright light he was working under, Ingrid noticed that his ears were kind of nice. Ingrid had never really noticed much about ears before, couldn't say what exactly made Joey's nice. She leaned a little closer. That was when she got the idea— not an idea, more of an urge—to give his ear a quick little kiss. She was just about to do that, her lips so close—although Joey, bent forward in concentration, seemed oblivious—when the basement door opened and Chief Strade came in.

Ingrid rocked back, so hard she almost fell off the stool.

"Hi, kids," he said, facial expression and voice neutral. "What's doing?"

"Not much," said Joey, reaching for an even smaller screwdriver.

"Joey's customizing my Blades," said Ingrid.

The chief's mouth opened as though he were about

to say something—maybe something funny; Ingrid could see that in his eyes. But the look faded quickly, and all he said was "When you've got a moment, Ingrid, I'd like a quick word."

Joey glanced up. "About what?"

"Is your name Ingrid?" said the chief.

Ingrid followed the chief upstairs and into the kitchen. Ingrid saw the first snowflakes of the year drifting down outside the window. Chief Strade opened the woodstove and tossed in a log.

"There's been a little hitch," he said. "Not with the steroid investigation. That's a slam-dunk—they're all headed for prison. This is about the kidnapping."

"I don't understand."

The chief leaned against the table; its legs creaked under his weight. "I'm having trouble fitting it all together," he said. "The problem is that everyone's got an alibi for where they were on MathFest morning."

"They do?"

The chief ticked them off on his huge fingers. "The Krakens were deer hunting the whole weekend in Pennsylvania."

"All of them?"

"The Krakens don't miss deer hunting—although that's going to change," said the chief. "They've got plenty of witnesses—clerk at the Motel 6 they stayed at, other hunters they met up with, state game wardens at a weigh station. Even had their picture taken—the three of them grinning like idiots around a dead buck."

"What about Rey Vasquez?" Ingrid said.

The chief shook his head. "Worked the seven-to-five shift at the hospital that day, E.R. duty. Never left the building."

"Then who?" she said.

"That's the question," said the chief. "We know it wasn't Sean Rubino. Course he wasn't the only low-level kid the Krakens had out there. I turned up two more at the high school and a trainer over at Bump's Gym, but they all alibi out on that Saturday morning, and none of them even heard of you. Plus the DNA—the nail clippings are Carl Junior's all right, and we've collected DNA from the others, but those hairs in the Yankees cap don't match up with any of them."

"So there must be more people in the ring," Ingrid said.

"Not that I can find," said the chief. "And Carl three is singing like a bird, ratting out his dad and granddad as fast as his droopy little mouth can move. I don't think there's anyone else, Ingrid."

Ingrid felt funny, like the floor had shifted under her feet. "What are you saying? That you don't believe me?

You don't believe I was kidnapped?" Were they back to that?

The chief gazed down at her. He had a big rough face, a face that should have been scarier than the faces of any of the Krakens or Rey Vasquez. But somehow it was not. "I believe you, Ingrid," he said. "The laneway behind one thirteen—had to have happened that way."

"But who?" said Ingrid.

"Whoever wore the Yankees cap." He thought for a moment or two. Something crackled in the woodstove. "Do you like jigsaw puzzles?" he said.

"No."

"Probably pretty far down the list of fun things to do nowadays," the chief said. "But I loved them when I was a kid. I remember this one puzzle, five hundred pieces, the USS *Constitution* in action. You know the *Constitution*?"

John Paul Jones? Or did his ship have some other name? But something about the Revolutionary War, Ingrid would have bet almost . . . Oops. The War of 1812, maybe? "Um, in general," she said.

"There was this one piece I couldn't get to fit," the chief said. "Looked like the end of a cannon, with smoke coming out. Must've taken that baby apart and put it together fifty times. No luck. Finally I sent that stupid piece to the manufacturer with a note asking for help. Know what came back?"

Ingrid had no clue about that, or about where the chief was going with this whole story, not particularly gripping so far.

"An apology," said the chief. "The cannon piece came from another puzzle, a packaging mistake."

"Did they send you the right one?"

"Nope," said the chief. "By that time they'd discontinued the *Constitution*. But I didn't care."

"'Cause you knew?"

"Exactly."

"And the Yankees cap?" said Ingrid.

"Piece from a different puzzle," said the chief. "But we're not letting on about that."

"So whoever did it feels safe?"

The chief nodded. "One more thing," he said. "No going anywhere by yourself, okay?"

"Okay."

Joey came up the stairs, Ingrid's Rollerblades in hand, a grease stain on his forehead. "Ready to try 'em out?" he said. "You're not gonna believe the difference."

The chief looked at his son, squinting slightly as though trying to sharpen the focus.

"On the way back from the bike path," he said,

"make sure you escort Ingrid home."

"Escort?" said Joey.

"Go with," said the chief. "Open door. ''Bye, Ingrid.' Close door."

"Um," said Joey. "So, like, you're saying . . . ?"

TWENTY-SEVEN

After school on Wednesday: last soccer practice before Saturday's championship game against the Central Valley Warriors, one of the biggest U13 powerhouses in the whole state. But for some reason the girls from Echo Falls didn't seem tense, were even kind of loosey-goosey, turning lots of cartwheels and seeing if anyone could do a handstand on a soccer ball, all this happening while snowflakes drifted down. At first there were just a few, like the day before, but this time they didn't peter out. Instead the sky darkened, the clouds sagged low, and snow fell hard, coating the field in minutes. That made the team even loosier-goosier. Snowballs started flying.

One grazed Julia's shoulder as she stood huddled in her fur jacket by the bench.

She blew her whistle. "That's it," she said. "Practice over."

"But we haven't worked on anything yet," Stacy said.

"Can't work in this slop," Julia said. "Does it always snow so early around here?"

"Sometimes earlier," said Ingrid; she loved the snow.

Julia glanced at the surroundings with distaste.

The girls called home. Some cars were already driving into the parking lot, headlights and wipers on. Soon only Stacy and Ingrid were left, their parents unable to change from the scheduled pickup time.

"Come on," said Julia. "I'll drop you off."

"Oh, that's all right," said Ingrid.

"We can wait," said Stacy.

"Then I have to wait too," said Julia. "And that's not happening."

They walked over to the Boxster, only car in the lot. Julia popped the trunk, a tiny one, with barely enough room for the soccer ball bag she tossed in.

"You'll have to squeeze up a little," said Julia. Ingrid ended up sitting in Stacy's lap, not for the first time.

"Move your stupid elbow," Stacy said.

Julia turned onto Hospital Road, fishtailing slightly on the slick pavement.

"I'll need directions," she said. "Who's first?"

Stacy gave Ingrid a little jab, meaning *answer*. Stacy had no clue about direction; Ingrid had been that way until very recently, but now she was trying to learn the town.

"We're kind of in opposite ways," she said. They came to the stop sign at River. "Right for Stacy, left for me."

Julia went right.

Ingrid was surprised to see that Julia drove Mom style, leaning forward and gripping the wheel tight. But maybe it was just because of the snow; the wind was rising now, blowing the flakes sideways through the air in long, billowing curtains.

"Nice car," Stacy said.

"It's all right," said Julia. She turned up the heat.

"What was it like playing for Team USA?" Stacy said.

"I was just an alternate at the end of one season," Julia said. "I never got in any games."

"So was that tough," said Ingrid, "or were you just happy to be there?"

Julia rubbed her gloved fingertips on the fog creeping up the windshield. "Neither," she said. "Soccer was over for me by then."

"Because, like . . ." Stacy said.

"I had other plans," Julia said. "Grown-up ones."

"But what about loving the game?" Ingrid said.

"Loving the game?" said Julia.

Another little jab on the back from Stacy, this one probably meaning *shut up*. But Ingrid barged on anyway. "Yeah," she said. "What happens to the loving the game part when you stop playing?"

"Good question," said Julia, in the Lower Falls neighborhood now, turning up Stacy's street. "Best answered by someone who loved the game."

"What did you do after that?" Stacy said.

"In what sense?" said Julia.

"Like for a job," said Stacy.

"Started an Internet company, actually," Julia said.

"Wow," said Ingrid.

"How did that work out?" said Stacy.

Julia's hands got even tighter on the wheel, the bony parts predominating. "Even you children must be familiar with the general history." She pulled up at Stacy's house, gave it the briefest glance.

"Gonna open the door or what?" Stacy said.

Ingrid let her out, got back in.

"Later," said Stacy.

"Yeah," said Ingrid, closing the door. Julia drove off, fishtailing again as she turned back onto River. Ingrid buckled her seat belt, noticed that Julia wasn't using hers.

"You didn't love soccer?" Ingrid said.

Julia glanced over. The snowfall had bleached the color out of everything, except for her eyes, greener than ever. "Rather persistent, aren't you?" she said with a little smile. "It's a game, Ingrid."

"I love it anyway," Ingrid said. Or maybe because.

"Good for you," said Julia. "We won't argue. I make it a rule never to argue with someone who's on a roll."

"I'm on a roll?"

"You scored that goal against Glastonbury," Julia said.

"A fluke," said Ingrid.

The bridge appeared on the left, its old lampposts and ironwork all white and somehow airy, like an icing sculpture that one little push would bring crumbling down.

"And reading between the lines of this local rag of yours, I gather you've been vindicated," Julia said.

"Vindicated?"

"Meaning found to be right in the end."

Which was kind of the definition Ingrid would have guessed. "Vindicated how?" she said.

At that moment Julia's cell phone rang. She tugged it from her pocket, checked the caller ID, answered right away. "Hello?"

Whoever was on the other end sounded pissed and

had one of those commanding voices. Ingrid recognized it: Mr. Ferrand.

"Today?" said Julia. "But you said—"

Mr. Ferrand's voice rose.

"The report's at my place," Julia said. "I can fax it over."

A few short barking syllables from Mr. Ferrand.

"Yes," said Julia, "right away." She clicked off and turned to Ingrid. "Mind a quick detour?" she said, sounding different than Ingrid had ever heard her, sort of subdued; a vertical green vein had appeared on her forehead, throbbing just beneath the skin.

"No problem," Ingrid said.

They were almost at the bridge. Julia took a quick left, fishtailing even more this time, and crossed the river. Maybe she wasn't a very good driver. Down below, the river flowed fast, swallowing up the falling snow. Julia turned north on 392. The houses got farther apart, the town line not far away. They were actually getting pretty close to Grampy's.

Where were they in the conversation? Oh, yeah: *vindicated*.

"Vindicated how?" Ingrid said.

Julia glanced at her. Those eyes, impossible to read, but no one had ever looked at her quite this way—it was the kind of look adults gave other adults, not kids.

"What we discussed at Moo Cow," Julia said. "I

assume the powers that be now acknowledge you were kidnapped after all."

"Yeah."

"Which must be a relief."

"Yeah."

"So it was all about this steroid ring."

"Uh-huh."

"They knew you were onto them and they kidnapped you."

"That's what I thought," Ingrid said.

The Boxster lurched forward, as though Julia had made a mistake with the gas pedal; she really wasn't much of a driver. "You thought?" said Julia. "Meaning you don't think so now?"

Oops. Hadn't the chief said something about this? *Piece from a different puzzle—but we're not letting on about that.*

"Um," said Ingrid. "Yeah, I do. Like before and now. Same thinking." Sticking to the story—but what was the chief's point again?

"So it was all about the steroid ring, as you said the first time," Julia said.

"Uh-huh," said Ingrid, trying to remember what other instructions the chief had given her. Oh, yeah: *No going anywhere by yourself, okay?* She was being good about that.

"Uh-huh meaning yes?" said Julia.

"Uh-huh," said Ingrid. She meant it as a joke but nobody laughed except her—only a little one because of the rule about not laughing at your own jokes.

Grampy's barn appeared on the right, all soft edged and blurry in the snowfall. Then the farmhouse itself came into view, a smoke plume rising from the chimney and getting torn apart right away by the wind. Just before they drew even with the house, Julia slowed down and turned left onto a narrow road. It led through a grove of evergreens and ended in front of three little houses, kind of crooked, with screened-in porches and shutters, more like cottages, really. Something in her mind about cottages, but what?

Julia parked beside the nearest cottage; Ingrid saw that the other two were boarded up.

"Just be a moment," Julia said, taking the keys from the ignition.

"You live here?"

"Temporarily." Julia opened the door, got out.

"Is this the old Prescott farm?"

"So I've heard." Julia closed the door—it made a lovely solid thump—and went into the cottage.

Ingrid sat in the Boxster, snowflakes landing on the roof and windshield with tiny thuds. Behind the cottage, she saw another car, this one not fancy, just a plain four-door car, Ford or Chevy or something like that, plus a rusty tractor, lying on its side, and empty fields stretching toward distant woods. The old Prescott farm—where Carl Kraken Senior had lived, sometimes playing cowboys and Indians with Grampy, games that ended with that noose-around-the-neck thing, until Grampy took charge.

Ingrid peered through the growing snowflake webs on the windshield, saw no movement inside the cottage. Julia was sending a fax to Mr. Ferrand. How long did that take? Ingrid had never actually sent a fax. Kind of a funny word, fax, did it come from—

Whoa. A memory came crashing in, a memory of Mr. Samuels and Grampy's board of assessors problem: *Always a neighbor in cases like this.* And the neighbor who'd ratted out Grampy, the owner of the old Prescott farm—was that Julia? What had Mr. Samuels found out? Something about DRF Development that turned out to be a shell for Black Coral Investments, or was it the other way around, and Black Coral Investments was the shell? Black Coral Investments, based down in the Caribbean, safe from Uncle Sam, on the island of . . . Anguilla.

Ong Willa. Where the Ferrands had gone for their getaway weekend, where they had friends named Ernst and Alicia. What did all this mean? Ingrid didn't know.

Should she simply ask Julia—*Hey, did you try to get Grampy's taxes raised?* Good idea or not? She didn't know the answer to that either.

Ingrid glanced out at the cottage. Or tried to: the windshield was completely snowed over now. It was getting dark in the car, dark and cold. Her gaze fell on the glove compartment.

The next thing she knew, her hands had somehow taken over, flipped the glove compartment open, and were rummaging around inside. Not much there—owner's manual, maintenance book, registration card, gas pump receipts, road maps for Connecticut and New York states, ticket stub, all very tidy, no surprise.

Ticket stub. She had another look at it: box seat, Red Sox versus Yankees, August 2 of last summer, seven o'clock start, Yankee Stadium. Yankee Stadium, home of Yankee-cap wearing Yankee fans: links in a chain.

Ingrid got out of the car. Quick glance at the cottage: door still closed, nothing moving behind any of the windows. Her body seemed much more decisive than her mind all of a sudden. The wind was blowing harder now, whipping right through her soccer warm-ups, the driven snow stinging her face. Ingrid walked behind the cottage, the snow covering her cleats, circled the plain old four-door car and stopped by the trunk.

Locked, of course, but trunks could be popped from

the inside. She tried the doors. All locked too. Ingrid really wanted to pop that trunk, but if there hadn't been an old pitchfork leaning against the back wall of the cottage, the whole thing probably would have stopped right there. An old pitchfork, the handle all cracked, the metal rusty, the tips of both the outside—what was the word? tines?—chipped off.

Ingrid took the pitchfork and jabbed it at the driver's-side window. Nothing happened. Smashing car windows was bad, unless you had a real good excuse. Ingrid was far from sure about that, but her next try with the pitchfork was more like ramming anyway.

CRASH! Broken glass all over the place. But maybe not too loud, with the way the wind was getting screechy. Ingrid took another look at the cottage. Two windows at the back, one downstairs, one up, both darkening now, reflecting the storm. She unlocked the door from the inside, opened it, leaned in, popped the trunk. And as she popped the trunk, her eye was drawn to a few CDs scattered on the passenger seat. One of them was *Elton John's Greatest Hits*. She picked it up. "I Guess That's Why They Call It the Blues" was cut four.

Ingrid walked around the car again, opened the trunk wide. She saw: a carpeted interior, a spare tire on the left, a roll of duct tape. She reached under the hood, felt the locking mechanism. Doing that made her lean back slightly, brought her gaze up to the back of the house.

Julia's face appeared in the window, a pale oval, almost as white as the snow.

TWENTY-EIGHT

nd then Julia's face was gone.

A jolt went through Ingrid. She bolted away without a thought, like one of those prey-type animals that survive by speed. And maybe like them too, she headed first in the wrong direction, toward those distant woods. It was only after ten or fifteen yards that her brain checked in and she realized where she had to go. Ingrid wheeled around, her cleats digging through the snow, and took off on a long diagonal past the farthest cottage, through the fringe of evergreens, across 392—not a car in sight—and into Grampy's fields. One thing about Ingrid: She could run, and now she ran her all-time fastest, everything flying by in a blur. She looked back only once, as she reached the far side of 392, and through a gap in the evergreens saw the cottage—door hanging wide open, no one in sight.

Ingrid crossed Grampy's fields to the long driveway, sprinted past the shed and the barn, around the house to the back door. Locked? Not Grampy. He came from another time. Ingrid threw open the door.

"Grampy! Grampy!"

No answer, house quiet, a low fire burning in the kitchen grate.

"Grampy! Where are you?"

She ran through the house—living room, dining room, all neat and tidy, never used by Grampy, then up to his bedroom, kind of messy.

"Grampy!"

No Grampy. She ran back downstairs, into the kitchen. Where could he be? She spun around. That fire had to mean—

And then Ingrid was airborne, slipping on a pile of unopened mail. She landed hard, face-first on that grate in the floor. Under the grate lay the envelope that had been out of reach the time she tried to straighten up Grampy's mail. Now so close she could read the front: *Urgent, Personal and Confidential.* And there was no stamp. Deep inside, Ingrid felt something shifting, like those plates way down under the earth's crust. Her mind tossed up a memory fragment: that glass of milk slipping from Julia's hand at Moo Cow.

She reached through the grate. The letter was still two or three inches out of reach. Ingrid rose to her knees, pulled at the grate. It didn't budge. She got a better grip, yanked with all her strength. The grate came ripping out of the floor, screws and all.

Ingrid grabbed the envelope—no stamp? what was that all about?—and tore it open. Inside was a single sheet of paper. She unfolded it.

What she saw made her feel faint, actually dizzy for a moment or two. At the top was written:

> *Want to see her again? Put the farm on the*
> *market by five o'clock today and keep your*
> *mouth shut.*

Below that was a digital photograph. It showed a kid lying in the trunk of a car, arms bound with duct tape. The eyes and mouth were taped too, but anyone who knew Ingrid would know the kid was her.

Whatever it takes.

Those deep-down plates stopped shifting and locked into place. Two puzzles, as the chief had suggested. Puzzle one, the steroid ring; and in her hand was the final piece of puzzle number two, filling in the biggest hole in her story: motive. It all made sense. *Ransom—no note.* Now she had every—

Ingrid heard a sound, looked up.

Julia stood in the doorway, the pitchfork in her hand.

Ingrid backed up a step. "Grampy?" she said, not screaming the name, which was what she felt like, but calling in a normal voice so Julia would think he was in the next room.

Those green eyes went to the letter in Ingrid's hand, to the piles of unopened mail, to the torn-up grate, back to the letter. Ingrid could almost feel Julia thinking, like her mind was a powerful high-pressure system pushing into the room.

"Give me that letter," she said.

"Grampy?" Ingrid said again.

The green eyes shifted, paused, came back to Ingrid. "Nice try," Julia said. "You've taught me something."

Ingrid didn't speak.

"The meaning of the saying 'too smart for your own good,'" Julia said. "That's you."

Ingrid shook her head. "I think it's you," she said.

She should have stayed with the nonresponse. Julia's face, so striking, got all twisted up in a terrifying way. Then she bounded across the room, so fast. Ingrid darted toward the dining room. Julia swung the pitchfork, caught Ingrid on the side of the leg. Ingrid went down, tried to scramble away on her hands and knees. Julia dove on top of her, the pitchfork coming loose, clattering on the bricks in front of the fireplace. They rolled right over it, ended up with Julia on top. She grabbed for the letter, balled up now in Ingrid's hand. Ingrid wouldn't let go. Julia gripped Ingrid's wrist, forced her hand into the fireplace, closer and closer to the flames. Ingrid felt the heat, hotter and hotter, unbearable. She let go of the letter. It fell into the fire, flared up.

"Step one," said Julia.

She reached for Ingrid's throat.

And then: "What the hell is going on?"

That voice came from the doorway. Grampy, all covered in snow, a bundle of firewood in his arms.

"Grampy! Help!"

The logs fell to the floor. For a moment Grampy looked a little confused. Then he said, "Hey, good girl. You caught the thief." A strange interpretation of what was going on, but that was Grampy. He came forward. "Get off her," he said, his voice low and growly.

Ingrid, down on the floor, felt Julia's body tense.

"Careful, Grampy, she's—"

Too late. Julia rose, grabbed the pitchfork. Grampy kept coming forward. Maybe he believed a woman couldn't hurt him. Maybe he believed no one could. He reached out to take the pitchfork away from Julia. She drove it at him, almost missed. Only one of those outside tines, a broken-off one, got him. It sank deep into his shoulder.

Everything went still, except for the faces of Grampy and Julia. His got all white. Hers got triumphant, like she'd just proved something. That made Ingrid go a little crazy. She jumped up and charged at Julia, her hands squared into fists. They both fell. Something hit Ingrid in the face. The room got noisy, went black, white, black again. When it settled down, back to normal, Grampy was holding the pitchfork and Julia was running out the door.

"Grampy, your shoulder." Blood was seeping through his jacket.

"No time for that," said Grampy. He went to the broom closet, took out the .357.

From outside came the roar of a big engine. Grampy and Ingrid went to the back door in time to see the Boxster speeding down the driveway toward 392, fishtailing all over the place, tires spinning wildly, snow flying.

"Come on," said Grampy. "You'll have to drive."

"What are you talking about?"

"Only got one arm," said Grampy. "Temporarily. Can't drive and shoot at the same time."

"But Grampy. Let's just call the police."

"Call the cops?" said Grampy. "Are you nuts?"

"But I can't drive, Grampy."

"Sure you can. It's just like the tractor."

He'd taught her to drive the tractor. Plus what no one knew was that she'd actually had a little adventure with Grampy's ancient Caddy during the Cracked-Up Katie episode.

"But what about your shoulder?" Ingrid said.

"Just grazed me," said Grampy. "And what makes you think we got time for all this jawin'? You gonna trust me or not?"

Ingrid trusted Grampy one hundred percent, which was how she ended up behind the wheel of the pickup, Grampy beside her with the .357 in his hand.

"Nothing sudden," said Grampy. "That's the secret of driving in snow. Slide it into D."

Ingrid, perched on an old blanket, slid it into D.

"Now go."

Ingrid went.

They headed up the driveway. Way ahead, Julia was turning onto 392. Maybe she didn't know the nothing-sudden rule, because the Boxster spun around in a complete three-sixty, banging off a telephone pole. The car sat in the middle of the road, rocking back and forth.

"Step on it a little," said Grampy.

Ingrid stepped on it. The rear of the pickup drifted out by itself, a very weird feeling.

"Ease off," said Grampy. "Don't touch the brake. Steer right into the slide."

Ingrid eased off, didn't touch the brake. She steered into the slide, which seemed like a wacky idea. The pickup straightened out, all by itself.

She trusted Grampy.

Up ahead, the Boxster was moving again, slower now.

"Snow," said Grampy. "One of those equalizers." He rolled down his window.

"We're not actually going to shoot the gun, are we, Grampy?" said Ingrid.

"Somebody breaks into your house and you don't shoot?" said Grampy. "What am I missing?"

"There's other—"

"Step on it."

Ingrid stepped on it. The distance between the Boxster and Grampy's pickup began to shrink. No other cars on the road, snow flying all around, up, down, sideways, the sky growing dark.

"Where's the headlight thing, Grampy?"

"Don't need 'em," said Grampy. "Lived here all my life."

The bridge appeared on the left, white and filigreed like a ghost shape. Grampy leaned out the window and fired a shot, an orange blaze in all that white.

"Don't, Grampy," Ingrid said. "How are you going

to hit anything in this?"

"Maybe you got a point," said Grampy, lowering the gun. "But step on it."

Ingrid put a little more pressure on the gas. Was Julia watching in her rearview mirror? The silhouette of her head seemed to shift, and the Boxster speeded up.

"She's going to take the bridge," Grampy said, "head for the interstate."

It didn't look like that to Ingrid. Julia was going way too fast for any kind of a turn, not in this. But at the last second, the Boxster swung to the left, just making the turn onto the bridge. Way too fast: the rear of the car slid far far out, and then the Boxster swung, round and round. It smashed into the rails on one side with a horrible crack, shot back across to the other, then flipped over and took flight, high into the air, tumbling and tumbling, first up in a long arc that was kind of mesmerizing and then down and down, starting to vanish in all that streaking snow and vanishing for real into the river.

"Oh my God."

Ingrid turned onto the bridge, stopped the pickup, jumped out. She ran to the side, looked over the rail. No Boxster. No Julia. Nothing bobbing to the surface, nothing to see except the river, black and roiling like it was in some huge temper, whirlpools getting born like funnels down to nowhere. Ingrid got the feeling the river was telling her something—something Oz-like about witches and melting away.

Grampy walked up and put his hand on her shoulder. She felt a little dampness on her neck. Grampy's blood?

"We've got to get you to the hospital," Ingrid said.

"I'll drive," said Grampy, "now that the shooting part's over."

TWENTY-NINE

Chief Strade took Joey and Ingrid to Benito's, best pizza in town. They ordered the Vesuvius, a large thin-crust with everything.

"On the house," said Benito, but the chief paid anyway.

"We could get practically anything free if we wanted," Joey told Ingrid.

The chief turned to Joey. "But?" he said.

"But?" said Joey.

Ingrid gave him a little kick under the table.

"Oh yeah," said Joey. "Not a good idea."

The chief nodded. He handed Joey a five-dollar bill.

"Go play video games," he said. Benito's had a video game room at the back.

"None of them are any good here," said Joey.

"Maybe they got some new ones in," the chief said.

"They never—"

"Do me a favor," said the chief. "Go check."

"Check on the video games?"

"Something wrong with your hearing, son?" said the chief.

"Huh?" said Joey. "What—"

Another kick under the table, harder this time. Joey went to check out the video games.

The chief laid some papers on the table, turned them so Ingrid could see.

TRANSCRIPT OF INTERVIEW WITH MR. TIMOTHY FERRAND. PRESENT: CHIEF GILBERT L. STRADE, MR. FERRAND, MR. BRAMWELL FLINT OF WHITESHOE AND FLINT, ATTORNEY FOR MR. FERRAND.

Strade: What is your interest in Black Coral Investments?

Flint: That would appear well beyond the parameters of your investigation, chief. I don't see why my client—

Ferrand: It's not a problem, Bramwell. This is an informal talk, after all, and I want to do everything I can to help.

Flint: Very well. May I repeat for the record that
            no oath has been taken?

Ferrand: We currently have no interest in Black
            Coral. The company, to the best of my
            understanding, is defunct.

Strade: Did you ever have an interest in Black
            Coral?

Ferrand: Briefly. A minority interest.

Flint: I don't believe Mr. Ferrand is at liberty to
            name the other investors.

Strade: Not a problem. What was the relationship
            between Black Coral and the late Julia
            LeCaine?

Ferrand: Why, none whatsoever, to my knowledge.

Strade: Must be some misunderstanding. I was
            under the impression that Julia LeCaine
            borrowed in excess of one million dollars
            from Black Coral several years ago to
            finance an Internet start-up.

Flint: May I take a moment with my client?

Strade: Not a problem.

Interview resumes.

Flint: I believe Mr. Ferrand can clarify the
            misunderstanding you referenced.

Strade: Great.

Ferrand: The company Ms. LeCaine founded was
             the borrower, not Ms. LeCaine personally.
             I'm sorry if in the interests of accuracy I
             perhaps misled you slightly. Not my
             intention at all.

Strade: Not a problem. Is it true that Ms.
             LeCaine's company went bankrupt last
             spring?

Ferrand: I believe so.

Strade: Was the money ever repaid to Black
             Coral?

Ferrand: Not to my knowledge.

Strade: None of it? Not a penny?

Ferrand: As far as I know, none of it, no.

Strade: What was your thinking in hiring
             someone who owed you more than one
             million dollars?

Flint: Mr. Ferrand wasn't owed it personally and
             she did not owe it personally.

Strade: Ah.

Ferrand: Ah? What does that mean?

Strade: Just ah. Please go on.

Ferrand: I came to feel the need for long-range
             corporate strategy. Ms. LeCaine is—

excuse me, was . . . this is so, so . . . I just
can't . . .

Strade: Take your time.

Flint: Some water, Tim?

Ferrand: Thank you. As I was starting to say, Ms.
LeCaine was a strategic-planning expert.

Strade: Funny—speaking here as just a blue-collar
guy—how a strategic-planning expert can
have a company go belly up so fast.

Ferrand: There are many variables, of course.

Flint: I'm sure you're familiar with bubbles.

Strade: Right. Bubbles. How did the unpaid debt
affect your relationship with Ms. LeCaine?

Ferrand: It wasn't a factor.

Strade: Is it possible she still felt the burden of the
debt and worked extra hard for you,
maybe crossing the line at times?

Ferrand: Julia was a very hard worker. I don't know
what you mean by crossing the line.

Strade: Perhaps anticipating things you wanted, or
things she thought you wanted.

Ferrand: I'm not—

Flint: You're asking my client to read her mind,
chief. I'm not sure that's reasonable.

Strade: Things she thought you wanted, like

Aylmer Hill's farm.

Flint: It's my understanding that there's no
            evidence backing up this girl's story.

Strade: Her name is Ingrid. No, there's no
            independent evidence.

Flint: All you really know is that they had a
            violent argument.

Ferrand: So sad. A terrific kid. She and Chloe are
            practically sisters. On an unrelated matter
            I would like to say how completely
            shocked I am by the behavior of my
            former caretaker and his family. I hope
            they're punished to the full extent of the
            law.

Flint: Have you got any more for Mr. Ferrand at
            this time?

Strade: No.

Flint: Then I would like to read this brief
            statement from my client into the record.
            Quote. My wife and I are distraught about
            recent events, especially the suggestion
            that they relate to real-estate interests of
            the Ferrand Group. It is true that we
            explored acquisition of the Hill property,
            but our partners were Mr. Hill's own son
            and daughter-in-law, Mark and Carol. Mr.

Hill declined to sell and the discussions
ended amicably. It was a normal business
dealing in every way, conducted in
accordance with the strict ethical standards
that have always characterized the Ferrand
Group. End quote.

Ferrand: Good to see you, chief.

Flint: A real pleasure.

Strade: Yup.

Ingrid looked up. Chief Strade was watching her.

"Well?" he said.

Ingrid had a feeling she'd just caught a naked glimpse
of how the world worked, a quick peek behind the curtain. No funny little man playing wizard—it was a lot
more complicated than that.

"You tell me," she said.

"I believe it all happened just like you said," the chief
told her. "But even if we had that note, nothing suggests
that there was more than the single perp, now deceased."

Joey came back holding a small pink stuffed monkey
with hostile little eyes.

"What the hell's that?" said the chief.

"The prize for getting to level ten," said Joey. He
handed the thing to Ingrid.

* * *

The Gobbler Bowl game started at ten. Echo Falls versus South Harrow, a rivalry that went back to 1899. Ingrid got up at seven—had to be at the field early to grill burgers for the Boosters—and went downstairs. No one in the kitchen, but Mom already had the turkey in the oven—the smell filled the house. Grampy, shoulder all sewn up, wouldn't be at the field—he'd had it up to here with football, even the Gobbler Bowl game—but would stop by the house later. He'd promised to bring deep-fried yams he made himself, some recipe from way back, inedible.

Ingrid went over to the table. What was this? A Boxster brochure, with a dealer's card attached. The dealer's name was Buddy. Buddy had written a little note. *Hey! Mark! Check out page 8!!* Ingrid flipped to page eight: gleaming Boxster on a mountain road, handsome young dude at the wheel, hair flying free. Dad had been pretty cheerful the last few days. He'd gotten a big raise from Mr. Ferrand. Ingrid tossed the brochure in the trash.

She heard that familiar clang from the basement, went down to see. Ty lay on the bench press, stripped to the waist, pumping iron. Four twenty-fives. With the bar, that made one forty-five: a little less iron, but still plenty, in Ingrid's opinion.

"Is that a good idea before the game?" she said. Ty was starting for the Red Raiders on Gobbler Bowl Day, amazing for a freshman. Everyone said the boys who played in the Gobbler Bowl remembered for the rest of their lives.

Ty raised the bar into the cradle, sat up. His muscles didn't look quite as big as the last time she'd seen them, not quite as defined.

"Why not?" he said.

"Maybe you should be saving your strength."

Their eyes met. His were distant. He reached for his BIGGER, FASTER, STRONGER T-shirt and put it on, but not before Ingrid saw that his back was less pimply. "Pretty funny coming from you," he said.

Ingrid ignored that. It was a special day, after all, and maybe he was right. "You nervous?" she said.

"No way."

"I play better when I'm nervous," Ingrid said.

"That's soccer," said Ty. "This is football." But his hands were trembling; she could actually see it.

"I read this survey," Ingrid said. "Ninety-nine point nine percent of NFL players say they play better when they're nervous." Complete fabrication.

"Yeah?" said Ty. "Where?"

"Where what?"

"Where was this survey?"

"You know. One of those sports magazines at Dr. Binkerman's."

"Like *ESPN the Magazine?*"

"Yeah," said Ingrid. "Like that."

"Sure it said the NFL?"

Ingrid nodded. "The big boys," she said. "The big boys of autumn." Maybe she had a future in sports broadcasting.

Ty looked thoughtful. "What time is it?" he said.

"Around seven thirty."

"I better start getting nervous," Ty said.

"In a hurry," said Ingrid.

Their eyes met again, and all of a sudden they were laughing, just laughing and laughing like crazy little kids, tears on their faces. Somewhere in the house Nigel started barking maniacally.

"Hey," Mom called down. "What's going on?"